Painting the Town Red . . .
with Blood!

The Virginian smiled, realizing Edge's instincts were the same as his own. If he were to die, the half-breed would not be far behind in the plunge to purgatory. So he was poised, too, to take at least one of the enemy with him.

The Winchester exploded a shot that drilled into Cox's skinny belly and knocked him flat onto his back. The scream that came from deep inside him sounded of terror rather than pain.

Steele looked down at Cox as he hit the street and clawed at the center of the rapidly expanding stain on his lower shirt front. Muttered, "Seems in this town it's not so much who you know but what you know that counts, feller."

Cox had stopped screaming, but he could not hear the Virginian, for Steele spoke against the sharp cracks of two more rifle shots. He was already dead then, the spasmodic jerking of his body and limbs triggered by an involuntary reaction of his out-of-control nervous system.

Edge came up the street from the corner and said: "I don't know if I should be seen around you, Reb. Way you're getting to be the death of men in this town."

EDGE AND STEELE
MATCHING PAIR
by George G. Gilman

PINNACLE BOOKS NEW YORK

EDGE MEETS STEELE: MATCHING PAIR

Copyright © 1982 by George G. Gilman

An original Pinnacle Books edition, publishing for the first time anywhere.

First printing, October 1982

ISBN: 0-523-41894-9

Cover illustration by Bruce Minney

Printed in the United States of America

PINNACLE BOOKS, INC.
1430 Broadway
New York, New York 10018

for:
B.K.
a favorable girl in the
nicest possible way.

MATCHING PAIR

Chapter One

The man called Edge was facing the way the train was going. Beside him sat a Frenchman with the name Bardot stenciled on his valise. Across from the Frenchman was a fat hardware drummer who had introduced himself to the girl as Harry Grade. The girl seated beside Grade and across from Edge was Belinda West. Who talked a great deal.

The half-breed gazed out of the dusty window of the jolting day car at the monotonous vista of the Colorado Plains spread to the south of the Union Pacific track and tried not to listen to what she was saying. Which was not possible. For she broke off in full flood, leaned forward to tap him on a knee with a fist, and demanded to know:

"Am I boring you, Mr. Edge?"

The combination of a glaringly bright sun, brilliantly blue sky, and ruggedly parched land—which was all that could be seen from the window of the clacking car—could make a man's eyes ache within a few minutes. Belinda West was not painful to look at for any length of time. And, Edge allowed to himself as he shifted his gaze back to her, under different circumstances maybe the sound of her voice would not have grated on his ear so much.

She was no taller than five feet three inches and was a blue-eyed blonde with the fresh complexion and slender figure of a healthy eighteen-year-old. The gentle curves of her body were only subtly hinted at by the loose fit of the high-necked white dress she wore. But the look in her eyes was close to being brazen.

"No, Belinda. I was just checking to see if your home town was in sight yet."

The start of a frown was swept away from her round, button-nosed, full-mouthed face to be replaced by a toothy grin

1

that made her look even younger than she was. But did not cause the half-breed's conscience to trouble him.

"Goodness, it's not yet the middle of the afternoon, Mr. Edge. Even if the train is on schedule, which as often as not it isn't, we won't get into Stormville before evening." Now her tone became mock rebuking. "And I trust you are not anxious for the train to reach Stormville because that is where I get off? And from where you will ride on to Denver without my company?"

"No, Belinda."

He returned to his stoic scrutiny of the landscape that slid aridly by the window. And was aware of the girl peering hard at him—perhaps trying to spot some sign that the short and evenly spoken reply held a hidden meaning. That he was indulging in sarcasm or, even worse, was patronizing her. And, seeing the shadows of a frown come and go from her youthfully pretty face, Edge knew he had passed the test.

The face she had started to frown at so anxiously was, he knew, to her mind, very handsome. But, he also knew, it could equally well be seen as ugly. It was that kind of face of that kind of man.

Lean, with angular features. The skin a dark shade of brown and deeply cut with many lines. The heavily hooded eyes, permanently narrowed, a light blue and coldly piercing in the manner they surveyed any and everything. The nose hawklike, with flared nostrils. The mouth wide and thin lipped. High cheekbones and a firm jawline. The tautly fleshed face framed by jet black hair that fell in an unkempt tangle to his shoulders. The same color as the two days' growth of bristles that sprouted on his lower face and neck—these just a little longer above and to either side of his mouth to form the mere suspicion of a Mexican-style moustache. A cruel-looking face of a man about forty with both Hispanic and Anglo-Saxon blood in his veins.

He was six feet three inches tall and weighed in the region of a lean two hundred pounds. His mode of dress was simple and would serve equally well for riding a horse as a train. A gray Stetson and a black shirt open at the neck to reveal a string of dull-hued beads encircling his throat. No neckerchief. Black pants and riding boots without spurs. Around his waist an unfancy gunbelt with a standard Frontier Colt in the holster on the right side—the toe ties not fastened while he was sitting down. Wedged between his left thigh, the front of his seat, and the side of the car was an early-model Winchester.

Unseen, because it was hung from the string of beads at the nape of his neck and concealed by his hair and shirt, was a leather pouch in which nestled a straight razor. Which often served other purposes than shaving.

He guessed that Belinda West preferred older men—especially those who she felt were able to protect her. But no matter how much this girl fantasized about this man with the unmistakable stamp of brutality upon him, she would never be able to conceive the extent of the carnage he had wrought with these weapons he carried.

Now, as the big Baldwin locomotive began to haul the string of five passenger cars and a caboose up the start of the first slope of the eastern Rockies, Edge experienced a mild stab of self-anger. As he realized that he was just as guilty as he imagined her to be of indulging in flights of fancy.

They were just two passing strangers from totally different worlds brought temporarily together by the accident of having facing seats on a train trip.

He had been aboard first, from Columbus in Nebraska, entering an already crowded car. By the time Belinda West boarded the train at Julesberg across the Colorado line, the seat opposite Edge was the only one vacant in the car—back to the engine and wedged between the side and the fat drummer who needed constantly to mop at his fleshy face with a spotted handkerchief to keep sweat from dripping off the point of his chin and on to his shirt.

That had been early this morning, when Harry Grade had helped the girl with her two valises get settled in the seat. Then had tried hard and often to engage her in conversation, to which she contributed only polite monosyllables. Until, perhaps an hour after she boarded, she told him in a sharp voice, loud enough for many of her fellow passengers to hear, to kindly stop pressing his leg against her leg.

The drummer had protested frantically that the seat was too narrow and it was the motion of the car that caused the close contact, and that it was not his intention to make improper advances toward the young lady.

Edge had been awake for a long time—since the Negro conductor had shouted the announcement that the train was approaching Julesberg. But it was at this point that he elected to sit straighter in his seat and to push his hat off his face and on to his head as he delved into a shirt pocket for the makings. Also nodded a curt and unsmiling morning greeting to the girl in the virginal white dress, the city-suited drummer, and the Frenchman.

Belinda West had not been able to conceal her intrigued interest in Edge from that first moment of seeing his face. While Grade had been frightened into sweating silence by the coldness of the half-breed's gaze as it moved briefly across his own eyes. And the Frenchman appeared petulantly disappointed that a quarrel which might have enlivened a dull trip was curtailed before it could get started.

Edge rolled and lit the cigarette and appeared to the trio of passengers closest to him to be as impervious to them as when he had his hat over his face, apparently asleep.

Grade and Bardot were familiar with the half-breed's brooding impassiveness that did not invite talk, for both had been on the train before he boarded, and in a short space of time the foreigner abandoned the smiles and nods with which he had met each chance glance from Edge, while the fat salesman withdrew into a piqued silence of his own.

And so the three men seated midway along the middle car of the train traveled like deaf mutes until Belinda West came aboard at Julesberg. When the garrulous drummer got cold-shouldered by her and made the error of thinking that the taciturn Edge was concerned by the attention he paid the girl.

She made the same mistake and her opening barrage of talk was designed to assure everybody that she was certain she had maligned the poor drummer and that she accepted his explanation. Then, after the fat man had gratefully accepted her apology and the passengers ahead, behind, and across the aisle from the group returned to whatever occupied them before the verbal flare-up, she quickly followed her opening salvo with more fast-spoken words.

Began to chatter about the discomforts of railroad travel. Which she knew a great deal about, since she rode the train frequently between her home town of Stormville and Julesberg, where her dearly loved Aunt Carrie lived.

Edge at first heard what she was saying without actually listening to her. While he smoked his cigarette and looked at her quite simply as a young woman rather than a person: sexually attractive and mildly arousing, but unattainable in the present circumstances. Easier on the eye than the fleshy salesman who had previously occupied the window seat before he surrendered it to the girl.

Now the drummer tried again to establish the groundwork of a relationship with her, by interjecting an eager comment each time she paused to draw breath before prattling out more mundane details of her small-town life. Until she told him to kindly mind his own business and that she was talking to the gentleman seated across from her.

The drummer was piqued again, then frightened again. Piqued by the girl who frowned at him and then frightened by the half-breed, whose glittering blue eyes did not reveal the surprise he felt as he looked up from crushing out the cigarette beneath a boot heel. He said nothing as he sat back in his seat, and Belinda West presumed this to be acceptance of her invitation to be interested in her. And he found himself almost involuntarily contributing the kind of brief encouragements that the drummer had supplied so eagerly before.

She was that kind of young woman, he realized, with the facility in the right situation for manipulating the people around her, especially men. Confident of her good looks and pleasing personality. Experienced, even at such a relatively tender age, in the ways a man could be tempted, toyed with, and then either rebuffed or kept interested.

When she was through telling him the highlights of her life and outlining her family tree, she started to question him and soon was drawing from him elaborations of the single-word responses he at first gave her.

He felt drowsy with the heat and the wearying effects of the long train journey. Was aware of Belinda West as more than merely a sexually attractive young woman now, but because of her candid interest in him could not rid his mind of lascivious images of her. And, as if anxious that the sharpness of his imaginings might be impaired should the link of talk be severed, he began to answer her freely.

Until, close to the middle of the hot afternoon, he discovered with a mild shock that he was responding to questions about his long-dead wife. And her voice as she spoke of her own experiences of grief took on a harsh tone to his ear. And he called himself every kind of daydreaming fool. While he tried to shake his mind free of unbidden fanciful thoughts about Belinda West. By looking away from her animated face and attempting to pay no attention to what she was saying.

But Beth was long gone. Just a fading memory that had momentarily come into sharp focus. And this girl was in the here and now. And he was back on the hook of her youthful but strangely sophisticated brand of charm as she took up where she had left off: allowing him to peer out of the window in the certain knowledge that he was still disconcertingly aware of her presence.

"Of course, I could not claim to know how you felt when you lost your wife, Mr. Edge. But I lost my mother and saw how her death hit my father. Goodness, Mother did not die in such tragic circumstances as your . . ."

Her mother had died three years previously, and she used the springboard of that event to launch into a chattering discourse on a hundred and one happenings that took place at about the same time.

Which did not call for any contribution from Edge until the afternoon had receded from the encroachment of evening and the Negro conductor came down the car to light the lamps. When she interrupted herself to ask the railroad man:

"Should we not be at Stormville by now, George?"

The conductor answered, "You know we should, Miss West."

"Did I not say we would surely be late arriving, Mr. Edge?"

The half-breed accepted a light for his freshly made cigarette from the Negro's taper and let one nod of his head serve as acknowledgment to him and a reply to the girl.

She was as muddle-headed as she was loquacious and—just as had happened before on many occasions during the day—an interruption caused her to lose the thread of what she was saying. But, just as before, she was able to fasten upon a new subject without the slightest pause for thought. "Goodness, we have talked so much about the past, Mr. Edge. What of now and the future? I am returning home from seeing my Aunt Carrie in Julesberg and will continue with my dull life. What of you? You do not look to be a salesman like this gentleman. Nor a tourist, which is perhaps what our other fellow passenger is? You are traveling from Columbus to Denver. For what? What will you do at Denver? If I am not being too inquisitive."

She smiled and bobbed her head at each city-suited man in turn. The drummer looked pointedly away with a disdainful sniff, while the Frenchman shrugged his shoulders and spread his hands to indicate his lack of understanding.

With the coming of night and the lighting of the lamps, the window offered only a distorted reflection of the interior of the car. So Edge was gazing directly at the woman now, through the drifting smoke of the cigarette angled from a corner of his mouth as he replied: "It was just outside of Columbus that I caught up with a man named Al Falcon, Belinda. And shot him. Only law office I know of will pay money for his corpse is at Denver. So that's where I'm taking it."

The girl caught her breath, the drummer wrenched his head around to stare at Edge, and the Frenchman was ready to be afraid if it seemed that it was fear of the half-breed which had sparked the reactions of Belinda West and Harry Grade.

Then the moments of shock were gone and the drummer uttered a louder sniff of disapproval as he folded his hands in his lap, closed his eyes, and feigned trying to get to sleep. The Frenchman was relieved. The girl was excited.

"So you're a bounty hunter, Mr. Edge?"

"Right now I am."

"Where is he—I mean, the body of the man you—killed?"

"In a coffin in the caboose."

"What did he do?"

"Some robbing and killing."

"And you tracked him from Denver to Columbus and—"

"No. I first heard of him at a town called Ridgeville over in Montana. Where he headed up a bunch of men who robbed the local bank and killed three people. Later killed another man."

"And you got on his trail and—"

"We were just both heading in the same direction and I was moving faster than he was. Happened to meet up near Columbus and I found out who he was. Didn't find out until after I'd killed him that there's a big reward posted for him in Denver. So never will find out if anybody at Ridgeville would have paid good money for his carcass."

"Goodness, imagine you being that, Mr. Edge?" she said in a mildly breathless tone of admiration.

And the drummer revealed he was not really asleep by grimacing his repugnance for the half-breed's line of business and the manner in which his speaking of it aroused the woman.

"I've been lots of different things," Edge answered. "And maybe I'll be something else again after the money I collect in Denver is all spent."

"Oh, so you are not—"

She was obviously more intensely interested in this aspect of his life than any other she had brought to light during the trip from Julesberg. Had until now unfailingly pounced upon something he said about himself to spark a recollection and a recounting of an event from her experience. And was suddenly irritably disappointed when the door at the front of the car swung open and the conductor came through to call:

"Stormville comin' up, folks! Stormville in five minutes! Thirty minute stopover in Stormville for them folks that wants to eat supper at the depot restaurant! Stormville! Stormville!"

The uniformed Negro left the car through the rear doorway as passengers began to stir. Standing and stretching, delving into bags or pockets for whatever they felt they needed to freshen themselves up for the meal halt. This as the volume of talk rose as people spoke of their hunger and anticipated the relief they would feel at being off the clanking, jolting, fetidly crowded train even if only for half an hour.

Not so Belinda West, who looked about to vent a curse. While the drummer mimed the act of eating for the benefit of the Frenchman, who was puzzled by the sudden burst of activity. And Edge decided he would remain aboard, having eaten his fill of railroad-depot food.

"You didn't shock me, you know. Well, maybe for a moment. And now I wish I had not talked so much about myself. I bet there are a thousand stories you could tell that—"

Edge peered out of the window again, needing to shade his eyes with a hand from the reflections caused by the interior lights as he saw the lights of the town around a curve in the track.

"I wasn't trying to shock you, Belinda," he cut in on her. "Just answered that question the same as all the others you asked me. Which is something I don't generally do."

Stormville was encircled by night-darkened hills. Seemed to be comprised of two streets which intersected each other at their midway points. The railroad depot was isolated by several vacant lots from the northern end of what looked to be the main street.

He pulled his face away from the window and saw that in common with most of the passengers, Grade and Bardot had got to their feet and were shuffling along the central aisle— eager to be close to the head of the line for supper at the depot restaurant. The girl remained in her seat, gazing at him with moon-eyed wonder. She swallowed hard before she said:

"I'm really flattered, Mr. Edge. That a man like you felt able to confide in a woman such as I."

"Was that what I was doing?"

"I'd like to think so, Mr. Edge. You see, at home, father and my sister think I'm nothing but an empty-headed child who talks too much. I'm never taken seriously."

"A child you're not, Belinda."

A beaming smile took command of her face. "I'm nineteen next birthday.

"About what I guessed."

"But you're not going to make an issue of me being young enough to be your daughter?"

"Ain't no denying it, Belinda."

Her face clouded with the threat of a frown. This as he reached down with both hands to grasp the girl's two valises. And drew another gasp of shock from her when he added:

"But that's also old enough to share my bed."

Chapter Two

The train jolted to a stop along the depot platform and Belinda West looked frantically toward the group of people at either end of the car as Edge gripped the handles of her valises and unfolded to his feet.

"Easy, young lady," he told her with a smile that failed to reach his narrowed eyes as she stared up at him, chewing on the inside of her left cheek. "You knew I was bound for Denver and you were going to get off here at Stormville. And the train would be crowded with other people all the way. Figure there was no harm in what each of us was thinking for most of the time. Ain't often I get the chance for playing those kind of games."

The tension drained out of her with a sigh and she showed him a wan smile as he stepped out into the aisle and held up her bags to show that he intended to help her with them.

"Comes from being treated like a child so much at home. And at Aunt Carrie's. Got to be that I think everyone will be the same to me. Even strangers."

The car was rapidly emptying as the passengers spilled out on to the platform and hurried across it, into the brightly lighted building. And Belinda West was talking fast again as she trailed the much taller and much older man who carried her valises.

"Still and all, it wasn't any game that barrel of lard salesman was playing, Mr. Edge. He really was pressing himself against me to get some kind of cheap—"

"He's a traveling man and it's expected of him to chase the ladies, Belinda," Edge cut in as he shouldered open the door at the rear of the car which the Frenchman had allowed to swing closed. "And he was like me. On a crowded train, what could happen?"

11

"I still want to thank you for being there to frighten him off me, Mr. Edge!"

She had to shout to make herself heard. For the engineer opened a safety valve on the locomotive's boiler. To hiss steam under high pressure noisily out into the night. Where it billowed like a brief, rolling mist along the platform between the train and the depot building. And momentarily enveloped the man who stepped from a patch of deep shadow into the shaft of light from a window. The man of whom nobody but Edge took any notice—because nobody else was aware of being on the narrow line between life and death. Had not the slightest expectation of seeing such a man—with a gun in his outstretched hand, aiming to kill.

The half-breed was on the top tread of the car steps when he glimpsed the gunman in that instant before the steam hid him. And he froze there for another instant, as the girl bumped into him with a soft gasp of surprise. Then he dropped both valises and they hit the backs of the Frenchman's legs. To tip him forward and into the fat drummer.

"What the heck?" Harry Grade demanded as he started to turn.

"*Excusez-moi,*" Bardot apologized, and also began to come around, as ready as the drummer to be angry.

"Mr. Edge?" Belinda West asked. Then vented a high-pitched scream when she saw him draw the Colt from the free-hanging holster.

Grade and the Frenchman saw the move too. And several other passengers whose attention had been captured by the drummer's snarled query.

"Watch it, Floyd!" a man warned, and his voice was almost as shrill as the girl's scream.

Edge, the Colt aimed and cocked, had to believe that Floyd was the man who was just becoming visible through the clearing steam. For if that wasn't so, there were at least three of them and that was too many.

Women screamed and men cursed in the area from which the warning had been yelled—down the platform toward the rear of the train.

Edge and the man he now saw clearly in the light from the

depot window squeezed their handgun triggers within a fraction
of a second of each other. But the half-breed was the calmer of
the two at the moment of firing, less disconcerted by the shrilly
shouted caution. And his aim was perfect, his hand rock
steady. To blast the bullet across a range of fifteen feet on a
slightly downward trajectory so that it drove accurately into the
intended target. Which was the man's chest, left of center and
slightly above the midway point.

"Floyd!"

The man who was starting to stagger backwards with a
bullet in his heart and limbs that in less than a second would be
limp, had to be Floyd. Edge realized this as he detected the
grief in the voice of the man who shouted the name, at the same
instant as he felt something snag at his shirt sleeve.

Belinda West said huskily, "Goodness, I'm shot."

Edge did not see Floyd back hard into the depot wall and
then slide down it to the platform, dead before he sat at the
angle and toppled slowly to the side. He did hear a thud
behind him, which he guessed was the girl falling to the floor of
the car. What he did see was Floyd's partner, and in the wake
of the girl's crumpling form there was a burst of gunfire. And
the shrieks of panic that accompanied the frenetically wild
shooting.

The man had a revolver, which he was fanning with the heel
of his left hand while the index finger of his right curled tight to
the trigger. In a half-turned, half-crouched position on an open
area of platform which expanded by the moment as passengers
scrambled to get as far away from him as possible.

The bullets thudded into the timber of the car's construction
and shattered a window. A shout that changed key to become
a scream perhaps indicated one of the bullets came to rest in
another victim of the Colt revolver.

But Edge saw on the periphery of his vision that many
people on the platform had sprawled to the boarding. Seeking
to get under the spray of rapidly fired bullets because the
nearest cover was too far off. It was not possible to see if any
one of them was oozing blood. And immaterial, anyway, as he
triggered a second shot from his own Colt. Fired from the hip
again. On a slightly less steep trajectory. The bullet aimed for,

and finding, the bulging belly of the man fanning his revolver. Who drew himself erect and flung his arms wide to the sides in response to being shot. With an expression of angry disappointment on his face for a moment. But then he screamed his pain and snatched both clawed hands to his belly, the Colt slipping from his fingers. And covered the blossoming dark stain on the lower part of his shirt front—first with his hands and then more completely with his upper body as he folded double before he fell hard to the platform boarding. Whimpering now, and shaking as if he were cold.

The hooded eyes of the half-breed, glinting in the light from the depot, raked from left to right in a complete survey of every shadowed area within his range of vision. While the gun in his right hand—cocked again—maintained a steady aim on the man enduring the agony of a bullet hole in his belly and the vulnerable tissue below the surface.

The steam from the opened safety valve was still hissing, but the sound was less loud now. Voices were shouting, but from some way off. But coming closer, the sense of what was being yelled even more difficult to grasp because of the counterpoint of running footfalls. Behind the depot building, on the street in the center of Stormville.

Edge discounted the din and the people making it. Just as he paid no attention to the train passengers who got to their feet or emerged tentatively from the areas of cover into which they had lunged when the shooting began. And spent perhaps a further three seconds in an almost frozen attitude on the car steps—just his eyes moving along their sockets in search of a third gunman intent upon killing him.

But then there was too much activity on the narrow platform between the train and the depot building as the newcomers from town demanded to know what happened and the passengers competed loudly with each other to give their version of events. People milled about, as if they were afraid to remain stationary for fear of being static targets for the other gunmen who might be among their number. Or, more likely, were too excited to stand still.

Edge neither knew nor cared. Simply acknowledged that the crowd in ferment provided too good a cover for him to spot any other men who might be gunning for him. And elected to challenge the unknown rather than to withdraw.

So he eased the hammer of his Colt forward and slid the revolver back into its holster. Stepped down on to one of three areas of platform left clear by the raucous and animate crowd. At the center of the two others, a man was dead and a second man was badly injured.

The half-breed stooped to shake the shoulder of the Frenchman, who was down on his knees with his back arched and his head resting on the platform, face in his hands. But the lightest touch was sufficient to cause Bardot to topple to the side and unfold to his full length on his back. To reveal a hole in his throat, just beneath his Adam's apple. And the large pool of blood which had drained out of it to form on the platform while he was precariously poised in such an odd position.

The sight of the hapless foreigner drew a swell of noise from the crowd—gasps and screams and choked exclamations. Then came a near silence which was broken by the whimpering of the man with a bullet hole through his intestines, next by the footfalls of Edge, and then by the shuffling of many booted feet—as the press of people parted to allow one man to approach the other.

Somebody yelled shrilly, "Belinda! My Belinda!"

Some people stepped aside to open up a passage for him. While he had to shoulder forcefully between others who were surging forward to see what Edge intended to do to the man he had shot in the belly.

The engineer, brakeman, and a trio of uniformed railroad men from the depot were engaged in a rasping-voiced conference while the fireman and conductor scowled their irritation at not being included.

Edge ignored everything and everyone as he dropped to his haunches beside the wounded man. Who was a match for his own age. Much older than Floyd, who had been little more than a kid. The man was in a great deal of pain, but there was hatred as well in the way he bared his gritted teeth and screwed up his eyes to look at the half-breed.

"Floyd's dead and you ain't got long, I'd say, feller."

The man had to swallow hard before he was able to rasp, "There's plenty more where we come from."

"A big rock, uh?"

"Uh?"

"You crawled out from under, feller."

The lines of the scowl and grimace deepened into the weathered and heavily bristled face of the anguished man. "From all over, Edge. Al Falcon had lots of friends. A hell of a lot more than you got days left to live, I reckon. Maybe even minutes, bounty hunter."

The half-breed nodded. "Obliged to you."

The badly wounded man managed to vent a gasping laugh as Edge rose to his feet. Then squinted up at him, his eyes pained by the lights from the train and the depot, to mock: "Me givin' you the warnin' won't make no difference. Floyd was just too young and itchy to get you for putting pay to Al. Rest of his buddies, they'll take more care to . . ."

The man's voice trailed away when he saw the half-breed draw the Colt from the loose-hanging holster. And there were gasps of shock and low-voiced curses from the circle of watchers— who backed off quickly, those at the front bumping into those at the rear.

"They'll either kill me or they'll die, feller."

"All aboard!" the Negro conductor yelled, still embittered after being told the result of the platform conference. "Train's behind schedule! No meal stop! Train's about to leave! All aboard!"

The engineer and fireman were already on the footplate of the locomotive while the brakeman and depot staff were urging passengers to heed the conductor's calls.

"It's one of my rules," Edge continued, and concluded, after the Negro finished shouting. And squeezed the trigger of the Frontier Colt. To blast a bullet into the squinting face of the suddenly terrified man from a distance of three feet. To drill a hole in the center of his forehead and through his brain. So that he was jerked out flat on to his back, spasmed once and became totally inert. Glazed eyes staring sightlessly up into the pitch black sky above the glow of kerosene lamps.

There were stretched seconds of total verbal silence in the wake of the killing shot. Broken by the conductor, who started:

"Come along, folks! All aboard who's goin' aboard! Train time and we ain't—"

"Mister!" a man whose voice Edge recognized cut in sharply to silence the Negro and the hum of talk and shuffling of feet that the renewed urge to board had started. "Leave the iron where it is and reach for heaven! Or don't do like I'm telling you and go to the other place!"

"Father, don't be so foolish!" Belinda West chided.

The Frontier Colt was back in the holster with the loosely hanging ties. Edge froze again, as unmoving as most of the audience, who were as surprised as him by the new turn of events. But most of them were in a position to see the man who was threatening him from behind. While he gazed unblinklingly at a poster advertising the attractions of Denver that was pasted to the depot wall.

"You aiming a gun at me, feller?" he asked evenly while his ice blue eyes glinted with evil intent.

"You bet your butt I am, mister!" There was no fear in the man's voice—as there had been when he had shrilled the name of his daughter perhaps a minute ago. "And I know how to use it, so best you do as I told you and reach!"

Edge had both hands down at his sides, fingers slightly curled, his right palm just below the jutting butt of the Frontier Colt in the holster. He did not move either hand the merest fraction of an inch. Replied in the same unemotional tone as before, "Then use it, feller."

"What?"

West's gasped response was all but masked by the low-keyed reactions of the watchers to the half-breed's bold invitation.

"Use it and kill me, feller. If you don't kill me, you're dead."

"He only gives folks the one warning, Mr. West."

It was a new voice to speak loud enough for Edge to hear this evening. Yet it was not new to him. A voice from out of the past. Heavily loaded with a drawl that made it sound as if the speaker had only left his native Virginia yesterday.

"So we meet again, Reb," Edge said as Adam Steele

stepped into view on the periphery of his vision. "Been a long time."

"Sure has, Yank. But I prefer rare meets."

"Always seems to be blood running when you're around, feller."

"This beef has nothing to do with me."

"You want to tell West here that he could be the lamb to the slaughter?"

"All aboard!" the conductor shouted, a little frantically, as the noise from the locomotive changed key.

"What the hell is going on here?" West demanded. "You know this man, Adam?"

"We had a disagreement over horseflesh a while back, Mr. West," the Virginian answered.

"Let's leave those sleeping dogs lie, Reb," the half-breed suggested and slowly turned his head to look over his shoulder at where the glowering man with a derringer in his fist stood in front of his daughter. "Stakes are higher here."

Belinda West, who had some blood on her right temple and a little staining the shoulder of her white dress, reached around from behind her father and plucked the small gun from his grasp.

Adam Steele said through teeth bared in a grin, "Well done."

Chapter Three

Adam Steele was of an age with the man called Edge. And had maybe suffered to the same extent and killed as many men—and women—in war and peace. But they had little else in common. Certainly shared no bond that should have kept the half-breed standing on the platform, not threatened anymore, as the big Baldwin locomotive hauled the line of cars away from the depot and the rest of the passengers scrambled to get aboard the moving train.

Certainly in appearance they were totally dissimilar—if it mattered.

The Virginian was just a half inch above five and a half feet tall, his lean build belying the strength he could command if needed. And he was undeniably good looking, the aging process—which seemed to regress when he displayed a boyish grin—having added more than it subtracted to a basic bone structure which in his younger years had given Steele a certain nondescript and shallow handsomeness.

His features were regular and he was clean shaven. His eyes were black as coal and his hair, which he wore neatly trimmed, was almost an unrelieved white with just a hint of its former red color showing in the sideburns.

There was, in both his bearing and style of attire, more than a hint of a topdrawer background. And he was, in fact, the only son of one of the richest plantation owners in the state of Virginia. But the long-ago War Between the States had robbed him of his birthright and, although he had adjusted fully to the drifting life that had become his, he still felt the need to cling to certain aspects of what once had been.

This night, in this town of Stormville, he looked the complete dude. For his black frock coat, gray city suit, white Stetson and boots and shirt, and the multicolored vest were all crisply new and stiff from being recently in a local store. Or complete, anyway, at first glance from a stranger.

And Edge was not a stranger—as the platform became more sparsely populated in the rapidly clearing steam and smoke of the train's departure, he took note of the torn and scuffed buckskin gloves, the slit in the outside seam of Steele's right pant leg, the worse-for-wear kerchief around his neck, and the well-preserved but time-scarred Colt Hartford revolving rifle canted to his left shoulder.

For his part, the Virginian with the remnants of the grin still clinging to his face knew that the glinting eyes of the half-breed were reading the signs—aware from the violent aftermath of their first meeting of exactly what he was seeing.

A rifle in the hands of an expert marksman. A neckerchief that was, in fact, an Oriental weapon of strangulation—made so by having diagonally opposite corners weighted. The seam of the pant leg slit so that access was allowed to a throwing knife stowed in a boot sheath. The gloves? . . . Perhaps worn to keep blood off his hands. Or maybe regarded as lucky charms, in the belief that they somehow mysteriously kept the man who wore them from spilling blood.

During the frenetic activity of the train's abrupt departure and then as the townspeople for the most part drifted away from the depot with nervous backward glances, Adam Steele watched Edge switch his gaze back and forth—between himself and the West father and daughter.

When the noise level had fallen so that it was possible to hear the spoken word at a normal conversational level, Belinda West asked, "Now, father, perhaps you would kindly explain why you——?"

"My intention was to arrest you, mister!" the stoutly built, balding, round, and ruddy-faced West cut in, ignoring his daughter as he glowered into the impassive face of Edge. "As a duly appointed deputy sheriff in the absence of Stormville's regular peace officer."

"For what, father?" Belinda demanded insistently.

West continued to stare fixedly at the half-breed. "For the most cold-blooded killing I ever did see in my entire life!"

"You live in this town?" Edge asked of Steele as he swung

his head around to locate the Virginian in a gesture that also served to dismiss West.

"No. Just waiting for Sheriff Gale to get back. He's the only one authorized to pay the bounty on the man I brought in. Why?"

"Don't you turn away from me when I'm talking to you, mister!" West snarled in high anger.

"Father!" Belinda hissed urgently.

"Don't you think you should have the girl's wound seen to, Mr. West?" Adam Steele suggested.

"And what about the dead, Nathaniel?" the most elderly railroad man asked—the one with the most gold braid on his uniform.

"Would like to know when the next train for Denver will be through here?" Edge asked, shifting his gaze from the Virginian to the most senior railroad man. "Figure you know that, feller?"

A rapid nodding of the head. "Certainly do, sir. Three more days. Scheduled to reach Stormsville at midday. Leave thirty minutes after that."

"By which time Sheriff Gale will be back in town," Steele pointed out to West. "So I reckon it would be wise of you to leave whatever needs to be done by the law over this to the regular peace officer."

"I think so too, father," Belinda added. And histrionically massaged the area of the nicked skin on her temple. "My head does hurt more than a little."

"Just so he knows I'm not afraid of him," her father growled, and drew a brief glance and curt nod from the half-breed, who interrupted his survey of the railroad track stretching westward from the depot to supply the acknowledgment. West then went on in a moderating tone. "If nobody else has done so, I'll have Joe Hart come down to pick up the dead. Come on, honey. Let's get you home so Sam can take a look at that nick. See if Phil should be—"

"I'm sure I'll be fine if I can just stetch out for a while, father."

"I'll bring the young lady's baggage, Mr. West," Adam Steele offered. "If I'm still invited to dinner, that is."

The man who had placed an arm around his daughter's waist paused before steering her away from the scene of violence. To share an intrigued and uncertain look between Steele and Edge. Then: "Of course you are still invited, Adam. And I appreciate your offer. But I can manage."

Edge ended his study of the night-shrouded track beyond the lights of the depot to ask, "Your telegraph line go all the way to Denver, feller?"

"Sure enough does, sir," a younger uniformed man answered. "I'm the operator."

"Name's Edge. There's all my gear still on the train and—"

"I'll get right on to it, sir," the young man said eagerly. "I'll have the Denver depot hold your property—"

"And there's a coffin in the caboose which I don't figure they'll want to hold since there's a body in it. Likely smells by now."

"A coffin with a body, sir?"

"You got it. Obliged if you'd have the Denver depot get in touch with the Denver law to pick up the corpse. And say I'll be by on the next train west to pick up my money."

The West father and daughter had gone from sight and now the railroad men went into the main depot building, the telegraph operator worried about how to word the message, while the man who was apparently the manager promised to help him and the less neatly dressed porter trailed them automatically.

"You still not drinking liquor, Reb?" Edge asked.

"That's right."

"No hard feelings about the horse?"

"It was one to one, Edge. Shook me up a little, but then I reckon I came as a surprise to you."

They had first encountered one another in the Sierra Madre foothills in Mexico. Parted company at a town called Southfields. A lot of killings later.

"You don't use the saloon then? This town has a saloon, I guess?"

"Called the Rocky Mountain Hotel," the Virginian supplied. "I'm staying there."

"Can afford to buy myself a drink. If you're staying there, coffee should be free."

"Things a little tight until you called on Falcon, Edge?"

"I'll get by, Steele."

"I'm just asking. Not offering anything. Have the same problem until the town lawman gets back."

"Hotel give credit?"

"If you know the right people."

"Like the town banker?"

"We could both have the same luck there, Edge."

A wagon and team had been heard coming down the street and now rolled into sight around the end of the platform. Bumped across the track and rolled toward the two men on the other side of the gleaming rails. Which gleamed a little less brightly as the lamps in the depot restuarant went out and an immensely fat woman of uncertain age waddled out and slammed the door. Stared resentfully at the half-breed and complained in embittered tones:

"Don't know how a body is supposed to earn a living when folks scare other folks to death with shootings. So there ain't no one left to eat the food I prepares."

She was so intent upon showing Edge the full extent of her bad feeling for him that she tripped and stumbled over the corpse of Floyd in the angle of platform and depot wall. She cursed at and kicked the obstruction, then hurried away, mumbling angrily to herself.

"Don't pay no mind to old Ada, mister," the man driving the flatbed with the two-horse team in the traces called as he halted his rig directly across the track from where Edge and Steele stood. He tapped the side of his head with two hooked fingers as he climbed down from the wagon. Made sure the woman had gone from sight and earshot on her way back to town before he went on. "She ain't got all she was born with. Now, what's the situation here?"

He dragged three rolls of burlap off the rear of the wagon and draped them over his shoulder. A tall, broadly built, easy-smiling man of about fifty with a great deal of untidy red hair and an unkempt beard that was mostly white. Dressed in heavily stained and much patched work clothes.

"Guess you're Joe Hart, the Stormville mortician." Edge

said as the man came across the track and swung up on to the platform.

"Sure enough am, mister. How you doin', Mr. Steele?"

"Fine Joe."

Edge stabbed a finger at each of the men he had killed. "Have to owe you for those two, feller. The Frenchman there, he got shot by accident. Not by me."

Hart dropped a burlap shroud beside each body and shook his head. "Sure to be enough money between the three of them to take care of the buryin' expenses, mister." He squatted beside the corpse of Bardot and with easy strength rolled the dead man up off his rump with one hand while he slid a billfold from the hip pocket with another. Grinned at the thickness of the fold and after checking the contents added, "What'd I tell you."

"Owe you for him and him," Edge insisted flatly, with a stab of the forefinger at Floyd and his older partner again.

"Okay, suit yourself!" Joe Hart growled.

And before the half-breed could answer, Steele said, "He usually does."

His voice low, so that the Virginian and Edge did not hear him as they started along the platform, the mortician murmured, "Like somebody else I know, runt!"

The clacking of a telegraph key sounded as the two men went by an open doorway. And each of them sensed, without needing to see, the watching eyes of the railroad men. Who had looked up at the sound of approaching footfalls, to glimpse with a mixture of reproach and nervousness the pair of bounty hunters pass the doorway of the telegraph office.

"What luck's that, Reb?"

"Nathaniel West has two daughters, Yank," Steele answered as they went around the side of the main depot building and stepped down from the platform and on to the end of the main street of Stormville. "Worships the ground both of them walk on. Samantha took a shine to me. Looked to me like Belinda was with you until the shooting started back there."

The half-breed gave the Virginian a sidelong look and received a slight shrug of the shoulders in response.

"You just like watching trains come and go?"

They were beyond the vacant lots now and stepped up on to a covered sidewalk that stretched across the frontages of a line of shuttered and darkened stores. Heading toward the midtown intersection, where a few wedges of lamplight supplemented the glow from the cloud-shrouded new moon.

"Jonas Gale is going to have to pay me five hundred dollars when he gets back to town, Yank," Steele answered as Edge took out the makings and began to roll a cigarette. "Provided Walt King is still in the jailhouse. And King is like your meal ticket. He has friends. Was at the depot to check on who was arriving in Stormville."

"Real glad you didn't lend a hand, feller," the half-breed growled as he paused to strike a match on a drugstore door-frame and light his cigarette. "Means I don't have to say thanks to you."

"Knew that's the way you'd want it."

"So maybe I have to say I'm obliged to you for not butting in, Reb?"

"Forget it."

"Already have."

Adam Steele showed a fleeting smile in the darkness of the roofed sidewalk. He had not changed at all, this Iowa farm boy become a drifter who would as soon kill a man as not for whatever reason that man chose. And be totally untouched by what he had done, or, more accurately, what he had been forced to do. The complete loner, only ever truly happy in his own company, and so inclined to be sour tempered in the company of others. Self-sufficient and at his most embittered when events beyond his control forced him to accept help. Hating much in the world but hating perhaps most of all to be in the debt of another.

And the Virginian would not have taken exception to what Joe Hart had murmured—had the epithet not been added. For it had become increasingly more apparent when they were last together in the area of the Mexico border that they were two of a kind—a matching pair in virtually everything except physical appearance. Had the makings of a perfect partnership in all but that one respect—they had suited themselves for too long to do more than suffer the influence of another on the way they did what was necessary to survive.

The main street, the cross street, and the intersection were deserted and the town was outwardly silent, the footfalls of the two men rapping against the boarding of the sidewalk the only sounds to disturb the quiet. Until, as they reached the batwing entrance of the Rocky Mountain Hotel, Joe Hart's flatbed wagon rattled over the railroad track and started up the street. And the clock on the wall above the street entrance to the depot struck the hour of seven.

"It always this quiet or did the killings upset everybody?" Edge asked, glancing with seeming indifference down each length of street that led off the intersection.

That between here and the depot was lined by stores and business offices, with a continuous run of roofed sidewalk to both the east and the west. The buildings mostly of timber and single story, with here and there a false front.

The southern length of this main street was flanked by a mixture of frame and stone and brick premises. Without sidewalks fronting them, but some with stoops. A church and a meeting hall. A livery stable and a wagon repair shop. A corn-and-seed merchant and a school house. And, right out at the far end, the cemetery, across from the undertaking parlor to which Joe Hart had headed after passing the two men without acknowledgment.

The cross street was of two unequal lengths and widths. To the east side of the intersection it was narrow and lined with small frame shacks built close together and directly on to the street. While the stretch that curved away to the west was flanked at widely spaced intervals with large, elegantly designed houses set in well-planted gardens enclosed by fencing.

"It's suppertime," Adam Steele answered as he pushed open the batwing doors and led the way into the saloon. "In a town where everyone minds his own business."

"A coffee, I guess? And what's your pleasure, stranger?"

The saloon was deeper than it was wide, with the bar down the left-hand side and twin rows of chair-ringed tables down the right. A stairway angled across the rear wall, with a dais jutting out from beneath it. There was a piano with the lid closed on the dais and the entire rear of the saloon was in semidarkness, for just two ceiling lamps near the front were lit.

Directly under one of these lamps two men were seated at a table playing five-card draw poker. Beneath the other, the bartender stood behind his counter.

The card players were as dudishly dressed as Steele, but in more garish colors and in suits that were not so newly purchased. Both in their late twenties, with blond good looks, lean builds, and a style of posture and movement that was not entirely masculine.

"Good evening, Mr. Steele," the taller of the two greeted. "How many cards, Billy?"

"Hello, Mr. Steele. I'll take three if you please, Nicky."

Their voices were deep and rich in tone. The smiles they shared between the Virginian and the half-breed were close to being simpering.

"You guess right, Grealy," the Virginian told the middle-aged, powerfully built, totally bald bartender whose ruggedly carved, darkly stained face seemed to be set in a permanent grimace of distaste for everything and everyone he came across.

"One beer, one whiskey, one glass," Edge answered.

"Coffee for the dude!" Grealy roared without turning around. Then stepped along the counter a pace and drew a beer into a glass he took from below. Took a bottle of whiskey from a shelf behind him and set it and the foaming, full glass of beer down in front of him.

"You want me to put it all on your bill?"

"Just the coffee, Grealy. Mr. Edge likes to pay his own way."

Steele and the half-breed bellied up to the counter, aware of the glowering looks that had replaced the smiles on the handsome faces of the card players.

"Or I go without, feller," Edge said as a plain and very thin girl of about twenty came through an archway at the rear end of the counter and set down a mug of steaming, aromatic coffee. "Unless my credit's good. Which it is now."

The plain girl in the shapeless dress seemed not to have attended to her hair in a very long time. And she slouched and shuffled from the archway, directed a sullenly reproachful look that excluded everyone except Adam Steele, and then made an equally slovenly exit.

Grealy fisted a meaty hand around the glass and draped another over the top of the liquor bottle. And his expression darkened as he rasped, "Who says?"

"Trouble, Nicky!" Excitedly anxious.

"Of no concern to us, Billy." Coolly calm.

Edge took a dollar bill from out of a hip pocket and set it down on the counter top. Asked evenly, "You can make change?"

This as Steele, the Colt Hartford still canted to his shoulder, went to the far end of the counter to get the coffee which the girl, who obviously did not like him, had refused to bring him.

"One slug of hard liquor, mister?"

The Virginian sat down at a table on the fringes of the light from the two lamps, rested the rifle across the tabletop, and cupped the mug in the palms of both gloved hands to sip at the coffee.

Grealy surrendered his hold on the glass as the half-breed reached for it. Picked up the dollar bill but did not push it into the pocket of his leather apron as he watched Edge drink half the beer and set down the glass.

"Half a buck's worth, feller."

"No trouble, Billy." Still serenely calm.

"I'm glad, Nicky." Relieved.

Grealy topped up the glass with liquor to within a quarter inch of the rim. And growled, "There's a two-drink limit if this is your last dollar, mister."

He pocketed the bill and fished out five dimes, which he dropped into the half breed's cupped hand.

Edge let the coins slide into a shirt pocket and carried his drink toward the table where Steele sat. And had enough trust in the Virginian not to look back over his shoulder when footfalls sounded on the sidewalk out front and halted at the threshold. For they were the footsteps of a woman, and Steele smiled and raised a hand from his mug to touch the underside of his hat brim.

"Good evening, Samantha. I thought supper would be late after what happened to Belinda."

Edge sat on Steele's left, so that he was able to see the woman at the batwing doorway and the three other men in the saloon without having to make a point of looking. Of the woman, all he could see was her head and shoulders above the doors and her booted feet and dress hem below. Saw that she was also a blonde, but with darker than blue eyes. Was a match for her sister's height and was perhaps ten years older. A little fleshier in build than Belinda, but not unattractively so.

"Be ready in another half hour, Adam," she said, her smile for the Virginian darkening a little while she spared a brief but appraising look for Edge. "Dr. Phil checked her over and said she'll be fine after a night's rest."

"That's fine."

"Not the only reason I'm here, Adam. Belinda's told father exactly how things happened at the depot and he feels he has blundered . . ." Now she looked longer at the half-breed, contrite on behalf of her father. ". . . and he sends his compliments, sir, and asks if you will join us for supper."

Edge touched his hat brim now. "I'll look forward to it."

"In thirty minutes then."

She turned away from the batwing doors and stepped across the sidewalk and down on to the street.

From beyond the arch in back of the counter came a harshly whispered, "Rich bitch!"

Grealy growled, "Seems like every flat broke drifter through Stormville has an in with the West females."

And he slid the whisky bottle along the counter top with precise skill, so that it stopped level with the table where Edge and Steele sat.

"Women!" the tall Nicky said with a sneer and a shudder. "What a much better world it would be without them, Mr. Grealy."

"A much emptier one," Billy pointed out as he dealt another hand of no-stakes poker. Then looked toward the other occupied table. To call, "The offer still stands, Mr. Steele. And is extended to your friend now that Mr. West of the bank is behind him. Draw, stud, or any other game you care—"

"Grateful to you again," the Virginian answered. "But I

don't reckon I'd be up to playing any kind of game with you and your partner."

"Likewise," Edge added. "And with West already behind me, you fellers wouldn't have a chance. Especially in the sort of games where you deal from the bottom."

Chapter Four

The two faggots enjoyed the jokes, their laughter resounding off the walls of the ill-lit saloon that was too big for the patronage it had.

But Grealy had to do a double take before he felt able to let go of the shotgun he kept under the counter, and return his big hands into sight. He had seen their kind before, but in cities rather than small backwater towns like Stormville. And had learned to treat them as dangerous—especially not to poke fun at what they were. For they were likely to lash back with more than words—commanding as they did the strength of masculinity mixed in with the wiles of womanhood. And so the big bartender with his bald head sweatily reflecting the lamplight made sure the laughter was not false and a cover for the start of some vicious move by the two card players before he shifted his attention to the other occupied table.

And realized that his guarded misgivings about the gleeful responses of Nicky and Billy had been superfluous: Adam Steele and Edge were still watchfully suspicious of the men, whose hilarity had now subsided to an occasional giggle as a new hand of cards were dealt.

They continued to be on their guard, he was sure, as they engaged in a desultory conversation. But were not merely wary of the colorfully attired faggots. Also with seeming indifference but, Tom Grealy was certain, with an underlying readiness to react to a threat, the glinting slits of the blue eyes and the less dangerous—looking coal black ones maintained a survey on the batwing entrance to the saloon. And the archway in back of the counter. The stairs across the rear wall. On Grealy himself.

And the bartender, who had been in his trade for a lot of years in a lot more places, knew he had seen more of their kind than of faggots.

31

In towns of all sizes, from two-shack railroad halts to places as big as Houston or San Francisco. And on the trails between.

They had meet before, this Adam Steele and the one called Edge. Since that time, the dude with the Virginian accent had been married and had run a store in a small town in Texas. Then there had been some kind of trouble about a whole lot of money that got buried back in the War Between the States. And something about hostile Indians and a bunch of religious people. The army was mixed up in it too.

Grealy could not get it all, for neither man was a loud talker—when he said anything. Which was not often, and when he did it was baldly laconic and assumed the other man could fill in the blanks with ease if he so chose.

The taller, Edge, who had the look of a Mexican to him, had been involved in a kidnapping down on the Mexico border. Then there was something about a girl who bought him a saloon. A crazy guy who built a boat in the middle of a desert. Some Apache fighting, a time spent on the trail with a man scheduled to be hanged and a run-in with a bunch of outlaws at their bolt hole in the timber country of Montana. Somehow a troupe of traveling actors was mixed up in that.

So they were not professional bounty hunters. Just drifting saddle tramps to Grealy's mind. Restlessly unsettled since the war, he was prepared to guess. For both had been in the fighting—the way they called each other Reb and Yank. Skilled in fighting and staying alive, untouched by the merest twinge of conscience as they rode the violent frontier land in search of trouble from which they could profit.

Just bounty hunters for the moment. Edge having run into and shot dead in Nebraska a man who tried to kill him. Not knowing of the five hundred dollar reward—if his terse and quiet spoken words were to be believed—until after events forced him to put a bullet in the heart of Al Falcon. An accident, maybe. And a fortunate one for Edge, since he was almost flat broke when the shoot-out took place. Had to sell his horse to raise the train fair and eating money to get to Denver.

The dudish Adam Steele told a more positive story about his capture of Walt King, who was a wanted man in almost every state and territory west of the Mississippi. He had played some cards with King at Leadville and a week later in Climax had seen a wanted flyer on the man issued by the Territorial Marshal's Office. By the time the Virginian got back to Leadville, King had left. He trailed him to Cripple Creek, then Pueblo. Finally caught up with him on the open trail when Stormville was the nearest town where King was listed on the flyer as wanted—for robbing the grocery store five years earlier. Of ten dollars and fifty-five cents. And killing the old man who ran it at the time.

So Stormville was where Steele brought King to three days ago. Only to find that Sheriff Jonas Gale was out of town and his part-time deputies were not authorized to pay the bounty money.

Tom Grealy relished hearing what he did. For a great many people had been curious about the Virginian with the fancy rifle and how he had managed to capture the violent criminal who was now locked up in the jailhouse. A close-mouthed little runt who got lucky was the general opinion. Who kept his mouth shut because he had nothing of which to talk proudly about. A strutting dude who caught the eye of the elder West girl. And so had to be given the virtual freedom of Stormville because Nathaniel West was rich and therefore important. Who spent the last of his money on a whole new outfit of city slicker's clothes so he wouldn't dirty up the carpets and furnishings in the West house when he went courting Samantha. And who kept himself to himself when he was not at the West house—like he considered himself too good for anyone not as rich as they were.

The bartender had been as guilty as anybody of indulging his intrigued curiosity about Adam Steele by filling in a background to the man that was all bad. Now, as the Virginian and the taller stranger rose from the table—the move triggered by a distant single chime from the railroad depot clock while the hands of the one in the saloon pointed out the time of seven-thirty—Grealy experienced an uncharacteristic flush of pleasure. This as he anticipated spreading the true story about the rifle-toting little dude. And his equally taciturn buddy, of course.

Having the real lowdown on the both of them had to be

good for business, especially if he paced the telling of the stories and embroidered them to fill in the gaps. Dressed them up for the ears of the citizens of this hick town, most of whom had never lived anywhere much different. Unlike the widely traveled Tom Grealy himself. Who had come across so many men like these in the hundred and one saloons and barrooms and dance halls where he had worked.

Slow-to-talk, fast-to-shoot gunmen who needed to smell danger on the air they breathed and taste it in the food they ate. See it in every shadowed corner. Hear it in every new sound. Maybe even touch it on the women to whom they made love. For unless they felt menaced by the threat of sudden death they could not feel truly alive. And so they rode their aimless trails in a paradoxically dispassionate pursuit of the excitement they craved. Like addicts in need of a drug which they knew would eventually kill them.

The big-built, bald-headed bartender had seen plenty of dead ones. Had watched some die. Which was why he had not bothered to go down the street to the depot after the shooting this evening. Was not surprised to hear about two of the men who were shot dead. They had been drinking here in the saloon during the afternoon. And he had recognized their type.

But these two . . . this Steele and this Edge. They had something extra going for them. Or against them. Were a little different from your average run-of-the-mill saddle tramp with a gun for hire. Or maybe a lot of things that made them very different.

Grealy had never seen quite such nonchalant watchfulness in men before—so highly developed a quality of appearing to be totally at ease while anyone who took the trouble to test the atmosphere would know for certain that just beneath the surface these men were as taut as a stretched guitar string. Which if snapped was capable of creating untold havoc.

How could he have been so wrong about Adam Steele these past three days? Tonight the Virginian was precisely as he had been before and yet now he caused a disconcerting feeling to churn in the pit of his stomach.

He was with Edge! Much more obviously the type, with his Western garb, his build, the cut of his features, the bristles on his face, and the unfancy gun on his belt. And it was as if the invisible light of menace that emanated from the newcomer shone directly upon those aspects of the Virginian's character that he shared with Edge.

Tom Grealy identified the unsettled sensation in his stomach as plain and simple fear. And knew he would not dare to tell more than the plain and simple truth of what he had overheard—while Steele and Edge were still in Stormville and able to dispute what he said.

The half-breed had brought the bottle of whiskey from the end of the bar and now he set it down in front of Grealy. Who reached for it with a big hand that shook from a spasming nerve.

"Careful, feller," Edge warned evenly. "Wouldn't want the liquor to go the same way as the eaves."

"What's that?" the bartender asked huskily.

"He means take care not to drop the whiskey, Grealy," Steele explained.

There was no reproach in the expression or tone of either man and Tom Grealy subdued his nervousness and was ashamed of having experienced it. He glowered as he growled:

"This is my place! People sit around in here yakkin', am I supposed to stick my fingers in my ears or somethin'?"

"You tell him, Pa!" the sullen slattern yelled from beyond the archway.

"I'm tellin' both of them!" he snarled, the anger of his overreaction growing wilder.

"Take it easy, feller," Edge placated flatly.

"You can't tell him to keep his hair on, mister," Billy put in, with a pointed look at Grealy's bald head and then a short gust of laughter.

"Don't talk us into other people's trouble," Nicky urged and collected and neatly stacked the deck of cards in the center of the table. Stood up and added: "Come on, let's get some fresh air. Take a ride before we turn in, perhaps?"

The bartender switched his glaring attention to the faggots and was about to snap a parting comment at them as they headed through the flapping batwing doors. But Edge said:

"Can't tell you to do anything, feller. Like to ask you to

keep listening to your customers, though. And let me know if any strangers to Stormville make mention of me. Or the two men I shot at the depot. Or Al Falcon."

Grealy's temper improved. But only to the extent of becoming contemptuous of the two men he had been ashamed to be afraid of. He growled: "Tell you what I told your friend when he asked somethin' similar, mister. I'd need somethin' on account to do a chore that ain't in my usual line of business. He's flat broke and you ain't much better off as I recall."

Edge nodded, his lean face devoid of expression. "Just the fifty cents you know about feller. So let's leave it this way. Something bad happens unexpectedly and I find out you could have given me the word, something bad will happen to you. Won't be unexpected in your case, will it?"

The slits of the eyes under the hooded lids looked like slivers of ice as they gazed steadily at Grealy's ruggedly sculptured, darkly tanned features from out of the shadow of the hat brim. The bartender needed to swallow hard before he could challenge:

"You don't scare me, mister!"

"You could have fooled me," Edge countered as he turned away from the bar and started for the batwing doors. "But you don't. Let's go eat, Reb."

"I hope the food chokes you, Steele!" the girl shouted as the Virginian moved in the wake of the half-breed.

"Maybe you could tell Jeanne that I never bite off more than I can chew, Grealy?" Steele said to the bartender.

The doors flapped closed behind him and the sounds they made all but masked the string of obscenities Tom Grealy rasped out.

The half-breed was leaning against a sidewalk roof support, in the process of rolling a cigarette. Asked of the Virginian: "Was it something you didn't do that got you in so bad with her, feller?"

"I gave her a tumble but then had Samantha West fall for me."

"Beggars can't be choosers, but they sometimes get picked, uh?"

Steele stepped down off the sidewalk and Edge trailed him

after lighting the cigarette. Over the intersection and on to the western stretch of the cross street.

"Least Jeanne Grealy and Sam West are both old enough for the cradle marks to have gone from their asses, Yank."

"I'm not putting you down, Reb. In the same boat myself, I figure. And if I get the chance to give the baby sister a rattle, I'll let you know about the craddle marks."

The Virginian did not smile. Said seriously: "Be grateful if you take things easy with her, Edge. Way I hear it from Sam, she talks and acts a lot older than she is. But she's likely to run home and cry on her old man's shoulder if something happens she doesn't like."

"Figure it's not my interest you're protecting, Steele?"

"That's right. I wouldn't want to get cold-shouldered by the Wests because I'm associated with you. And you step out of line with the kid."

They had reached the far end of the street and were out front of the largest and most elegant house in Stormville. A two-story stone-and-frame house with a great many windows glinting in the weak moonlight. Standing in an extensive garden filled with plantings, from neat beds of flowers to carefully sited groves of trees.

The door in the arched porchway was open and Samantha West was silhouetted against the light that spilled out of it.

"Is it the woman or the high life you don't want to lose, feller?" Edge asked, shiftin his gaze away from the house to pointedly survey the dudish outfit the Virginian wore. A garb which, seen on this street out front of this house, made the rifle canted to his shoulder look even more out of character than before.

And now Steele did smile, the expression serving as a self-controlled acknowledgment to the woman's enthusiastic waving and an admission that the half-breed had guessed right. He said as he opened the gate in the picket fence and gestured for Edge to go ahead of him under the trellis arch: "If women like her were a dime a dozen they would be overpriced, Yank. There's no way Ben Steele's son can put a value on the opportunity to sample the kind of life he used to live. Except to say that it could perhaps cost a man his life if he—"

"Please hurry, gentlemen!" Samantha West called. "Supper is about to be put on the table and it does seem to me that Mr. Edge has not yet even washed up."

"Hell, seems I've already blotted your copybook, Reb," the half-breed murmured lightly as he and Steele were midway along the cement walk between the gate and the porch.

"A little dirt won't be the death of you, Yank," the Virginian replied softly out of the corner of his mouth.

"As long as I don't do it to you."

Chapter Five

The West family made an occasion of the supper meal which made Edge feel uncharacteristically uncomfortable. For although he was newly washed up in the bathroom filled with modern conveniences, he was still unshaven and garbed in the only clothes he possessed.

The father and two daughters dressed for supper and were, of course, as clean as they were neat, seated at the oval table in the upstairs dining room, which was furnished in Queen Anne style. Waiting to be served a meal of onion soup, fricassee of chicken with vegetables, a cold compote with maple syrup and cheese. With white and red wine to drink. Port or brandy to finish.

A pretty young black girl to serve the food, under the grim-eyed supervision of a Negro butler.

Belinda, with a small dressing on her minor head wound but otherwise showing no sign of being hurt in the shooting, told him about the meal as she took his arm so that he could escort her up the stairs. From the room below where everyone had sipped glasses of punch while the half-breed washed up.

Adam Steele mentioned during the buzz of talk that followed the saying of grace, while the soup was being ladled into dishes, that the luxuriously furnished room was Queen Anne in style. Which led to a discussion about period furniture and how the big house on the Steele plantation had been filled with pieces of Chippendale.

". . . but of course, sir, I was too young to appreciate it," the Virginian was saying easily while Samantha gazed moon eyed across the table at him. Her father was obviously preoccupied and making an effort to appear interrested, and her sister waited impatiently for a suitable opportunity to change the subject.

And Edge, who never slurped his food under normal circumstances, felt it necessary to have to concentrate on not doing so
at this meal he was eating in such elegant, candlelit surroundings.

"Oh, Adam," Belinda cut in as her father nodded an
acknowledgment of what Steele had said while the Virginian
drank some soup. "I think it is really marvelous how you and
Edge—goodness, I wish you had a given name I could call
you—have become such friends."

Steele shot her a perplexed frown.

Samantha laughed. "You'll get used to my little sister. Going
off at a tangent in a conversation is just one of her many
endearing charms."

Belinda grinned. "Goodness, I didn't mean to. And I'm not,
anyway. What I mean to say is that Adam comes from such a
totally different background from Edge. Edge was born and
raised on a small farm in Iowa. He told me all about it on the
train ride from Aunt Carrie's. He had a young brother who
was murdered by some men who were under the command
of—"

"One of my younger daughter's not so endearing habits is
that she has a tendency to talk to excess, Mr. Edge," Nathaniel West cut in on Belinda, with an indulgent smile on his
rubicund face as he looked at her. Which he replaced with a
rueful expression as he switched his blue-eyed gaze to the
half-breed.

Edge spoke first. "It seems she stopped talking for long
enough on the train for me to say more than I usually do."

"Quite so. And she has already told her sister and I much of
what was said and done on the train journey. That you
protected her from the unwelcome attentions of another male
passenger."

"He really was most objectionable, Daddy," Belinda em-
phasized, and shuddered.

And was ignored except by her sister, who made a face that
expressed tacit criticism and warned her not to overplay her
hand.

"I reacted instinctively at the depot, Mr. Edge," West went
on. "While I was still shocked by seeing my daughter's face
covered with blood. Not knowing the wound was such a

relatively minor one. I also was not cognizant of the reason for the shootings. And in my capcity as a deputy sheriff of this town, I felt it my duty to arrest you. I apologize."

He beckoned for the butler and the girl to remove the empty soup dishes from the table.

Edge said, "For doing your duty, feller?"

"What?"

"You apologize for doing your duty?"

Nathaniel West had started to show how relieved he was to have said what he felt he had to. While Belinda was beaming her delight that she had got her own way again. And Samantha was lost once more in some female fantasy about Adam Steele. The Virginian showed he was not entirely detached from his surroundings as he savored the aroma of the chicken that the butler had hauled up on a dumbwaiter—vented a low sound of disgruntlement at Edge's question and tone of voice.

"Now, Edge . . ." Belinda began.

"Really, Mr. Edge, I don't . . ." From Samantha.

"No, sir. Not as such. I mean—how I should have put it?—I should not have pulled a gun against you without—"

"As long as you don't do it again, Mr. West, I guess I won't have any cause to kill you."

"Goodness, Edge—"

"Well, really—"

"Sir, I invited you to my house so that my apology could have more substance than mere words and I would have expected you to have the decency to—"

Nathaniel West was no longer spluttering as he got into his stride, recovered from the shock of having an aspersion cast on his integrity and now deeply insulted by the implied threat to his life at his own supper table. But curtailed what he was saying as the half-breed rose slowly from this table with its starkly white cloth cover and fine silverware glinting in the candlelight.

In getting to his feet, Edge was careful to ease back his chair so that it did not tip over. And to drop his napkin on the warm plate the Negress had set down before him.

"Just need to say two things," he drawled as all of them looked up at him. "Me and the Reb, we had some time together a while back. Didn't make us friends. Just ain't enemies. Second thing, I don't need to stay in the house of a man who only asked me on account of his spoilt brat of a daughter told him—"

"Edge!" Belinda shrieked, and a tear squeezed from the corner of each of her big blue eyes.

"Well, really!" Samantha blurted out yet again.

Nathaniel West sprang to his feet, knocked his chair over backwards, and caused the suddenly terrified black girl to drop the salver of meat she was about to place in front of him.

"Quit your bawling and clean up the damn mess!" he snarled. And in the same tone, to Edge: "So get out of my house, sir! And you're more welcome to leave than to enter it! A man who would shoot to death another who is wounded and helpless!"

Belinda was wailing now, and beating her fists on the table as tears raced down her cheeks. Almost hysterical in her temper tantrum. The black girl was also crying, down on her hands and knees, piling the pieces of meat back on the salver while the butler rasped rebukes at her. Samantha had her hands over her ears and her eyes screwed tightly closed—her face drained of color as she tried to pretend none of this was happening. Adam Steele was impassive until West finished ordering Edge from his house. When he drew back his lips from his teeth to demand of the scowling, rasping butler:

"Lay off of her, mister! It wasn't her fault!"

The Negro was abruptly afraid, mouth and eyes wide and standing in a frozen attitude, as if literally petrified by the tone of the Virginian's voice and the look on his face.

"Please, Adam, at a time like this, how my household staff—"

It was a sound from beyond the room that caused Nathaniel West to curtail what he was saying now, as the half-breed swung away from the table to go to the double doorway.

A gunshot. From quite a long way off. Heard clearly because of the quietness of the town at night. And the fact that West's voice was the only sound within the room, Steele's censure having silenced the butler and the black girl while Belinda was sucking in air to power another barrage of wails.

But then the initial, isolated gunshot was followed by a

fusillade of others. Accompanied by a series of shouts. Then the beat of galloping hooves.

West barked at his daughter, "Quit that howling, girl!"

Edge pulled open both doors and glanced over his shoulder as he heard another chair thud to the carpet. And saw Steele was on his feet, grim faced and in the act of whirling from the table to head for the doorway.

"It sound like it's coming from the jailhouse, Reb." the half-breed guessed.

The scowl took a firmer hold on the features of the Virginian as he hurried by Edge, crossed the landing, and took the stairway two steps at a time. Down in the hall, he snatched his frock coat and hat from the stand and his rifle from where it leaned against the wall nearby. Wrenched open the front door and did not close it behind him after lunging out of the house. His footfalls sounded on the cement walk, then receded along the street.

The shooting was ended and nobody was shouting anymore. The beat of galloping hooves as at least three horses were hard ridden away from the south side of Stormville faded from earshot.

"Least I have the manners to say thanks and good night, feller," Edge said. Nodded to each daughter and added, "Ladies." Then went in the wake of the Virginian, but at a far easier pace.

The Wests and the servants all began to talk at once, in low tones that were for the most part rasping. The half-breed was down in the hall, his hat on his head and gunbelt slung around his waist—knotting the ties of the holster around his right thigh—when the banker bellowed:

"Just clean up the mess and have cook fix something else, I told you! And I told you girls to stay here and wait for me to come back!"

The doors of most of the houses along Stormville's high-class residential street were open, some with couples or entire families silhouetted on the thresholds. The more adventurous of the town's rich citizens had emerged from their houses and were on the street, hurrying toward the already thronged intersection.

"What is it, Nat?"

"It certainly is a troublesome evening for us, Mr. West!"

"You take care, you hear! It's Jonas Gale's job to take risks!"

"I've never known the like of it!"

"You think—"

"What—"

"Who—"

"Nathaniel—"

"Mr. West—"

The flabbily built banker hurried by the strolling Edge in a waddling run. The little derringer in his hand. He was sweating, breathless, and irascible. Swept his head from side to side as he roared, "How the hell do I know anything until I've checked it out?"

Edge rolled a cigarette and hung it unlit from a side of his mouth as he went on down the street and crossed an empty section of the midtown area to step up on to the sidewalk fronting the Rocky Mountain Hotel. There leaned against a roof support and lit the cigarette as he peered along the southern stretch of Stormville's commercial street. To where the crowd had gathered on an area out front of the church. A crowd that was noisy with questions and restless with movement as the people jostled for a better vantage point, the center of their attention the facade of a building that was set back a little from the street between the church and a livery stable.

Then the focus of interest was briefly directed elsewhere, when Adam Steele led a gray gelding out of the livery and swung up into the saddle. Heeled the horse forward and steered him across the intersection toward the front of the hotel where Edge stood.

The crowd returned to what had occupied them before, and became silent as a man began to address them. The voice of Nathaniel West could be recognized, although the sense of what he was saying did not carry to the hotel, where the half-breed said to the Virginian with a wave of his hand:

"Sounded like they went thataway, feller."

"There's nothing wrong with your hearing, Edge," Steele answered as he swung out of the saddle and hitched the reins to the hotel rail. "That's the way they went sure enough. Way I'll be heading soon as I get a few things from my room."

Several exclamations of shock sounded among the crowd who were listening to West in his capacity of deputy sheriff.

"You want to bed down in the hotel, Tom Grealy won't give you any argument about credit," Steele went on as he crossed the sidewalk and paused halfway through the batwing doors. "They jumped him as he was taking Walt King his evening meal. Shot him in the back. He died before he was properly through telling me about it."

"He see who they were?"

"Nick Conners and Bill Short."

The doors flapped closed and the Virginian's footfalls resounded against the walls of the empty saloon as he went to the rear and up the stairs. The crowd began to disperse from the front of the jailhouse and Joe Hart came down the street aboard his flatbed wagon.

The rich people, many as elegantly dressed as Nathaniel West and Adam Steele, turned left to go back to their homes and satisfy the curiosity of their families and neighbors. While the poorer citizens of Stormville—blacks, Latins, and Orientals for the most part—made a right turn to head for the crudely built and cramped shacks of the town's east side.

Edge remained where he was, smoking the cigarette and apparently oblivious to the many surreptitious looks directed at him from both sections of the community. The eyes that flitted briefly across his tall, lean, unmoving form expressing a gamut of emotions from mild reproach to loathing.

More footfalls on the stairway and then the floor announced that Steele was on his way out of the saloon. With his back to the batwing doors and his gaze impassively watching West as he approached the hotel, Edge said: "Seemed like a lot of people didn't like you before, Reb. Some of them look like they hate your guts now. And I'm tarred with the same brush."

The Virginian came through the doorway, having changed the frock coat for a more well used sheepskin coat, and his white hat for a gray one.

"We both brought trouble to town, Yank. I'll maybe see you if I'm back before the train comes through."

He stepped off the sidewalk, unhitched the reins from the rail, and swung astride his gelding. On the southern street, the Stormville mortician was loading the burlap-shrouded corpse of Tom Grealy on to his wagon, struggling under the weight and bulk of the big bartender's body.

"Adam?" West called, still breathless and sweating, as he hurried to cross the intersection before the Virginian could wheel his horse and heel him into the start of the trailing chore. "I'm told Grealy was alive when you reached the jail? And that he spoke to you?"

"It won't be law business until I recapture my prisoner and bring him back, Mr. West," Steele drawled evenly. Then snarled, when the incensed Stormville banker and deputy sheriff reached out to grasp the bridle, "Let it be or get dragged!"

West snatched his hand back. And complained with a motion of his head, "Adam. I might have expected that of him, but you? . . .

"The Reb's a bad loser, feller," Edge supplied. "Makes him testy."

"There's still five hundred dollars in the pot, Yank." He heeled the gelding into a walk. "Not lost until it's won."

"Seems to me that a King in the hole wasn't enough. And you lost to a pair of queens."

The irritable and confused Nathaniel West was ignored by both men as Steele looked back over his shoulder without reining in the horse, as a grin that matched the expression which had a tentative hold on Edge's features spread across his face.

And countered: "Least I didn't get off the gravy train."

Chapter Six

Adam Steele demanded and got a gallop from the gelding, and the pumping hooves of the horse raised an elongated cloud of spiraling dust across the intersection and down the center of the southern street.

Nathaniel West had swung around to go angrily back home by then. And Edge had turned to go through the batwing doors to enter the saloon. So it was only the red-headed, white-bearded Joe Hart who coughed on the dust as the Virginian rode by him. Then directed a string of rasping obscenities after him.

Beyond the town limits Steele eased his mount down to a much slower pace, and cursed the coldly grinning half-breed—then himself for allowing Edge to needle him. Felt even worse about giving in to the impulse that had caused him to race the horse out of Stormville, for no good reason. The gesture simply a safety valve for the ill temper the man had aroused in him.

The open trail curved gently from its start at the end of the street, veering from south to west around the hump of a thickly wooded hill. Then climbing steadily and quite steeply as the heights of the Rocky Mountains began in earnest.

There was just a mild breeze detectable against the flesh of his face, but the high and thin clouds were being scudded fast across the sky in a northeast to southwest direction. So that the moon was intermittently obscured or veiled. Which would have posed problems for the Virginian had it been necessary for him to seek signs of his quarry. But there was no need of this, for he knew exactly where Walt King and the two men who broke him out of jail were headed.

So all he had to look for—or sense in the manner of an animal preyed upon by others—was some sort of early warning of an ambush. In the event that King expected to be followed and

47

decided to remove the danger rather than try to outrun it. And watching, listening, and using his mysteriously developed sixth sense for a lurking threat came automatically to Adam Steele. Be he on a crowded, sunlit city street or riding alone along a nighttime mountain trail.

Thus his mind was free to roam and receptive to thoughts that he might wish remained locked in his subconscious.

He had been wrong when he spoke of not getting off the gravy train. For in leaving the West house and Stormville in a manner that made no allowances for the feelings of the father and two daughters, he had certainly ended a very comfortable and easy time. Maybe even the best, in terms of creature comforts and cultural elegance, since those times before the war that he had always taken for granted.

But at what cost?

A whole string of compromises, which is what that sonofabitch Edge had spotted right away. The Wests were not his kind of people. What kind of people were? Steele actually shook his head and vented a grunt of annoyance in the night as this notion sprang from out of the back recesses of his mind to threaten to sidetrack him.

The Wests, like so many of the families who lived on the high-class street of Stormville, were the new rich. Who had not yet learned to use their money in the proper manner, were more inclined to buy with it than spend it. And, the Virginian was forced to admit, they had bought him.

Samantha had seen him and wanted him. So Daddy had bought him. And he had allowed himself to be purchased. His price tag was comprised of having his credit underwritten by West in every business in town and being able to wine and dine on the best of everything amid the sophisticated splendor of the house at the end of the street.

In return, all he had to do was be an amusing escort for the dull-witted, halfway pretty, childishly infatuated daughter. Who he would not normally have looked twice at after tipping his hat to her.

He shook his head more vigorously and uttered a louder grunt of dissatisfaction with himself—and everybody else.

Hell, Edge was not the first to see the extent to which he

was humiliating himself for a taste of the finer things of life. Everyone in town, from Jeanne Grealy to maybe even Nathaniel West himself, had been aware of what he was doing.

Was he the only one who did not know what he was doing? He could hear now, like an echo, the words he spoke to Edge just before they entered the West house: *There's no way Ben Steele's son can put a value on the opportunity to sample the kind of life he used to live.*

Hell, that must have given the half-breed a charge. When he said it and during the start of the meal—as it became increasingly apparent that the cost of what he was enjoying was his self-respect.

He had a bad taste in his mouth and he spat a stream of saliva to the side. Which did not help. What was done was done and there was no way to eradicate the past. He had tried often enough, when the experiences had been far more harrowing than recent events.

The war. The lynching of his father. The killing of his best friend. Women worth a thousand Samantha Wests won and lost.

"Shit!" he said aloud, angry that his mind was on the brink of desperately dragging up anguished memories of the long ago. In a last-ditch attempt to crowd out thoughts of Stormville, the Wests, and the man called Edge.

If only it had not been the glinting-eyed, taciturn man who drew what heritage he had from a Mexican father and a Scandinavian mother. Who had the benefit of only basic schooling in the Iowa farming country where he was born and lived until the start of the war.

Who fought for the winning Union side.

Who made the rank of captain of cavalry.

Who had been the injured party in the horse-shooting incident through which they had first met.

Adam Steele never rose above the rank of lieutenant in the Confederate cavalry. And had been guilty of being a yellow bushwhacker on that blisteringly hot day in the Sierra Madres when Edge rode into his rifle sights.

Edge had a bigger frame than Steele and was consequently

stronger. Was maybe tougher because his life—at least the early, formulative years—had been harsher.

Shit, he thought, but did not speak aloud now, as he heard a horse whinny and reined his own mount to a halt. He was really reaching now for reasons to explain why he should feel the need to be on the defensive whenever the damn half-breed was around. Hell, it was almost as if he wanted to think himself as inferior to Edge.

This final disquietening thought on the subject came into and was rapidly ejected from his mind as the Virginian swung out of the saddle and slid the Colt Hartford from the scabband, as part of the same series of smooth movements. This as the scudding cloud left the new moon starkly clear against the black infinity and its blue-tinged light fell unobstructed over the foothills of the Continental Divide.

He was on the fringe of a stand of aspens that had once been far more extensive. Before a wide swath of the timber had been felled to provide land for a sugar plantation. Which stretched to north and south over a distance the Virginian was unable to judge, was limited about a mile to the west by a towering cliff face.

The crop had been allowed to run wild on the plantation, which had obviously not been worked for a number of years. Which was why the Virginian reacted as he did to the horse whinny from somewhere in the canebrake to the south. And led his gelding by the bridle now, the rifle canted to his left shoulder, index finger curled around the trigger and thumb resting on the hammer. Moving out from the timber and staying close to the twelve-foot-high wall of canes on the south side of the trail, which cut diagonally across the plantation toward the end of the escarpment that reared up to the west.

Perhaps a quarter of a mile out across the canebrakes, he smelled the smoke. This as a fresh layer of cloud was blown across the face of the moon. And a stronger gust of wind swayed the cane and neutralized the acrid taint he could no longer be certain he had detected.

In the almost pitch dark of the mountain night he was able to hear the eerie sounds of the canes being brushed against each other by the strengthening wind—but not his own footfalls or the thud of the gelding's shod hooves on the trail.

Another quarter mile—halfway across the overgrown and weed-choked plantation—and he reached the house and its outbuildings. Situated some fifty yards back from the trail and surrounded by a fence that was in a bad state of repair and which had fallen down in some places. Which probably meant the buildings were in a similar condition. But from the trail he could see them as no more than dark shapes against a dark back-drop. A single-story, flat-roofed house with taller, pitch-roofed barns flanking it, to form three sides of a square, the rear of the house facing inwards.

In the area between the fence and front of the house was a well and signs that there had once been a garden laid out. A former shade tree, scorched from a lightning strike and smelling of rot, lay leafless across the ground. Saplings were growing from around the stump.

The Virginian took in the general scene at a single glance, then concentrated his attention on a narrow strip of light that showed at the front of the house. Low down. A dull red glow. Firelight. Marking the crack at the base of the front door.

Against the rattle and rasp of cane on cane he caught the sound of a horse whinny again. The animal obviously disturbed by the wind and the effect it had among the high cane and perhaps the dilapidated timbers of the barn's construction.

The narrow line of light rose in intensity and faded as the fire was fanned and then bypassed by stray drafts of air that came and went from the room behind the door. A room which had no windows or windows that were securely boarded, for no other flicker of light showed in the dark facade of the house.

Steele thumbed back the hammer of the Colt Hartford but kept the barrel resting lightly against his shoulder as he led the gelding to a corner of the fence. Hitched the reins to a post and then moved along the trail to where the top section of a stretch of fence was broken and hanging. Swung a leg over it and stepped into the front yard, close to the top of the felled and rotting tree. He lowered the rifle now and fisted his right hand around the barrel as he advanced along the tree, on the side away from the house. Tensed to hurl himself down into the insecure cover of its decayed trunk at the first sign of a threat.

From its lightning-charred broken base he went with long strides to the well with its circular stone wall and roof held up by two posts. There was no rope wound around the winch and the handle was broken off.

The cloud passing in front of the moon thinned and disappeared. Very quickly, so that the bluish light became progressively but quickly brighter. The shadows deeper.

Far away, an animal roared at the moon. A mountain lion, maybe. Or an elk. Perhaps not an animal at all, but a sound effect of the wind moaning among a rock formation.

Whatever, it caused Steele to bob down and freeze in the cover of the three-foot-high well wall and roof support posts. A moment later he scowled at his own instinctive reaction to a noise that was harmless in itself and in terms of what made it. He was not normally so jumpy.

But he was not normally preoccupied with irrelevant side issues when he was engaged in a dangerous job—had only survived to the age he was by remaining totally single-minded in a situation such as this.

"Let's play a different game, Nicky!" Bill Short sang out from the area of the barn to the left of the houe.

"Let's do that, Billy!" Nick Connors agreed in the same gleefully excited tone.

"Like I Spy?"

"With My Little Eye!"

"Something beginning with A!"

"Adam!" Conners shrieked. "Adam Steele. It's Adam Steele, isn't it, Billy?"

There had never been a situation like this before. It had elements of a surreal nightmare as the two men who broke Walt King from the Stormville jailhouse called out to each other in shrill-voiced glee. Anouncing they were about to spring the trap into which the Virginian had so calmly ventured.

He crouched lower on his haunches as his eyes moved back and forth in their sockets. From the roof of one barn to the other—the house between not in sight because the well wall intervened.

The wind rustled among the canebrakes and moaned around corners of the three buildings.

King roared, "What the frig are you two crazy men yellin' about?"

There was the sound of the door being wrenched open as he finished the query. And Steele was aware of a larger outlet of firelight. Was about to risk a fast shot across the top of the well wall. But heard hoofbeats as a horse was galloped along the trail. From the east.

And he froze again, except to snap his head around and look back along the length of the fallen tree. Saw his horse still hitched to the corner fence post.

"Get back, Walt!" Short shrieked, suddenly grimly serious.

"It's Steele!" Connors added sounding panicky.

King blurted, "Shit" and slammed the door closed.

This simultaneously with the blasting of two rifle shots. Which directed bullets into the top of the well wall and showered Adam Steele with splinters and dust. Just as the horse raced into view on the trail—the rider crouched low in the saddle—was galloped the length of the front fence, and ridden out of sight beyond the tall cane to the west.

"Two of them!" Short yelled, and fired a wild shot toward the horseman.

Connors sent an equally useless bullet in the same general direction.

And Steele whirled on his haunches and lunged across the open ground to the stump and blackened, broken end of the tree. Heard the metallic sounds of repeater actions being pumped and both men cursing him as they saw his move. And they realized that in allowing themselves to be distracted by the rider, they had let the Virginian out of the trap of the isolated cover of the wall. Where he would have had to remain pinned down or been easy to hit when he made a run for it.

Now their anger with him and at themselves took control of them for a few frantic seconds. And they blasted a fusillade of shots at the tree, the bullets sending up a constant spray of decaying wood along the entire length of the trunk.

"Hold it!" Nick Connors shrieked. "Hold it, hold it, hold it!"

He was no longer firing his rifle and at the fourth attempt his command penetrated into the fevered mind of Bill Short.

Walt King demanded to know: "What the frig's goin' on out there? It sounds like the whole friggin' United States Army is hittin' us!"

"It's not just Steele out here, Walt!" Connors called back. "He's got a friend! Maybe the one he was with in the saloon."

"So friggin' do somethin' about the two of them!" King barked.

"We're not playing games anymore, Walt!" Short answered, sounding peevish.

"Cover me, Billy!" Connors ordered in a calm, even tone.

"You take care!" Short urged anxiously.

"Don't I always?"

Adam Steele lay on his side, curled up into a ball, in the cover of the solid tree stump. Grimacing as he peered down the length of the tree and saw how the volley of rifle fire had blasted through the rotten wood. Realized that if he had elected to seek the cover of the tree instead of the stump, he would probably have been hit. Knew for certain that he was not going to risk using the tree for cover in backing off from the dangerous buildings.

But the grimace was not entirely a visible sign of his response to a temporary lucky escape. He was also angry at himself again—for foolishly walking into the trap. For taking the bait of the firelight at the base of the door and assuming the three men were inside the house, resting up and warm, eating a meal or drinking coffee. Or maybe already fed and now sleeping.

Which was unlike the Virginian, who did not normally take anything for granted—especially not in a situation of potential lethal danger. Hell, there had not even been an instant when he sensed he was being watched before the first voice called tauntingly out of the night.

Then the mystery rider had shown up. Or was there anything mysterious about him? Steele did not think so. Nick Connors had almost got it right. It had to be that supercilious sonofabitch Edge. He was wrong to call him a friend, though. For the half-breed was nothing more than a pain in the ass. First screwed up the Virginian's peace of mind so badly he could not think the way he should in a life-and-death situation. And now he had showed up at the worst possible time to stress just how badly Adam Steele had been handling himself since the jailbreak.

When he should have ridden hell-bent for leather in pursuit of King and his rescuers. And not given Edge all the time in the world to get himself a horse and gear with which to pursue the pursuer. Which surely he would do, since he was only fifty cents short of being broke. And Walt King, free again, was five hundred dollars on the hoof to anybody who recaptured him.

When Steele reached this conclusion about the rider who had galloped past the house and his motives for being here, it strengthened his resolve to finish what he had started when he first found out he had been playing poker with a wanted man. And the grimace became a scowl of grim intention as he cleared his mind of all side issues. This as he eased himself around, careful to stay pressed close to the ground and out of sight of Short and Connors behind the tree stump.

Short, still in a barn, while Connors came out into the night, seeking to get close to Steele.

But from the front, either side, or by a circling movement to the rear?

Steele did not waste the nervous energy on straining to pick up some telltale sound that would warn of the direction of the man's approach. For the wind noises through the canebrake and between the buildings masked all but the loudest sounds. And Nick Connors would be going to great lengths to stay quiet until he was in a position to blast a killing gunshot at Steele.

The Virginian had gone through a 180-degree turn when Bill Short yelled:

"Nicky, what's that?"

Steele was also curious for a moment, as he heard the first of the crackling sounds that was louder than those of the wind. Then he caught the taint of smoke in the night air again, then saw it. And the dull glow of the flames that gave off the smoke. Was able to see this because in half completing the turn that would have faced him toward the front of the house, he was peering out over the yard surface to the west boundary fence and the constantly swaying sugar canes beyond.

"Shit, it's fire!" Connors shrieked.

And Steele snapped his head back and rolled his eyes to the extent of their sockets—to locate the man whose suddenly fear-filled voice revealed his position. Not so much out of the barn, as on it—held for a second in a rock-still attitude of being half in and half out of a hole on the pitched roof. His head turned in such a way that he was obviously looking at the the fire in the canebrake rather than at Steele.

But then the second was gone. And Connors snapped his head around to look down from his elevated vantage point at the Virginian—and saw him while Steele was completing his turn and struggling to aim his rifle.

Connors would have taken longer to draw a bead on his target—his rifle trapped under both hands as he made to haul himself out through the hole in the barn roof.

He knew this and so he went on the defensive. But shouted as he dropped back down through the hole: "The tree stump, Billy!"

Short's Winchester began to blast shots out of the other barn. And Steele pressed himself tight to the ground again. Eyes cracked almost closed by instinct against the flying splinters of wood. But open wide enough to watch the roof line of the other barn. Grimly aware that if Connors came up through the hole again, he would have a clear shot at the target while Short's barrage pinned him down.

Then the fusillade was over. Its end forced by the emptying of the repeater's magazine.

And Steele was ready for it. Was straining his hearing now, to pick out the dry click of a firing pin thrusting forward into an empty breech. He heard it. And grinned as a rasped obscenity from Short confirmed that the final live shell had been fired and its expended case had been ejected.

The Virginian pressed himself up on to all fours.

Short shrieked, "Get him, Nicky!"

Burning sugar cane could be heard crackling fiercely in the wake of the barrage of rifle shots. And the glow of the flames was no longer dull in the night to the west after the muzzle flashes of the shooting were curtailed.

Steele lunged into a dash across the yard, needing to hurdle the decaying tree trunk after the first two strides. He could hear both Short and Connors cursing. One as he fumbled to reload his empty rifle. The other as he raced to get into a position where he could get a clear shot at Steele.

The Virginian could not fail to be aware of both these men, and the danger of being shot dead by either of them, if he failed to gain the cover of the canebrake before a loaded rifle was aimed at his back and the trigger was squeezed. But he was more concerned by the threat posed by Walt King. Who had not yet taken a hand in the attempt to kill him. And who could have used the time since he slammed the door of the house to move secretly to any one of a hundred positions where he could aim and fire a gun at the running man.

And Edge?

It had to be the half-breed who started the fire. As a distraction which just happened to be of benefit to Adam Steele? Or purely to suit his own purpose. Which, if it was to capture and collect the reward on Walt King, would also have to entail killing the other contestant with the identical aim.

He plunged through a gap in the decrepit fence and crashed into the canes. Hurled himself to the ground as rifle shots cracked out and bullets made odd clicking noises through the tall vegetation.

"We get him?"

"I don't frigging know!"

"He fell down! I saw him fall down!"

"You wanna go see if he took the tumble himself or a bullet made him, Billy?" Connors snarled.

"Damnit, Nicky, don't get on to—"

"Or you wanna start worrying about that fire out there?"

"Oh, Jesus!"

Steele rose on to his haunches and turned to go back to the fringe of the canes. Used the barrel of the Colt Hartford to make a narrow gap through which he could see as much as he needed.

Which was the front of the house and the ends of the flanking barns. The house door securely closed while one of the big double doors of both barns stood slightly ajar.

Connors instructed, "Over here, Billy."

Steele rested his cheek against the side of the rifle stock and took aim on the doorway of the barn in which Short was hidden. He was surprised at how cool the rosewood of the stock felt to his face. And knew this meant that his flesh was sheened with the sweat of tension.

"Not the front way, Nicky!"

"Of course not the frigging front way!"

Steele eased his gloved index finger away from first pressure against the trigger. But continued to survey the facades of the buildings and an area of the yard in front of them along the barrel of the Colt Hartford.

Connors called: "You better get in here, Walt! Before long, there's not going to be anything left of this place but ashes!"

He was right.

The blue light of the new moon was providing hardly any of the illumination by which Steele could see so clearly now. For great palls of high-rising, wind-driven smoke were hiding the moon for most of the time while the roaring flames in the canebrake lit up the area that held his attention. Flames that were visible now as they raced through the tinder-dry canes, sending up showers of bright sparks that died in the air or started fresh fires ahead and to the sides of the main blaze.

King did not reply to Connors.

And for what seemed a very long time, as the heat pushed ahead of the flames made itself felt to Steele and oozed beads of fresh sweat from his pores, there were just the sounds of the raging fire and the wind that fanned it.

Then a horse snorted. But not in the barn. Out on the trail. Hooves beat at the ground. In the area where the Virginian had hitched his gray gelding to the corner fence post.

"Walt's running out on us, Nicky!" Short yelled from the barn with a hole in its roof.

"The sneaky sonofabitch!" Connors snarled.

Steele bared his teeth and vented a soft sound of fury. This as he used the rifle barrel to open a wider gap between the canes and altered the direction and focal length of his gaze.

Saw the familiar figure of Walt King astride the gelding, hunched low in the saddle as he thudded in his heels to demand and get a frantic, almost panicked gallop from the horse. Heading west along the trail, desperate to make it off the plantation before flying sparks set fire to the canebrake to the north.

But a greater danger to him than the threat of being encircled by ferociously blazing sugar cane was the Colt Hartford of Adam Steele. The muzzle of which sought to track to him and move fractionally ahead as he raced the stolen horse along the line of the front fence.

The set of the drawn-back lips altered from a snarl to a grin as the Virginian squeezed the trigger. But changed back again at the instant the shot cracked out.

For the man who should in another instant have been tossed off the horse with a bullet hole streaming blood from the side of his head veered to the right.

Not by accident. Nor as part of some evasive tactic against the threat of Adam Steele. Instead, to avoid colliding with the horse of another rider who had appeared out of the cane at the side of the trail. A rider who had his rifle out of the scabbard. But not to menace the escaping Walt King. Instead, aimed it across the firelit yard as he spoke a word to halt his mount. Aimed it from the shoulder with his face pressed to the stock, hat brim pulled low to make it even more difficult for his features to be recognized. But the length of his jet black hair, flying in the wind, made it certain in Steele's mind that the man was Edge.

"Get up!"

"Yeah, yeah!"

Two doors crashed open and more hooves thudded against hard-packed dirt as Connors and Short yelled the orders to their mount.

And Steele wrenched his head around in time to see the two men race their horses out of the barn. Angled toward him. Their rifles in the scabbards, but with revolvers aimed at him while they gripped the reins in their other hands. Their teeth and eyes glinted in the firelight as they expressed grins of delighted triumph. Sure of a kill after the shot had signaled

Steele's position to them. And now they could see him, as he thumbed back the hammer and swung the Colt Hartford toward them.

But they had looked away from the fleeing Walt King at the sound of the gunshot—a fraction of a second before they would have seen the other rider move into view.

The man astride the stationary horse fired his Winchester, pumped the lever action, and squeezed off a second shot. Just a sliver of time after Connors and Short fired their revolvers. And Adam Steele powered into a roll, choosing to try to evade the bullets of both men rather than risk being hit by one for the satisfaction of killing the other one.

He heard all four gunshots and felt the draught of air as a bullet came dangerously close to the side of his head.

Hooves continued to hit the dirt of the yard.

Steele completed the roll on his belly and again used the barrel of the rifle to open a gap between the canes. This as the fire reached the far side of the yard.

Nick Connors was slumped on the ground, his head twisted awkwardly to show that he had broken his neck after falling from his galloping horse. Blood was still oozing from a large and ugly exit wound in the center of his back. His horse leaped the fallen tree a full two seconds before the mount of Bill Short—this animal hampered by the weight of the man. Who had a foot trapped in a stirrup and was being dragged. Until the horse launched into the jump and the burden was wrenched free.

The man on the trail had moved his mount halfway along the front fence, away from where the fire started to die on the fringe of the canebrake, although it raged more fiercely than ever as the flames leapt the gap and took a hold on a barn. The loose horses went to either side of him as he slid the Winchester into the scabbard. Beyond him, the cane on the other side of the trail barred their way. And they turned east with high, snorting rears. To bolt away from the stink of smoke and charred earth.

The man cupped his hands around his mouth and roared: "Hey, Reb, if you're still in the land of the living, best you get the hell out of there! Way things are hotting up!"

"Maybe we should both hang around here and save the Devil a job," the Virginian rasped as he got to his feet and stepped out of the canes.

Edge saw him, touched the brim of his hat, and set his mount moving. Eastwards, in the wake of the two runaways. But slowly, with a hand gesture that invited Steele to ride double with him. But the Virginian had other ideas. And instead, he hurried in another direction—going into the barn with the wide-open doors out of which Connors and Short had burst to meet their sudden and violent ends.

The half-breed reined in his mount and watched impassively. Saw in the bright firelight that Adam Steele showed no sign of being hurt. So was thinking rationally and therefore had a good reason for entering the barn. Which would shortly go the same way as the other one as the fire raced through the cane at the rear of the buildings.

A horse snorted in there.

And Edge was struck by the same thought that had hit Steele earlier. That Walt King had stolen the gray gelding, so his own mount—the one on which he had ridden from Stormville—had to still be here.

The Virginian emerged from the barn astride a black horse, his Colt Hartford jutting from the forward-hung scabbard. Seated in a saddle that must already have been on the animal, for only a few seconds elapsed between him going in and coming out of the barn.

Now Edge heeled his horse into a canter along the trail that led off the eastern side of the plantation. Looked back over his shoulder once and saw Steele halted astride the black horse. Peering westward toward the cliff face that was no longer visible through the flames and smoke now that the canebrakes on both sides of the trail were burning. Moments later heard the beat of hooves behind him as the Virginian headed off the plantation in the only way open.

The half-breed was dismounted and lighting a cigareete in the stand of timber to the east of the plantation when Steele reached him. Reined in his fresh horse and said flatly:

"Careful what you do with the match, Yank. Reckon you've done enough damage for one night."

Edge blew out a stream of smoke and the tiny flame died as the night continued to be lit by the fires raging across the canebrakes.

"You look to be burning a whole lot slower than the sugar, feller."

"Am I supposed to jump for joy?" Steele countered, gazing stoically out across the blazing plantation.

Edge shrugged his shoulders. "It seemed to me you were in a tough spot out in front of the house."

"I was doing fine," Steele lied.

"With two of them dead and one on the run, there's no way we can go through it again. Oh yeah, and pretty soon there won't be any house and tree and—"

"I can go around the fire or I can wait for it to die, Edge. Whichever, I plan to bring in Walt King again. Be grateful if you'd attend to your own business now."

"That's you, Reb."

"What?" The Virginian snapped his head around to peer down at Edge, perplexed.

"Your lady friend was worried about you. And her pa staked me to what I needed to come out here and—"

"The Wests paid you to trail me?"

"In advance, in cash and kind." The half-breed ran a hand over the neck of the bay gelding, the horse saddled with a Western rig hung with all the necessary accoutrements for a long ride. And grinned, exposing his white teeth but not injecting any warmth into the glinting slits of his eyes. "It was a hard decision for them to make. Seeing as how they don't like me too well. Even the kid sister now. But there wasn't anybody else. Which is what the big sister thinks about you."

The Virginian grimaced as he was reminded about Samantha West and how he had used her infatuation with him to indulge his liking for luxury.

The half-breed, the cold-eyed grin still in place, glanced at the burning sugar cane and drawled, "Just tried to spread a little sweetness and light, Reb."

Steele sent a globule of saliva at the ground. And growled: "Which leaves me bitter and in the dark, Yank."

Chapter Seven

"About what, feller?"

"Why you let King ride right around you and off the plantation?"

"He was no danger to me nor you right then. His buddies looked set to blast you into hell and there was only time to see they didn't do that."

"West must have paid you well, Edge."

"A little cash plus the mount and gear and supplies."

"That all? And you let a man worth five hundred dollars back in Stormsville ride on by you?"

The cold grin had been replaced by impassiveness several moments ago. Now an expression that came close to a snarl twisted the mouthline and gave a more intense light to the glint in the narrowed eyes. "You know me better than that, Steele."

"I do?" the Virginian countered, unafraid of the taller man's attitude. And showing an expression that approached a smile, as if he relished provoking anger.

"I'm no thief. King belongs to you."

Steele nodded, acknowledging his agreement with Edge on both counts. Then gave the smile freedom to spread across his face as he said, "And the longer you have to take care of me, the more money you'll earn?"

"Guess so."

"Which means it's in your interest for King to stay on the loose and for me to track him?"

"Until the next westbound train comes through Stormville."

"Then we better get after him. Around to the south of the property looks the fastest way."

"After you, Reb," Edge said, and flicked his still-glowing cigarette butt into the fringe of the cane. Its red embers died in midair but soon the cane would be burned to charred stubble by the fire that moved inexorably across the plantation. In an hour maybe, unless the wind strengthened or changed direction. He swung up into the saddle.

Steele did not move on ahead. Instead, watched him and waited until he had moved the bay gelding up beside his black mount. Then, as both men heeled their horses off the trail and along the grassy strip between the timber and the canebrake, the Virginian asked, "How much cash did West pay you?"

Edge grinned. "You don't strike me the kind of feller who cares how much value somebody puts on—"

"I'm not," Steele cut in impatiently. "I've got good reason for asking, in the event King makes it to Silver Pass."

"They have a toll there?"

"They have a town there."

"So we don't have to look for a sign of where we pick up the trail to the west?"

"You have it."

"Twenty dollars. Prepared to make you a loan. Providing it ain't to buy any more fancy threads."

He glanced at Steele, who was wearing an old sheepskin coat and black hat. So that only the pants of his suit and the riding boots from his recently purchased new outfit were visible— showed signs of their rough treatment in his abortive attempt to recapture Walt King.

The Virginian scowled briefly and asked, "So I made a mistake? Are you right all the time?"

"No, feller. The older I get the more things I do wrong, seems to me. That older and wiser saying I heard so much way back doesn't seem to apply to somebody in my business."

"Anybody in our business isn't wise at all to ride into Silver Pass, from what I hear about that town."

"I never heard of it."

"Me neither, until I was on the trail of Walt King that first time. When I was told I had to catch up with him before he reached Silver Pass. Or I'd lost him until the next time he came out into the open."

"An outlaw town?"

They had reached the southern extent of the plantation and veered to the west. Pulled up their neckerchiefs to mask their mouths and nostrils from the smoke that the wind was gusting toward them. For a long time, until they were beyond the fire and skirting a vast area of blackened ground where just wisps of smoke rose here and there from smoldering debris, they had to concentrate all their attention on watching where they were going while astride horses that were strange to them. The animals constantly on the brink of panic as they snorted and quivered and tossed their heads in response to the smoke-thick air they sucked into their lungs.

The atmosphere alongside the vast area of burned-out cane-brake was bad to smell, but largely clean of smoke. And the horses became calm.

"Two towns in effect," Steele answered the question posed several minutes earlier, after he and Edge had removed the masks of their neckerchiefs. "Called North Pass and South Pass. King runs North Pass."

"Runs it?"

"That's what he claimed when I was bringing him in to Stormville. Threatened there would be all kinds of dire things happen to me when his men found out he was in jail and came to break him out."

"You mean you could've been raped by those two fellers if I hadn't? . . ."

The half-breed allowed the sardonic comment to hang unfinished in the acrid, tainted air when he saw that Steele was gazing off to the right, listening with little interest, if any at all.

And he peered in the same direction.

Saw that the flames were far to the east now. And the moon was again the predominant light source although still thinly veiled by the straggling, wind-scudded cloud. What it showed in the area the two riders surveyed was the scorched canebrakes with, close to their center, the fire-blackened heaps of rubble that were the remains of the house and barns. With a partially crumbled stone chimney pointed skywards like some simple memorial marker. But not to the memory of the two dead men who were sprawled nearby. Instead, to the folks who might still be alive, who had put so much time and sweat into establishing the plantation. Before circumstances caused them to abandon it.

"Looks kind of familiar, uh?"

"To you too?"

They knew a considerable amount about each other's backgrounds from their first meeting.

"Our place was a lot smaller."

"Ours was a great deal larger."

"But I got the money now."

"I'm not boasting!" Steele snapped, and wrenched his gaze away from the scene of fire destruction to see if the half-breed was scowling at him. And saw that the lean, deeply lined face was impassive.

"You figure King might have been?"

The Virginian quelled the threat of rising anger. "I didn't pay much attention to what he said. But Connors and Short did fine, despite what they were. Maybe better than a whole army of regular gunslingers could have."

"King's still free," Edge agreed, and did not pursue the point—irrespective of whether or not he was influenced by the suspicious sidelong glance Steele shot at him. Asked: "What about South Pass?"

"Story is it's run by a man named George Blood. Who, so everybody seems to agree, is the hardest man that was ever born."

"Everybody including King?"

"That's true. Walt King reckons Blood is full of bullshit. Only thing that seems to be certain is that the folks who live at Silver Pass are either North or South Pass people. There's no traffic between the two, except by strangers who go into the area without knowing the situation. Enough people told me that as hearsay. And King confirmed it's true."

They were beyond the western boundary of the burned-out sugar plantation now and needed to swing northward for a while. Riding along the rim of a deep ravine until they reached the trail around the end of the cliff. Where the ravine took a right-angle turn and the trail dropped down into it on a steep incline. It was wooded and darkly moon shadowed at the bottom of the sheer-sided trough.

There was a break in the talk until they were back on the trail and starting to ride down the slope, when Steele asked, "You happen to see if King was armed, Edge?"

"If he was carrying a gun, he wasn't advertising it, feller."

"He boasts that he never has killed anybody, so claims he has to be innocent of some of the charges against him. Reckons he has men to do his killings, so doesn't need use a gun himself."

Both riders raked the murky depths of the ravine with narrow-eyed care as the clop of hooves on the trail echoed off the confining walls.

"You don't believe him?"

"It doesn't matter, Edge. I just don't want to get shot to prove he lied."

Their voices resounded between the rock faces. And after this they engaged in another verbal silence for a long time. Watching and listening and testing the feel of the atmosphere until the echo of clopping hooves was curtailed. Each man riding with both hands on the reins, but with the right wrist resting on his thigh—inches from and ready to reach for the jutting stock of his scabbarded rifle. Tensed behind a surface calm, to lunge off his horse in a defensive move should the situation call for it. Afraid and not ashamed to be so. Experienced in controlling fear and using it to hone instinct and reaction.

The ravine petered out by the flanking rock faces splaying outwards and diminishing in height. This at the base of a broad, rocky slope that the trail conquered by zigzagging in a series of sharp turns.

"He sure didn't have a rifle, feller."

"Wasn't carrying a gun when I braced him."

They had reined in their horses at the start of the first stroke of the rising zigzag: Edge to roll a cigarette and Steele to drink from a canteen. Both eyeing the broad, high, steep slope impassively, knowing they would be safe from surprise attack by a man with a handgun until they neared the distant ridge.

The Virginian finished drinking, but the half-breed was still making the cigarette.

"You know how far to where we're headed, Reb?"

"A day's ride from Stormville is what I was told."

"A pass between what?"

"Two army forts that were abandoned years ago."

"You were told?"

Steele eyed Edge suspiciously in the flare of the match flame as the cigarette was lit. But the set of the half-breed's face did not imply criticism.

"On this trail?"

"That's right. And I was told it, Yank."

Edge nodded. "No sweat, feller. It sounds like a real interesting place to visit. Just that I didn't want to miss my train looking for a place your ex-prisoner dreamed up. And sold to a whole lot of other people you happened to come across. After King had passed through."

"A day's ride if a man doesn't sit around admiring the view. Or thinking up reasons not to go on."

The half-breed spat a flake of tobacco off his lower lip and growled, "*Touché*, Reb."

"French yet, Yank?" Steele answered as both men heeled their geldings up the slope.

"Maybe because I can't bring myself to say anything good about you in American, Reb."

"I noticed that, Yank. *Merci*."

"Forget it."

"Now I've said it, I intend to."

It took them almost three hours to reach the ridge, including two rest periods of about ten minutes each for the horses. And another two hours elapsed before they reached a point from which they were able to see their objective.

The first gray light of the new day was streaking the sky by then, as they rode out of the thick timber that totally draped the flat top of the extensive expanse of high ground they attained by climbing the zigzag trail. They halted at the side of what had once been a fort.

All that remained of the military post now was part of the stockade wall and the foundations of some buildings. These spread on the grassy crest of a long, gently sloping hill that was the southeastern side of a broad valley. The northwestern side, several miles distant but clear to see in the as yet unhazed light of the false dawn, was much higher and of solid rock, with drifted snow among its serrated ridges.

Some five miles to the north, the rock face began to curve

eastward, and lose some altitude. Then the ground fell sharply away before it reared up again, leaving what surely had to be Silver Pass as the only way out of the northern end of the valley.

The area at the high point of the pass was as desolate looking as the elsewhere along the ridges of the valley sides. But below this, on the trail that snaked up from out of the bottom land, was a small town. With the trail as its main street and several other streets spurring off and dead ending to either side.

No breakfast fires had yet been lit in South Pass, so there was no smoke to smudge the crystal clear air. And individual details of the town could be clearly picked out if the two men dismounting from their horses on the site of the old fort had been inclined to study the far off clusters of buildings.

But instead, as they ate a cold breakfast from the supplies in the half breed's saddlebags—those on the horse left by Walt King were empty—both Edge and Steele scanned the terrain closer to hand. Searching for the escaped prisoner riding the Virginian's horse.

They saw nothing that moved out on the trail or the rocky, spartanly featured ground spread to either side of it. Until the sun rose above the south-eastern rim of their world and the shadows began their regular slow crawl to mark the passing of time.

"Either he's been riding like a bat out of hell or he knows another way to North Pass from the south, Steele."

The Virginian nodded and yawned. And Edge, like he had been waiting for the other man to be first to show a sign of weariness, fisted grit from his eyes.

"One thing's certain, Edge."

"What's that?"

"If or when he makes it to North Pass, he'll stay there. For a while."

"There never was any rush."

"Except for you to catch the next train west from Stormville."

"If I go into that town as beat as I am and it's as tough as you say, it could be the train time won't matter."

"I'm happy for breakfast to be supper, Edge."

"And I could use a whiskey, but I never drink hard liquor until after midday."

"That'll be plenty long enough for me."

Each of them drank water from a canteen and then led his horse back into the timber. Steele, in the cover and shade of the trees, angled off the trail to the left. Edge went to the right. Then, out of sight one another beyond trees and brush, each could hear the small sounds made by the other in bedding down his horse and then himself. Unknowingly imitated each other in almost everything they did. Even to the extent of covering his face with his hat and sharing the shelter of his bedroll blankets with his rifle.

Then a pastoral quiet settled over the forest, the silence broken only by the bird calls and the scurrying sounds of small animals after these living things had accepted the intrusion of the two men into their world.

Men who breathed regularly in a shallow level of sleep that rested and refreshed them, but allowed them to be ready for immediate waking, total recall, and instant reaction if their instincts should warn of danger close by.

But Adam Steele woke up simply because he had slept as long as he needed. And it was the sounds he made in preparing to complete the journey to Silver Pass that roused Edge.

They did not communicate until they both emerged from the timber at the top of the grassy hill where the army post had once been situated. When the sun was an hour short of its noon zenith. About the time it would take them to ride easily down into the valley, along its bottom, and up to the South Pass section of the town that was now veiled by slickly shimmering heat haze.

Each man had used canteen water to wash off old sweat and trail dirt, but had not shaved. Just the dark-colored shirt was stretched taut over the half-breed's torso. The Virginian wore the many-colored vest over his lace-trimmed white shirt.

"Morning, Reb."

"And to you, Yank."

The heels of their spurless boots set the geldings to moving along the side of the former fort's crumbled wall and then down into the valley as the eyes and ears of the riders watched and listened for danger signs while the attitudes of the men seemed to suggest they were totally indifferent to their surroundings—and each other.

Steele asked suddenly, "Samantha West need to twist her pa's arm very hard to hire you, Edge?"

"I wouldn't know, feller."

"What do you know?"

"That I was in the saloon, getting close to the last of my fifty cents. Listening to your earlier lady love complaining about how everybody in Stormville is either stinking rich or stinking poor. Her father being shot dead didn't seem to bother her much."

"You've got it wrong, Edge. Jeanne Grealy's a whore and her father was also her pimp. They had me lined up as a customer before Samantha West put out for free."

The half-breed had rolled a cigarette and now he shot the Virginian a sidelong glance as he touched his tongue to the gummed strip of the paper. "For free?"

Steele grimaced. "All right, Edge. You showed me what kind of a sonofabitch I was for using Samantha's interest in me to get more than a share of her bedclothes. And I thanked you for it last night."

"You did? And I figured you were grateful for having me save your life." There was just a hint of mockery in Edge's tone. But then he added evenly: "Anyway, it was pretty plain to see I was being hired against the old man's will. And the kid sister was still smarting from me calling her a spoilt brat. But that was all to do with me. I'd say the only thing they hold against you is knowing me from another place."

"Grateful for the information."

Now Edge lit the cigarette with a match he struck on an outcrop of rock as he rode by it. Said: "I guess it wouldn't take hardly any effort at all for you to get your feet back under the West table again. Or your ass into the big sister's bed. Just for you to knock on the door could do it, maybe."

"The poor have just as many faults as the rich, Edge. And I've been long enough on both sides of the line to know. The good was more than the bad while it lasted—and even looking back on it. And I like West well enough not to want to think that he was simply indulging one of his daughters again when he hired you."

"Like I told you, feller," the half-breed answered sourly. "Only so far as it was me he had to hire. Because there was nobody else in town who wanted the job."

They rode off the slope and on to the level trail that followed the curve of the valley along the bottom land. And each man automatically took it upon himself to keep careful watch on the half circle of rugged terrain that the heat haze allowed him to scan on his side of the trail.

It was Edge who ended the long silence.

"Getting married, buying a store, and settling down for a while in that small town did more harm than good feller. Just because it all ended, I guess."

"Like you and your wife and the place you farmed in the Dakotas, uh?"

"Too long ago, Reb. I can remember it. Can't recall too much about how I was after it was over, though. Not that it matters. Different people do different things in different ways. In every kind of different circumstance."

"Especially at different ages, Yank."

"Figure that's true."

"Isn't it said there's no fool like an old fool?"

Edge showed a half smile around the cigarette angled from the side of his mouth. An expression that, like always, injected a brighter glint but no warmth into the blue cracks of his eyes. "One thing's for sure, Reb. I can't take too much of people crying on my shoulder. Danger of rheumatics setting in." His thin lips closed and compressed tightly for a moment before he added in a rasping tone, "At my age."

"Is that what I've been doing?" the Virginian asked, concerned and surprised.

"Getting to sound like a sob story, feller."

Steele shrugged, then grinned as he countered, "And an old one."

Chapter Eight

For a long time after the heat haze had retreated up the slope at the end of the valley—above and beyond the town—the terrain below the pass kept the buildings hidden from the approaching riders.

This because the streets of South Pass were laid out on a broad plateau, like a giant step down from the gap between the ridges, and the trail had to be followed to the rim of the level area before the town could be seen.

A ghost town was the immediate impression of each man as he got his first glimpse of the place. Which took no account of what Adam Steele had been told about it. Which was immaterial, since neither man ever trusted without question his first impression of anything—or anybody.

There was dust and rubble, neglect and decay. Broken glass and warped timber. Leaning walls and sagging roofs. Holed sidewalks and cracked awnings. Peeled wash and bubbled paint. Fallen fences and collapsed archways. The whole creating an atmosphere of melancholy desolation made to look the more mournful because of the bright glare the midday sun shed on it.

Then a small sound was heard.

And Edge and Steele reined in their geldings and each moved a right hand as they swung their heads to look fixedly to the right. But Edge did not draw the Frontier Colt from its holster and Steele let the Colt Hartford rifle remain in the scabbard. Neither man withdrew his hand, though.

As the sound came again and again and again. To be recognized long before the chime of the pocket watch struck for the twelfth and final time, and a man showed himself, holding the watch in the palm of his left hand. While in his right was an

73

army Remington aimed only negligently in the general direction of the two new arrivals.

A tall, thin man of about fifty. With dirt-ingrained skin and matted red hair. Dressed only in ragged pants and a broad-brimmed hat that hung down his back. His ugly feet were as bare as his prominently boned torso. He had stepped out of the doorless entrance of a stone shack.

"If you aim that gun at this feller, you better kill him right off," Steele said evenly as the man pushed the watch into a pocket and the childlike grin at hearing the chimes left his face.

"It's usually me who gives the one warning," Edge growled as the man switched his gaze from one stranger to the other and back again.

Then the skinny shoulders were shrugged and the juvenile grin took hold of the emaciated features again. This as the hand fisted around the Remington's butt dropped to his side and the gun was aimed down at the ground.

"Two more tough guys, uh?"

"Not tough enough to survive a well-placed .45-caliber bullet, feller," Edge answered with his face still impassive. "Which is why I object to having a gun aimed at me."

"Nor tough enough to stay alive after gettin' your neck stretched, I'll bet!" He tipped his head hard to the side so that it rested on a naked shoulder. Then pushed his tongue out and widened his eyes so that they bulged. Giving his impression of a hanged man. Then he vented a shrill, demented-sounding laugh. Which he abruptly curtailed as hoofbeats hit the street at the far end of town. To sneer: "What's done to dirty bounty hunters in this place. You guys think you're tough? Well, you come to the toughest town there is."

Now his voice had the same ring of madness that had been heard in his laughter, as he turned and looked toward the advancing riders, grinning again.

Edge and Steele were already peering along the street, right hands still close to the jutting stocks of their scabbarded rifles. Having reacted with no more than the briefest exchange of impassive glance when the crazy man revealed that the punishment he had enacted was reserved especially for one particular crime in South Pass.

Now, out of the side of his mouth, his lips hardly moving at all, Edge asked, "You sure you didn't mix up the north and south side of this town, Reb?"

"I'm sure, Yank," Steele replied in the same low tones. "Sure as I am that this isn't the kind of place I'd like to hang around in."

"We ain't really been branded yet. Let alone roped. Maybe some talk?"

"All right. But not until we're blue in the face."

"And got sore throats."

They did not shift their right hands and during the exchange had not relaxed their watch on the four men who were riding at an easy pace along the street toward them. Big, powerfully built, hard-faced, and mean-eyed men. Dressed in dark-hued, well-worn work clothing. Each with a gunbelt slung around his waist and a scabbard hung from his saddle. A revolver and rifle nestling in its respective scabbard.

The horses they rode were big and strong and well schooled. Their shoes sounded good and their coats looked in fine condition. Thus did the geldings have a better appearance than the unwashed and unshaved riders who were as unkempt and smelled as bad as the crazy man with the chiming watch. Their body stink not detectable to the nostrils of Edge and Steele in the unmoving, very hot air of early afternoon until they reined in their mounts some fifteen feet in front of the newcomers. On the center of the street between the crazy man's shack on one side and the standing rear wall and a pile or rubble that had been a larger building on the other.

"Trouble, Elmer?" the oldest—at fifty—of the quartet asked dully and like his partners did not shift his unblinking gaze off Edge and Steele.

Not one of them had a hand closer than the strangers to his gun, but all looked confident of winning a lethal fast-draw contest if this was what was called for.

Elmer noisily worked some saliva up from his throat. And spit it out in a foul-colored stream. Answered bitterly: "Hell no, Mr. Baxter. Just another couple of tough guys like the rest of you. Nothin' I couldn't handle on my own. There ain't no

point me standin' guard out here unless I'm trusted to take care
of things when strangers show up. Why, I might just as well—"

"You've supposed to send word to the hotel, Elmer," Baxter cut in with a sigh. "You been told time and time again.
Soon as you see anyone out in the valley, you keep watchin'
them and you send your woman to the hotel to let us know."

Elmer was suddenly shamefaced and Baxter sensed his change
of mood and now looked at him to ask bitterly, "Not this one,
too?"

"She wouldn't do like I told her!" Elmer came back quickly,
on the defensive. "I only wanted to beat up on her a little.
Teach her how a guy has to be obeyed. Must've been sickly, I
reckon."

Baxter sighed again. Instructed, "Go bring her out, Elmer."
And when the again crestfallen man turned to go into the
shadowed interior of the shack, switched his attention back to
Edge and Steele. Asked, "You men mind tellin' me your
names?"

"Edge."

"Adam Steele."

"Edge? Just like that? Nothin' else?"

"Not for a lot of years, feller."

Baxter had taken a dog-eared book from a shirt pocket and
was flipping through the pages. He paid particular attention to
two of them and then vented a grunt of satisfaction when he
pushed the book back into his pocket.

This as Elmer backed out of the shack, stooped and breathing heavily as he dragged a burden from the shade into the
harsh glare of the sun.

"Your business ain't our business, mister. Unless its manhuntin'.
For the law. With a badge or a wanted flyer in your pocket.
Ain't neither of your names on the list, but that don't mean
you're clean. So watch yourselves while you're in South Pass.
Because everyone here'll sure be watchin' you."

Temporarily, this was not true. For, the caution having been
given, all four South Pass men ignored the two newcomers to
look down at the burden Elmer had dragged from the shack.

An Indian girl whose age would have been difficult to
determine had she not been naked. For her face had been badly

beaten, the flesh swollen by contusions and caked with dried blood from many cuts. From the way in which one of her arms lay in the dust after Elmer let go of her, it was broken. The blood had not yet started to show that it was settling at the low points in her body, and she was still limp. So had not died long ago.

Her breasts had just been beginning to form and there was not yet any hair on her body when the crazy man killed her. So she was very young. A child even.

"You handle it, Ed," Baxter instructed "You guys want to give me your guns?"

The blond-haired South Pass man at the end of the line closest to the pathetically dead Indian girl unhooked the lariat from his saddle horn and tossed the noosed end to Elmer. Who, in what was obviously a chore that was not new to him, inserted the arms and head of the corpse through the noose. And tightened the honda to her chest with the rope under her armpits.

"Mr. Blood got anymore he don't want?" Elmer asked.

"I'll see him about it, Elmer," Baxter promised, as Ed wheeled his horse away from the line and began to drag the corpse along the street like it was a diseased cow destined for the lime pit. "How about it, you guys? One of the few laws we got in this town. Strangers ain't allowed to keep their guns until they ain't strangers no more. They don't obey that law, they die strangers. It's all the same to me and these boys."

"And me," the crazy man added with a harsh laugh, his hand draped over the gun butt that jutted from his pants waistband at his belly.

"And Elmer," Baxter allowed.

"What d'you think, Steele?"

"I think I'd prefer to die in a town where they treat their dead better than here, Edge."

And both men slid the rifles from the scabbards. Slowly, and gripping them loosely around the narrowest parts of the stocks. Behind the trigger guard of the Colt Hartford and the lever of the Winchester.

Edge turned his to the side and tossed it forward toward the youngest of the South Pass men. Who reached out lazily to catch it. While Baxter and the other mounted man gazed fixedly at Adam Steele, suspicious because he continued to keep a hold on his rifle.

"Here, Elmer," the Virginian drawled and leaned to the side, turning the rifle so that its stock was toward the crazy man. "It's important to me and I wouldn't want anyone to drop it."

Elmer looked to Baxter for guidance and received a nod. Went to take the Colt Hartford from Steele and was attracted by the sun-glinting gold plate screwed to the right side of the fire-scorched rosewood stock.

"Fancy gun, Mr. Baxter," he said as he gave the rifle up to the mounted man. "Got writing on it."

Baxter read aloud the inscription on the stockplate as Edge eased his revolver from the holster and tossed this in the same direction as the Winchester. The young man thrust out another hand in a similarly lazy manner to catch the Colt as cleanly as the Winchester.

"To Ben Steele, with gratitude, Abraham Lincoln."

"Benjamin P. Steele," the Virginian corrected.

"Yeah, okay. So why d'you call yourself Adam?"

"Thought I heard you say my business wasn't your business, feller?"

"Ben was his father," Edge supplied. "The rifle's all he had left to leave him when he died. The reason it's so important to him."

Baxter shrugged. "I was just curious. Like I say, just don't step outta line in South Pass and you'll be welcome here long as your money holds out."

He turned his horse around and the men flanking him did the same. Then all three started back along the street in the wake of Ed dragging the beaten-to-death Indian girl.

"Don't forget to ask Mr. Blood, Mr. Baxter!" Elmer yelled. "About a new woman for me."

"And don't you forget to send word to the hotel if anyone else shows in the valley," came the growled reply.

Steele drawled, "I can talk for myself, Yank. About my pa's gun or anything else."

"Me, too, Reb. About aiming a gun at me or anything else."

Along the street, a gun had been drawn. By Ed, who aimed it high to the side after reining his horse to a halt in front of a church with a bell tower.

The report of the gunshot and the clang of the bullet striking a bell that sounded cracked reached the south end of the street in unison. The strangers to town did not hear the door in the arched porch at the base of the tower open. Nor any words spoken from the threshold.

But Ed said dully: "Another one for burial, padre. Nothing fancy. She was a heathen."

A tall man in a much-the-worse-for-wear cassock came out on to the street and dropped on to his haunches. Loosened the lariat noose from around the Indian girl and then picked her up with both arms as Ed re-coiled the rope. Then fell in with the other three riders, who had caught up with him.

The padre, who was old, with a crinkled face and a ring of gray hair around the crown of his head, looked long and hard down the street and then swung around and carried the corpse into the church. He was trembling, perhaps sobbing.

Elmer spat some more yellow-stained saliva into the arid street surface and muttered: "Stupid bitch of a squaw wouldn't do nothin' but lay out flat on her back! A guy gets bored with that!"

"Yeah, feller," Edge agreed. "Like they say, variety is the spice of life. Maybe you didn't make the position clear to her?"

"Uh?" the crazy man grunted, perplexed.

But first Edge and then Steele had moved their horses forward and Elmer was left to peer at their backs as they allowed the geldings to set their own easy pace along the street. Then, before he swung angrily around to reenter the shack and resume his watch on the heat-shimmered valley curved to the south, he yelled:

"You guys see George Blood, you mention about a woman for me! Pretty damn quick! Seein' as how I won't be able to watch the necktie party!"

Nobody lived anymore in the tumbledown houses between the end of the street and the church. For they had dust piled by the wind against their doors or heaped inside where the doors were missing. And some had untrampled weeds growing as high as their roofs against the side walls.

The church was on a corner of a derelict side street, and as the two strangers to town rode across the intersection they could see the cemetery out back. A large area of irregular shape with a great - many graves spread across it without symmetrical design. Close to the rear wall of the church a man was digging a fresh grave. And was too far advanced with the chore for the hole to be for the burial of the Indian girl.

The man interrupted his labors and looked across at the intersection with a toothless grin when he heard the clop of hooves. And called, "Hey you guys, how you doin'?"

"Lot better than the feller you're digging that for," Edge answered.

"Whole lot," Steele added.

The gravedigger vented a throaty laugh. "You'll understand if I don't say to take care of yourselves?"

They rode on by, out of the man's range of vision and heard his shovel start to bite into the dirt again. Then had their attention captured by a louder sound. Reined their mounts to a halt and snapped their heads to gaze to the right. Just as when the first chime of Elmer's pocket watch had struck. But they were intensely aware of their surroundings—and their circumstances within them. So were able to restrain the instinct to thrust their hands toward guns that were no longer where they should be.

Which would have been unnecessary, anyway.

For the sudden sound was nothing more than that of the double doors of the church being kicked open. By the tall, thin, elderly, trembling, and tearful preacher in the badly torn and heavily stained cassock. Who stood on the threshold of his church, shaded by the arched porch from the glare of the afternoon sun. Holding in his arms the now blanket-shrouded corpse of the Indian girl. And as they looked at him, he extended his arms to their full stretch, presenting the body as the reason for the grief that was deeply inscribed into every line of his crinkled face and clearly seen in the tears that coursed down his cheeks.

"We heard about it," Edge growled, and Steele knew the half-breed was angry at having been alarmed by the unexpected sound. Knew exactly how he felt, for he was affected in the same way. But did not speak immediately and had time to calm his jangled nerves before he said:

"Maybe he's too choked up to speak, Edge. He looks like he's trying to tell us something."

In the ominous quietness of the former ghost town given new but perilous life by men who were more than a match for their reputations, sounds carried a long distance. And the gravedigger again curtailed his chore with the shovel to call from behind the church: "You guys won't get a peep outta the padre! On account of he ain't got a tongue no more!"

He resumed his work, and started in to whistle now.

Steele nodded his understanding of what the mute preacher was communicating and when the tear-reddened eyes shifted their look of pleading to the half-breed, Edge shrugged. At which the old man lowered his corpse-burdened arms and expressed total hopelessness before he turned his back on the strangers and went into the church.

"You know something?" Steele drawled as they started along the street again, riding between sidewalk-fronted business premises now.

"You're going to tell me, I figure?"

"This town could be hell if only the Devil lived here."

"What makes you think he don't?" the half-breed retorted, and nodded along the street.

To where a woman in a black dress had appeared from around a corner. Turning on to the main street from the side street to the right, where Baxter and Blood's other three henchmen had ridden out of sight earlier.

She stayed on the street instead of using the shaded sidewalk because she was forced to—had the noose of the blond-haired Ed's lariat around her neck. Pulled tight enough to be an uncomfortable threat but not to cause pain. And it was terror that formed the expression on the pretty face of the woman, who was in her mid-twenties, and a slenderly built Chinese.

Ed rose his horse slowly behind her, the coil of the lariat hung from his saddle horn as he cupped his hands to his mouth, touching the flame of a match to the end of a half-smoked cigar.

"Called George Blood," the half-breed went on. "And there's a piece of tail he's finished with."

The woman and her escort went on by—she with her head bowed after starting to look imploringly at Edge and Steele and receiving not a crumb of tacit comfort from them, and he ignoring them as he drew contentedly from the cigar.

Then Steele let out his breath and growled bitterly, "It's a place I've been destined to end up in for a lot of years, Yank."

"Trick is not to end up here, Reb," Edge answered as they reached the corner on the right and looked diagonally across the side street. To where three horses were hitched to the trail outside a once impressive frame building of two stories. It was in a bad state of repair now, but the painted lettering of its roof sign had not yet faded away entirely. Enough still showed to point out the name of the place as the Miner's Inn. "Figure we should celebrate getting this far without having our asses put in too tight a sling. And I won't mind if the whiskey's a little fiery. Just so long as it don't taste of brimstone."

He drew the tip of his tongue along the narrow gap between his thin lips as he veered his mount across the intersection.

"Make mine coffee, black as Satan, Yank," Steele countered. "And I'll drink to that. Sulphur, so good."

Chapter Nine

Just as the two swung out of their saddles at the rail of the saloon, a man spat a globule of saliva over the tops of the batwing doors. Which arced gracefully across the width of the one-step-high stoop and hit the ground midway between the booted feet of Edge and Steele.

"Hey, George!" the young man who had caught the half-breed's rifle and revolver yelled. "The two strangers that just rode into town are makin' tracks to come in here! You want them to stay out?"

Edge and Steele turned just their heads, to look up from the rapidly drying stain on the ground to locate the arrogantly scowling face of the twenty-year-old man who was chewing candy and dribbling sticky juice down his bristled chin as he spoke.

"Shit no, Floyd," came the sour-voiced response. "You have them two come on inside here. Ain't no better way to learn than by example is what my pa always used to say."

The youngster, who was dull eyed and had an unhealthy pallor, pushed open one of the batwing doors and executed an overemphasized and so mocking bow, gesturing with a curved arm for Edge and Steele to enter the saloon.

The two men hitched their horses and stepped up on to the stoop to go through the held-open door.

Edge said, "Thanks kid."

Steele added, "We don't tip."

Floyd growled, "Up both your asses," and let the door swing.

So that it would have banged into the back of the half-breed had he not stopped it with a hand.

"Temper, kid, or you may not be allowed another piece of

83

candy," Edge murmured as he scanned the saloon and its occupants.

"Language too," Steele put in. "Reckon you should go wash your mouth out with lye soap."

The Miner's Inn had not, in its heyday, been merely an impressive facade to lure customers into a place that failed to match the promise. And men with the imagination and the inclination and opportunity to give it free rein would have been able to visualize what it had looked like at the height of its prosperity.

A large room, as wide as the building and two stories high at the front. Divided into two sections by the broad staircase with curving banister rails that started to rise halfway to the rear, immediately opposite the entrance. The stairs giving access to a gallery that ran along the length of rear wall and down both sides. With a rail at the edge of the gallery and doors in the walls at the other side.

To the right of the stairway a small ballroom with a platform for the musicians in a corner and upholstered bench seats against the walls.

To the left of the stairs the saloon, with the bar running the length of the side wall and chair-ringed tables taking up most of the remaining floor area. But needing to share the space with the paraphernalia of roulette, the wheel of fortune, craps, and other games of chance.

The walls of the place were wood paneled, hung with mirrors and gilt-framed oil paintings. Three chandeliers were suspended from the ceiling. Drapes at the windows and carpets on the floor except in the ballroom area.

Wood was no longer polished, rails were broken in many places, upholstery was ripped, mirrors were cracked, paintings flaked, the chandeliers were veiled with cobwebs, and furnishing fabrics were tattered, holed, and faded.

The town smell of decay and dirt clung to the place. But the stinks of unwashed bodies, cheap perfume, liquor, and tobacco smoke were also strong in the Miner's Inn—generated by the group of people in the saloon section. Who all, except for Baxter and the fourth, unnamed, man of the quartet that had come to brace the new arrivals, peered at Edge and Steele.

Temporarily more interested in them than the card game that had earlier held their attention. A very tense game which had been played in total silence. Before Floyd brought it to an end with his question to Blood.

. Tense because one of the two players was destined to die soon. Lynched by the rope that reached down from the ceiling so that its noose turned lazily with warm air currents some five feet above the table top on which two five-card hands had been dealt.

It was obvious that George Blood was one of the card players and equally obvious which of the two he was. For he was expressing a broad grin of pleasure on his very ugly face. The fat face of a fat man who was perhaps six feet tall and weighed in the region of three hundred pounds. He had bulbous cheeks, bulbous neck, bulbous breasts, and a bulbous belly. And wore tight-fitting and light-colored clothing that did nothing to camouflage his obesity, so that the rolls of his fat strained the seams of the white pants, pale blue shirt, and bright red vest—had already popped buttons on the shirt and vest.

His complexion was close to the hue that might result from combining the colors of his shirt and vest—a blue-tinged red that contrasted badly with the bright green of his eyes and the dull yellow of his tobacco-stained teeth. His eyes were too small relative to the size of his head. And his teeth were irregular. He had a squashed nose, jug ears, and several double chins. In contrast, a fine head of curly black hair.

His age might have been anything from forty-five to fifty-five, since his fatness smoothed out the wrinkles from his skin and the thickness of his hair tended to make him appear perhaps younger than he actually was.

The man seated across the table from him was fifty or so. He was as tall as Blood, but with an average frame for his height. A black-suited, white-shirted, derby-hatted dude. With a tanned complexion and gray sideburns. And long-fingered smooth hands like those of an artist, a musician, or a gambler.

On his angular face was an expression of calm resignation and just a mild sheen of sweat as he shifted his blank-eyed gaze away from the newcomers to look down at his hand of cards on the table. Looking at them through the blue smoke that drifted up from the freshly lit cheroot jutting from the center of his thin-lipped mouth.

The members of the audience, aligned along the bar and the front wall—so that the two card players were completely isolated at the centrally positioned table—also sweated to a normal extent in the confined atmosphere of the saloon at early afternoon.

Men cut from a pattern similar to that of Baxter and Floyd and Ed. Aged from eighteen to over sixty. Hard men in hard times with holstered guns and sheathed knives on their belts. And craft and cunning in their eyes. Hatred and bitterness in their hearts—ready to be directed at whatever random target presented itself.

At the moment, the dude was playing cards with George Blood, at whom they looked again after brief and contemptuous glances toward Edge and Steele.

Maybe two dozen men. And half that number of women. These all under thirty and, in one way, as much of a pattern as the men. With the look of whores about them: the unsubtly revealing style of their dress, the way they carried themselves, and the lesser degree of hatred and bitterness which they harbored for a world that had treated them so badly.

One more Indian, two Chinese, a black woman, and a Mexican. The others white. None of them moved to display even professional interest in Edge and Steele as the card game and its participants reclaimed all interest.

Blood, large beads of sweat running out of his hair and trickling unheeded down over his fleshy face, kept the grin in place until he laughed. A strangely girlish sound that caused the rolls of his fat to quiver. Then he cut the sound and the movement abruptly, snarled: "Tough-talkin' strangers ain't welcome in South Pass, you guys. Figure I'll have to have you apologize to Floyd when this little piece of business is settled." He waved a pudgy hand over the table, then extended a thumb to indicate the noose suspended above. And vented another, shorter laugh. "Even if Floyd does tend to get a little big for his breeches sometimes. But ain't right strangers should put him down for it."

"Are we going to finish this game, sir? Or do you wish to enter into a lengthy discussion with these gentlemen?"

The dude was an Englishman with a refined accent that perfectly matched his calm demeanor and elegant dress. Even the way his fine-boned hands delicately stacked his cards and then spread them out into a line, still face down on the tabletop.

George Blood sighed, and even this caused his bulky flesh to tremble. Then he rasped as he spread out his cards in disarray, "Am I gonna enjoy seein' you swing at the end of that rope, Smith."

He flipped one of his cards over so that it was face up. It was the ace of hearts

"Smythe, sir. With a *y*, as I am getting weary of telling you."

The Englishman turned over a card and it was the two of spades. A tight smile flitted across his face—come and gone in an instant.

"Deuces are wild, you guys," Blood said, and turned over the two of diamonds.

Edge had taken the makings from a shirt pocket and was rolling a cigarette.

Steele spoke first, while the half-breed was running his tongue along the gummed strip of paper.

"That all we're allowed to know about the game?"

Smythe carefully turned over the king of diamonds and set it down in perfect alignment with his wild card.

Blood said: "Hell, that's right. How can you learn by example, you don't know what the frig is happenin' here?"

"You got it, feller," Edge drawled, and struck a match on the frame of a painting hung just inside the entrance. Then did a double take and saw through the grime of the years that the pictures depicted an orgy—with fellatio and cunnilingus engaging every subject. Which, he decided, confirmed his initial impression the Miner's Inn had been a cathouse long before Blood and his men brought their whores here.

"Shut your trap and you might get to hear somethin' you want to know, as my pa always used to say," Blood growled. With a short, beady-eyed glare at the half-breed. Then leaned back in his chair, picked his nose, and examined what his finger had found as he said: "This guy here come over Silver Pass from the north side last night. Claiming to be nothing more or less than a gambling man that got robbed by Walter King and the scum that live over to the north."

Smythe made a sound of impatience and reached forward a hand to turn over another card. But Blood fisted his free hand and thudded the heel of it down on the table, causing the cards to jump.

"Me first, you friggin' scum!" the grossly fat man roared in an awesome tantrum. "In this town, George Blood is always first with every friggin' thing! I told you that, bounty hunter!"

"I am not a—"

"Frig it, I'll kill you with my bare friggin' hands you don't do like you're told and listen!" Blood shrieked, the crimson color of his skin deepening by the second.

"What else can happen to me, sir?" the English dude posed evenly.

Blood licked his lips, swallowed hard, and squeezed his eyes tight closed. And by an effort of sheer will brought his temper under control. His color returned to what was normal for him and his voice was steady as he flicked open his eyes and looked at the Englishman for just a moment before he switched his gaze to Edge and Steele.

"Okay, this guy has had it. He knows he's gonna die and there ain't no way out of it for him. So what can he do, except needle me all the time. Make me lose my wig, which he knows I don't like to do so much. Okay, so I'm gonna stay as ice cold as he is. So he comes into South Pass and he checks out okay. His name ain't in Arch Baxter's little book and ain't no one here spots him for a hunter. So we let him have the run of town. Roll out the welcome mat as well as we're able. And we ain't bad at that, long as a man's got simple tastes."

He flicked his gaze between Edge and Steele and his eyes seemed to challenge them to say something.

"Came in here because I need a whiskey, feller."

"Sworn off liquor. Cup of coffee is all."

"You both gotta wait."

"That's fine, ain't it, Reb?"

"Fine."

"You bet it is." Then an embittered glare at Smythe when the Englishman vented another sound of impatience from deep within his throat. But still Blood kept his impulse to fury from having its way. "Okay. But we never thought to check him out with Elmer Flexner, who didn't see Smith or *Smythe* or whatever because he came in from North Pass instead of up the valley. And Elmer didn't come up the street until this morning." He shook his head and sighed. "To tell me about wastin' the Shoshone piece, I'll bet. But he plumb forgot after he spotted this guy and recognized him. From Virginia City, Nevada. Elmer, he saw this guy bring in two bodies and collect cash on them from the law office."

Now the beady green eyes of the sweaty fat man challenged the Englishman. Probably to deny the charge yet again. But Smythe simply removed the cheroot from between his lips, knocked ash to the floor, and replaced it dead center of his mouth again.

George Blood nodded and grunted his satisfaction with this. Then: "We got this rule in South Pass, you guys. Any of my men say a stranger is a hunter, he's guilty straight off. Because, like my pa was always saying, if you can't trust your friends, who can you trust? Okay, so bounty hunter here is set to hang. But since he's a gamblin' man as well as a hunter, I figured a little entertainment on the side wouldn't be amiss and . . ."

The cigar-smoking, blond-haired Ed came in through the batwing doors and announced brightly: "Elmer says to thank you, George. Figures the Chinese piece will suit real fine."

"Shut your trap, I'm talkin'!" Blood snarled. And had to pause to think where he had left off at the interruption. Then: "So I thought up this here card game. One hand of five-card poker. Deuces wild and nothing to draw. High hand wins."

"What?" Edge asked.

"I said high hand wins!"

"I reckon he means what does it win?" Steele offered.

"Oh, yeah. Well, if this guy wins, he just plain hangs. Gets put up on this here table with the rope around his neck. And I jerk the table out from under him."

Blood made a slashing motion across his own throat with the side of a hand. And grimaced.

"Guess I won't ask if I can be dealt a hand in this game, feller. Not the kind of pot I like to play for."

"I'm anti those stakes, too," Steele agreed with the half-breed.

"Most amusing, I am sure," Smythe rasped.

"And if you win?" the Virginian asked.

The badly stained teeth were displayed in another grin as Blood turned over another card, which was the two of clubs. "If I win, stranger, he gets strung up still. But the other way. By his ankles. Over with another, hunter."

The English dude's nerve began to crack now. His elegant hand trembled as he turned a card, and it fell crookedly. The queen of diamonds. Sweat showed as beads on his forehead and upper lip as he carefully aligned this third card with the first two.

"But it is not as simple as that," he said, as if he felt he would be better able to quell his terror if he was speaking. Was addressing Edge and Steele but stared fixedly at Blood's massive hand as it toyed with a fourth card. "When I'm hanging upside down, they'll cut off my testicles and see how long it takes for me to bleed to death."

He swallowed hard, but trapped a cry in his throat as Blood turned over the king of hearts.

"You forgot somethin', Smith," the fat man reminded, and the Englishman was now beyond a point on his emotional scale where he had the inclination to correct the mispronounciation of his name. "You forget that we're gonna gag you with your balls in your mouth. Show another, hunter."

This time the artistic fingers did not tremble as the dude's fourth card was placed face up on the table. The ten of diamonds.

Blood said, "Call it, Arch."

And Baxter, who had his back to the tension-charged room while he sipped at a beer, turned and took a couple of paces forward from the bar counter so that he could see the cards.

"You, George," the fat man's apparent lieutenant said dully. "Possible four aces, possible three aces, possible full house aces and kings. The hunter, possible pair, possible two pair, possible straight, possible flush, possible straight, possible straight flush."

"Appreciate it, Arch."

"You're welcome, George."

Baxter turned to the bar, back to the room, and resumed sipping his beer.

Blood turned his fifth card. Ace of clubs. Said, after he had eased with a tooth something from his nose out from under a fingernail: "Four of a kind can be beat, hunter. Even four aces. And you got the makin's there. If I have to tell a guy who claims he's a gamblin' man and not a hunter. Two of hearts or jack of diamonds and you got yourself the top straight flush. Royal flush, ain't it called?"

The Englishman eased his final face-down card to the edge of the table in front of his flat belly. Jutted it out over the edge with all four fingers of his right hand while his left moved to fold up a corner so that he could see the suit and value.

Every eye was on him and many of the watchers held their breath. And some let out the stinking air from their lungs in sighs when the dude's lips parted to display his very white teeth clamped to the cheroot. More did likewise and there was a shuffling of feet and some nervous coughs when the glint of a satisfied smile rather than the dullness of a grimace was seen in the man's eyes.

"It friggin' can't be!" George Blood roared, and wrenched his head around to stare toward Arch Baxter.

Who himself had swung around, his demeanor of calm confidence abruptly evaporated as he became the target of the fat man's fury.

And now all attention was transferred to Blood and Baxter, who stared at each other—one enraged and the other incredulous. All save for Edge and Steele. Who saw Smythe release the card. And then saw both the man's hands disappear into the sleeves of his suit jacket—right into left and left into right. His wrists twisted so that it was the inside of each forearm for which his clawed fingers reached.

The Englishman was both fast and smooth. Calm in the knowledge that he was certain to die. And confident that it would not be alone—that the gross George Blood was equally doomed for a violent end within the space of a stretched second.

His hands sprang apart and were flipped forward from his

body, each fisted around the butt of a miniature gun. In the
right a four-barrel Sharps derringer of .22 caliber. And in the
left a single-shot genuine derringer .45. One plainly made and
the other ornately decorated. Both capable of instantly killing
the fat man seated across the table from them. Who was the
only target in the mind of Smythe, whose mind perhaps was so
intently concentrated upon the desire to kill Blood that he was
oblivious to every other component part of his surroundings.

Edge knew how this could be. And so did Steele. Maybe
everyone in the sun-bright, rancid-smelling room had experienced the strange sensation of total detachment that such single-
minded craving can generate. Were even doing so at the same
moment as Smythe, perhaps.

Blood glaring at Baxter and Baxter gazing at Blood. One
demanding to know why the cards had fallen the way they did
and the other imploring innocence of involvement.

The hard men and the whores unable to draw their attention
away from these two because of the fascinating explosiveness of
the tacit challenge and the mute response. The watchers not
wanting to miss one detail of the outcome of this head-to-head
battle between the top man of South Pass and his first lieutenant.

Edge could only watch with the others, the razor in the
pouch at the nape of his neck useless in such a situation. For he
was some twenty feet away from the table where death was
about to strike.

Adam Steele was not so powerless.

The moves made by the Englishmen were spare and silent,
seen as just a blur. Likewise those of the Virginian.

But they were seen on the periphery of everyone's vision.
And in an instant Blood and Baxter had lost their audience, as
they themselves became part of the watching crowd. Whose
sole concern became self-preservation. In the face of the double
threat. From the guns in the hands of Smythe. And from the
throwing knife that Steele grasped—having dropped into a
crouch and drawn from the boot sheath through the gaping slit
in his pant leg.

The former silence was suddenly shattered. By men who
snarled and women who shrieked. By footfalls as cover was

sought. By the less intrusive sounds or revolver hammers being cocked as the guns were slid from holsters.

But before a single trigger could be squeezed, the noisy activity was abruptly curtailed. And for an instant it was like everyone had tunnel vision again and every pair of eyes were drawn to just one point now—the left side of the Englishman's neck. Into which the knife of Adam Steele had sank, forward of the midway mark. Just half the length of the blade in the flesh. Which was sufficient to penetrate the vital jugular and the windpipe. And to keep Smythe from maintaining his aim with the two tiny guns and firing them.

Edge said softly, "You ain't lost your touch with that sticker, Reb."

His words filled the silence of the tension-taut atmosphere. As Steele straightened up from the crouch into which he had dropped, and which he held while he hurled the knife with an underarm action.

The Virginian rasped the back of a gloved hand across his bristled jawline and answered, "Have to hope our position isn't any stickier than it was, Yank."

Only Edge heard this, for the saloon was almost riotous with noise and movement again. The new mood heralded by the spectacular death of the Englishman. Who sprayed a great gout of crimson from his gaping mouth as he toppled off his chair and his jerking muscles caused both forefingers to squeeze the triggers of his small guns. This as his hands slid off the edge of the table so that it was the floor that took the two bullets.

Everyone started in to yell then, and to try to find the cover they had first sought when they saw the Sharps and the derringer and the knife. But afraid now of the revolvers being drawn and waved by their own kind. Then George Blood brought this state of bedlam to an end when he lumbered to his feet and roared:

"Okay, you crazy people! Shut your friggin' noise! Quiet it down, will you?"

He flapped his thick arms and waved his meaty hands as he swung first one way and then the other, the penetrating glare in his small eyes issuing a command that was as strong as the vocal one.

The noise and the activity eased.

Floyd said excitedly, "I got the knifeman covered, George!"

Near silence.

Ed growled, "And if his buddy moves a friggin' muscle, I'll plug him."

Total silence, as Steele looked over his shoulder at the youngster, who was still chewing candy, and Edge glanced at the blond-haired man. The South Pass men were flanking the batwing entrance, each with a cocked Colt leveled from his hip.

"You want to tell him too, Reb?"

"Already made my point, I reckon."

"Don't like having a gun aimed at me, feller," the half-breed told Ed. "Try to give folks the one—"

"I said to quiet it down!" Blood snarled. "And that means every friggin' one! Until I find out what the friggin' hell is goin' on here!"

Edge and Steele returned their impassive-eyed gazes to the fat man after seeing chastened expressions replace the tight smiles of triumph on the faces of Floyd and Ed.

Blood nodded his satisfaction with the way his command had been finally obeyed. Then dropped back on to his chair with a sigh and mopped at his sweat-beaded face with a neckerchief, as if the effort of rising from the chair and remaining on his feet for all of fifteen seconds had drained him. Then: "Okay. Arch, what about these here hands of cards? You were supposed to have fixed the deck."

Blood had totally regained his composure now. Baxter was still a little anxious about the situation, obviously not trusting the grossly fat man to stay cool, calm, and collected.

And I stacked them just like you said, George," he answered, keeping his voice steady with an effort that could be seen but not heard. "Way I see it, he was a gambling man like he said and he figured a cold deck—"

"Gamblin' man and a hunter, Arch," George Blood put in and nodded. "Yeah, I'd say he was sharp. Never really did think you'd let me down, Arch."

Baxter had managed to extract the look of relief from his smile by the time the fat man glanced over his shoulder at him.

And the fleshy face of Blood was spread with a similar expression when he shifted the gaze of his tiny green eyes to Steele and said:

"I figure you gotta be faster with a blade than most men with a gun, Steele. That throw, it was almost magical."

"Wasn't me who had something up my sleeves, feller," the Virginian answered.

And Blood laughed, his whole bulky frame quivering like jelly, but it was an effort for him to give the sound a genuine ring. And quite obvious that it would have been easier for him to be trembling with delayed shock after his close brush with sudden death.

Some of his men laughed with him, and here and there a whore joined in. And the whole chorus of sounds had an odd tone: low down on the scale of hysteria as pent-up tension found an outlet.

"And you, Edge," the fat man blurted as he struggled to control the false mirth, as if he feared the strain of it would crack his wafer-thin composure wide open. "You just a big talker or you got any tricks to make Ed Rouse sorry he aimed a gun at you?"

The half-breed shifted his narrow-eyed gaze from the nervy fat man to look over his shoulder again. And saw that the blond-headed man with the cigar between his lips and the Remington revolver in his fist was also still charged with tension. Untrusting of the mood of George Blood. Perhaps knowing from past experience that in such a situation the top man in South Pass was likely to go off at a sharp tangent into any mood.

"George?" he asked, his gun hand shaking a little and his brow furrowing with a frown.

This as the dull-eyed, pale-faced Floyd acknowledged with a nod a signal from Blood and slid the Frontier Colt he was aiming at Steele back into the holster. Then backed off from the side of the batwing entrance, so that Rouse was left in anxious isolation, his eyes flicking back and forth in their sockets as he sought reassurance from others in the again quiet saloon that he had misjudged the fat man's state of mind and that everything was going to be all right.

The half-breed saw that nothing Rouse saw acted to calm his unease. And it was almost possible to read his racing mind from the expressions that came and went fast across his face, which was heavily beaded with sweat. Then he grinned and the cigar fell out from between his parted lips as he thrust the revolver back in the holster.

"Dumb move by me and Floyd," he said quickly, nodding vigorous agreement with himself. "Weren't for the dude here the hunter might've plugged you, George. And the dude and this guy are partners. We didn't oughta have pulled guns on them. Right, George?"

"What else didn't you oughta have done, Ed?" Blood asked, even toned now.

Edge looked at him and saw he was totally in control of himself. Just quietly and dangerously angry. Toying with a victim in a similar manner to how he had played the rigged card game with a man who was a slicker cheat than he was.

"About him." the fat man added, with a wave of his meaty hand to indicate the corpse of Smythe.

"Hey, that's right!" Floyd said eagerly. "It was you supposed to take his guns, Ed. You was the one let him in from the pass side of town and—"

"Shut up, Floyd," Blood interrupted flatly, and the candy-chewing youngster complied, looking frightened and with juice running down his chin.

"Shit, George, he wasn't wearin' no irons and I just figured the Winchester on his saddle was—"

"Reason I asked, Edge," Blood cut in again, "is that I'm real happy Steele here wasted the English guy. Under the circumstances, you understand? Hangin' would've been better. But under the circumstances, I was real grateful he done what he did. But under this new circumstance, I wouldn't like for no outsider to waste Ed. Ed being one of us."

"No sweat, feller."

"You bet. You and your buddy mind steppin' aside?" He put his palms together and then drew them away from each other, in a gesture to indicate the strangers to town should go in opposite directions. "Go to the bar. Have a drink. My treat."

"Obliged, but I pay my own way," Edge said, and went to

the left of the table, which was stained with blood and scattered with playing cards.

"Grateful to you, but the Yank owes mè, I reckon," Steele added as he went to the right.

Blood raked another piece of matter out of a nostril and as he examined it with a grimace, he said, "Arch, pay off Ed."

Rouse shrieked, "Noooooooooooo!" which started on a high, shrill note. And faded to a groan of despair in the wake of the revolver shot that drilled a bullet into his chest, left of center.

The .45 shell was fired across a range of perhaps thirty feet and was in the heart of Ed Rouse, who was dead on his feet less than a second after the order had been given. Which meant Arch Baxter was a very fast man with a handgun.

The corpse crumpled to the floor and the killer thumbed open the loading gate of his Colt and used the extractor rod to get the empty case from the acrid-smelling chamber.

Blood said, as he rose to his feet again: "Floyd, clear up the mess. Both messes."

Then he went to the other side of the table, breathing heavily as if from a great deal of exercise, and stooped with a steadying hand on the tabletop to draw the knife from the side of the Englishman's neck. He wiped the blood from the blade on his already red vest and came with the knife to the bar counter where Edge and Steele stood—in a space resentfully cleared for them by scowling henchmen of the fat man.

"I gotta make him coffee, George?" the bearded old-timer who tended bar asked sourly.

"If that's what the man wants, that's what the man gets, Harv," Blood growled, and laid the knife on the counter top as the bartender moved away, muttering under his breath. "Blades are okay, Steele."

"Grateful to you," the Virginian acknowledged, and replaced the knife in his boot sheath.

"And me to you. Pity about me havin' to waste Ed Rouse on account of him, though."

He looked genuinely contrite as he directed a glance across the saloon to where the candy-eating Floyd was dragging the body of Rouse out through the doorway and on to the stoop. And the remainder of the people in the saloon returned to doing what had occupied them before the rigged card game had started. Which was drinking, chewing the fat, or playing cards. But they would not have been so morose earlier.

Edge finished his whiskey at a swallow and said: "Rouse should have figured out those guns, feller. Smythe being an Englishman."

"What difference does that make?" Blood growled, as despondent as his men and the whores. Whether at the need to kill one of their own or because they had been denied a hanging, it was not possible to decide.

"They all have coats of arms. Ain't that so, Reb?"

"No, Yank," Steele answered. "Mostly just those that are entitled."

Chapter Ten

The grossly overweight George Blood began to tremble with belly laughter again in another abrupt change of mood. And managed to squeeze out between gusting bursts of chortling: "Hey, that's very funny, you know that? You guys are really funny!"

Then he swung away from the counter and headed for the batwing doors, still enjoying the joke. On the way out of the saloon crooked a finger in the direction of a very pretty Mexican girl of about twenty who had never been part of the crowd since Edge and Steele came into the Miner's Inn.

She rose and hurried toward him, like a dog trained to respond at once to a signal from her master. Hips swaying and breasts bouncing seductively as she veered to left and right between the tables. And was ignored by everyone except Edge and Steele.

The batwing doors flapped in the wake of Blood. And the girl a grimace of distaste on her finely sculptured features, held one of the doors open for Floyd to drag the corpse of the Englishman out over the threshold.

From the stoop, the madman snarled, "Move your friggin' ass, cow!"

She flinched as if the words had a physical force that stung her. And let the door go as she hurried to comply with the command.

The ancient bartender with the unkempt beard and the bloodshot eyes banged a mug of coffee on the counter top so that some of it slopped over the brim.

Steele confined his complaint to: "Seems you didn't have to make it at all, old-timer."

The old man spat out over the counter and on to the floor at the customers' side. Warned with relish: "Why don't one of you go try to make that? So that won't be wasted."

First he nodded to the doorway through which the girl had gone and where Floyd was dragging the corpse from the saloon. Then jerked a thumb toward the noosed rope hanging above the table in the center of the place.

"The big man's private supply, uh?" Edge asked.

"What do you think?"

"This coffee could be hotter," Steele growled.

"And the big man thinks the sun shines out of his ass, feller," Edge added. "So maybe you'd better make some fresh coffee, uh? And cook up a mess of something to keep our belly buttons out front of our backbones?"

The bartender spat out over the counter again.

Edge warned, "I'll know if you've done that into the food you've cooked for us."

The old man looked set to snarl a retort—perhaps a refusal. But the glittering slits of the half-breed's blue eyes and the steady gaze of the Virginian's black ones created an inhibiting fear as a lump in his throat. Which he had to swallow before he could tear his eyes out of the traps in which they had been held. And asked in a whining tone, "Arch, I gotta run around doin' what these guys tell me?"

Baxter—the fourth man who had come down the street to check the new arrivals—and two whores were at a table close to the far end of the bar from where Edge and Steele stood, drinking beer and talking in low tones. Not enjoying any of it from the frowns on their faces.

"Yeah, Harv, you have. Until George gets mad at them over somethin'."

The fifty-year-old, tall, thin, narrow-faced, slightly stoop-shouldered Arch Baxter withdrew from the exchange with a dull-eyed grimace he shared equally between the bartender, Edge, and Steele. But then the other man at the table said something to him in a whisper and Baxter added: "Or until they leave town, Harv. Head on out over the pass, like Johnnie just said."

There were many words and gestures of agreement with this, and waves of rancor were like currents of air wafting across the fetid saloon to buffet Edge and Steele as the Virginian drank his coffee and the half-breed signaled for his shot glass to be refilled.

"I heard that North Pass is a bad town to be in unless you have friends there." Steele said to Harv as the old-timer poured the drink.

"It's an asshole of a place, I can tell you, mister," Harv answered quickly. "Always was and always will be. Was where the paydirt was hit in the old days and—"

"Harv!" Baxter cut in with his dull-toned, bored-sounding voice.

"Yeah, Arch?"

"We would like for these guys to ride on over to North Pass. And they ain't likely to do that if you tell about it the way you usually do, are they?"

The old-timer had been warming fast to his subject. Eager in the way of the elderly to speak with authority on a subject he knew well. Having forgotten he was supposed to feel animosity toward those he was talking with. Now, having been censured by Baxter, he was shamefaced for a second or so. Then embittered, as if he felt the strangers had tricked him.

He spat out over the bar again and snarled, "Go to hell."

Then was as startled as every other South Pass man and whore when the batwing doors were flung violently open, and all looked toward the entrance to the Miner's Inn as George Blood stepped on to the threshold. A glower of anger on his fleshy face as he thrust out a meaty hand to either side to keep the batwing doors from banging against his belly.

"You're like friggin' kids, you know that? The whole friggin' lot of you! Kids around the friggin' cookie jar, scared you'll miss out because somebody'll get a bigger share than you!"

His tiny green eyes raked their penetrating gaze around the room and the fat man was not satisfied until every familiar face wore an expression of contrition that matched that which Harv had shown earlier.

Except for Edge and Steele, who had turned back to face the bar counter again and sip their drinks after glancing over their shoulders to see who made the forceful entrance.

"You guys!"

They looked at him again. And saw the anger go and a grin replace the glower.

"Cow, come on in," he called. And stepped to the side, to hold open one of the batwing doors so the Mexican girl could re-enter—carrying Steele's Colt Hartford and Edge's Frontier Colt and Winchester.

A buzz of surprised whispering erupted, then was immediately silenced when George Blood cleared his throat. And it sounded of genuine embarrassment, which was a match for the unfamiliar expression that took an unsure grip on his face.

Both strangers to town turned fully around to face the big, garishly attired man and the pretty Mexican girl who stood at his side. Guessing from the hushed expectancy that filled the sun-heated, rancid-smelling saloon that they were seeing a side of South Pass's top man seldom seen. Perhaps never before seen.

"So okay," Blood announced thickly, his small eyes gazing fixedly at a point in infinity which was midway between himself and Edge and Steele. "A man saves your life, you owe him everythin' you got is what my Pa always used to say. And this here guy Steele sure kept me from being wasted by the hunter."

"Forget it, feller," the Virginian said.

"Don't tell me what to do!" the fat man came back sharply, but remained staring into the middle distance. Angered by the interruption because it threatened to cause him to lose the thread of what he was saying. Then moderated his tone as Steele pursed his lips and vented a low sigh, and went on: "Now I reckon my Pa went a little too far on that one. So I sure as hell ain't gonna give you everythin' I got. But I am gonna give you back your guns. And I'm gonna throw a party for you. All you can eat and drink and screw."

He reached a hand to the side to caress the rump of the Mexican girl with the guns. And as he did so, he focused his eyes on Steele, then Edge, and altered his tone again, to warn: "Except the cow here. No one gets to screw the cow except me."

He stepped closer to her, so that he could reach a meaty arm around her, moved his hand up from her rear to insert it between her side and her arm to cup a breast.

Both Edge and Steele were certain there was something wrong with the broad smile that was spread across the pretty features of the girl. And this was confirmed when they saw, on the periphery of their vision, pitying looks on the faces of some of the whores. Women who as women could sympathize with one of their kind who had to put a brave face on it while enduring the humiliation she was subjected to—on pain of suffering much worse if she did not.

Blood pressed his face into the crook of her neck and sucked at the flesh and dark strands of her hair for a long time. While some of the watchers lusted, others leered, a few grinned, more grimaced, one laughed nervously, and two remained impassive.

Then he took his mouth and his hand off her to command, "Go give our guests their guns, cow."

To Edge and Steele after the girl had crossed the saloon and complied with the order: "You're both still strangers in South Pass, remember. With the privilege of carryin' guns, that's all."

The half-breed and the Virginian nodded briefly to acknowledge what was said to them and to thank the Mexican girl for bringing the guns. And could not fail to see the even briefer expression of desperate pleading from an abyss of despair that showed in the dark eyes of the girl—while her mouth continued to smile.

This as the fat man went on: "And you South Pass folks. I want you to be real friendly toward the strangers here. See they have all they want. But I don't want them or anyone else to have too much of anythin' until tonight. Party here in this place at sundown."

He beamed around at his audience and nodded like an indulgent father in front of his family when a chorus of enthusiastic cries and yells greeted what he had said. Then he crooked his finger at the Mexican girl, turned, and went out of the Miner's Inn again. Leaving her to open the batwing doors for herself after she had glanced around the noise-filled room. Frowning with fear, and directing another pleading look at the strangers a moment before following in the wake of the fat man.

"Like I was saying!" Harv announced loudly to Edge and

Steele as they bellied to the bar counter again. "North Pass was where the pay dirt was hit in this here mountain!"

In his own way, the old-timer behind the bar was as mercurial as George Blood. Had switched from hating the strangers to sucking up to them. Proud of being the only man in the saloon to have anticipated Blood's instructions on how Edge and Steele should be treated. And there was arrogant vanity on his bearded face and in his bearing as he addressed the strangers but swept his bright-eyed gaze back and forth over the others in the saloon.

Most of whom ignored him, as the stir of excitement in the place subsided but did not fade entirely. Those bucked by the promise of a celebration outnumbering the men and whores who continued to resent the intrusion of the strangers and how they had got on to the right side of the fat man.

"Reckon they've all heard your story, feller," Steele said to the old-timer as he scowled at failing to needle the South Pass men.

This as Arch Baxter and Johnnie led a minor exodus from the Miner's Inn. Men moving out through the batwing doors while some of the whores climbed the stairway to their cribs off the balcony. None accompanied by a man.

"And why should we want to hear it?" Edge asked as he took out the makings after holstering the revolver and leaning the rifle against the front of the bar counter. And meeting with his eyes a glance from Steele that said a great deal in a very short time.

That he knew it could be dangerous to appear overly interested in North Pass. That he was not a fool and resented being thought one. That if Harv wanted to run off at the mouth, there was no harm in listening to him. That Edge could take a walk and go all the way to hell if he wanted. That if it had not been for him and his skill with a throwing knife, the situation here might have been a whole lot different. And less favorable to them.

"If north is the way you figure to ride outta South Pass, handsome, there ain't no other way to go than through North Pass," a whore said.

She was drunk. Slurring her words, swaying as she rose

from a table and grinning a lopsided way as she banged against the bar counter and the two strangers looked toward her. Then she got the hiccups.

"Frig off, Nora!" the bartender snarled.

"Shuddup, you ball-less old bastard!" she countered, speaking fast between the hiccups.

She was a red-haired thirty-year-old with bad skin from neglect and a lumpy shape from overeating. The scent she wore could not mask the rancid smell of her filthy and sweating flesh. Her breath smelled even worse when she half fell along the front of the bar counter to come close to Edge. And invited, "Hey, you wanna get raped for a couple of bucks?"

Another hiccup and her full breasts moved in time, straining the fabric of her snug-fitting, sweat-stained blue dress.

"Nora, I'd want you to pay me ten times that much to even let you that close to me!" Harv said softly. Then roared with harsh laughter.

Edge finished the whiskey, set down the glass, and picked up the bottle. And his Winchester. Sensed the quizzical look Adam Steele directed at him as he said to the drunken whore: "Why not, lady? Been a long time since I got myself screwed."

He canted the rifle to his left shoulder and draped his right arm around the thick waist of the whore, his hand clasping the neck of the open whiskey bottle.

"Mister, this little girl is gonna screw you the best you ever been screwed," the whore said with enthusiasm.

She was a head shorter than the half-breed, who had to bend his knees so that he could turn his face into her greasy-smelling hair and rasp into her ear, "You ain't hiccuped in a while, lady."

She hiccuped. And proved just how good an amateur actress she was by not looking around at the now sparse crowd in the saloon to check if they had noticed her omission and correction.

"Little girl for Christ sake!" Harv blurted with a sneering grin. "They supposed to be made of sugar and spice and all things nice. And Nora, you sure don't smell like that's what you're made of!"

"She ain't so little, either!" a slender-bodied but sour-faced whore called from across the saloon.

"Go to hell, Sandy Powers!" Nora snarled, and hooked her

arm around Edge's waist to urge him toward the foot of the stairway. "Least I got me some tits bigger than my shoulder blades so as a man knows which way up I should be laid!"

The half-breed submitted to her urging, feeling the tension in her body at the strain of giving the performance.

But she was able to give a good enough impression of being in high humor as she joined in the laughter at her retort to the skinny whore.

"You'll take care of the horses, Reb?" Edge called as he allowed himself to be steered up the stairway. 'Might be a while."

"I'll see to it they get their oats as well, Yank!" Steele answered. "No rush."

"Sure won't be, feller. Never do bolt a screw."

The Virginian rasped, "Nuts."

Chapter Eleven

"You wanna another cup of coffee, or that food your partner ordered a while back?" Harv asked after Edge and the whore had gone from sight on the balcony and a door was slammed to signal they were in her crib.

"First I'll take the horses to the livery, feller. If you have a livery in this town." He took his rifle off the bar top.

"Sure we have, mister. We got everything a man and his mount needs. And some thing that ain't so much needed." He glanced at the stairway Edge and Nora had climbed. "Show you where the stable is, if you like."

He went to the far end of the bar, where he raised a section of the counter top to come out from behind. And as he did so he scooped something off a shelf. Which was a gunbelt with a revolver in the holster, which Steele did not see until the old-timer ambled back toward him, buckling it around his waist.

"Trustin' you people to pay for what you have while I'm away!' Harv growled with a less than hopeful look around the near empty saloon.

"Why pay to be poisoned by your rotgut when we can get it done for free at the hoedown later?" the dull-eyed, badly complexioned, still-chewing Floyd countered from the craps table, where he had been shooting a solitary game since returning after attending to the corpses.

"Young whippersnapper!" Harv snarled. "I don't know how you got to live as old as you are."

Harv held open the batwing doors for Steele without any hint of mockery, and as the Virginian and the old-timer stepped out on to the stoop, Floyd yelled:

"By stickin' my friggin' fingers down my throat every time I make the mistake of havin' a bellyful of your liquor, you crazy old man!"

"Ain't just your friggin' self you make sick to the stomach sometimes!" the old-timer called back into the saloon. Then was shamefaced again as he unhitched the half-breed's horse from the rail while the Virginian attended to the one Walt King had left at the sugar cane plantation. They were the only two animals still out front of the Miner's Inn in the blistering heat of the early afternoon. On a side street of South Pass that looked and sounded like the ghost town it should have been had not George Blood and his henchmen breathed vicious new life into it. "Sorry, mister."

"What for?" Steele asked as he led his gelding out into the center of the street in response to a gesture from the old-timer.

Harv fell in beside him, with one hand on the bridle of the half-breed's gelding. And gestured again, to indicate they were to turn right at the intersection, toward the pass that was reached on a steeply rising open length of trail that snaked up between a scattering of rock beyond the northern edge of town.

Steele did not bother to glance up at the facade of the Miner's Inn, since he had heard from the slamming of the door that Nora's crib was at the rear of the building.

"Actin' stupid childish as that Floyd kid!" Harv growled, and spat down at the street.

"Some people can get you going that way," the Virginian excused sourly, recalling how he had reacted several times to things the half-breed had done or said.

They turned the corner and the old-timer pointed along the street to the right.

"Red Gatling's Livery Stables is up there, mister. Corner of Mountain Road and this here street, which is Silver Trail. Or was. Ain't many folks call many places by the proper names they had once. Not anymore."

The voice of the bearded old man was a match in tone to the look of melancholy on his sweat-run and dirt-ingrained face. But, just as Nora had been putting on an act—Steele had finally realized when she hiccuped after Edge whispered to her—so this man was only going through a charade of indulging in nostalgia for a bygone time. This fact given away at close quarters by his bloodshot eyes that constantly moved in their sockets, surveying the facades of the flanking buildings.

Business premises to the left and big houses in fenced gardens to the right. Substantially built and well maintained at one time. But mostly now in a state of total neglect with just here and there signs that a store, an office, or a house was occupied still. Smoke from a chimney, a movement or sound behind a window that was not smashed, a length of sidewalk or a stoop that had been swept clean of dust, a smell of cooking wafting from an open doorway, and even—in one garden—a lovingly tended flower bed.

Harv kept up a running commentary as he maintained his surveillance for watchers and listeners.

"Doc Watkins works outta that office next to the old Chinese laundry there. He's one of the new people and I got my doubts about him bein' a proper doctor. The house there with the kinda pointed-topped windows—that's used as a kinda bunkhouse for the men. They're all new, of course. Mel Diver that used to have the hardware store way back, he sells notions now from what used to be the post office. Just scratches a livin' from the whores. That house there, with the flowers growin'—that's where George lives. Biggest house in town. Where Mr. Jack Volney lived in the old days. He's the man that first staked a claim in Silver Pass. Made his pile and then invested it in the plant to process the ore other men hacked outta the mountain. Went to live in San Francisco when the lode was worked out. They say he died the perfect death. Shot by the husband of the woman he was in bed with."

The bearded old-timer laughed long and loud at this, as he and Steele led the geldings down the center of the street between a totally abandoned house and a derelict stage depot. Then glanced back over his shoulder and continued: "Them flowers was started to grow by the little Shoshone girl that George give to Elmer Flexner after he was done with her. The Mex girl, she gives them just as much attention as—"

"Be best if you'd call her Mexican if ever you mention her to Edge," the Virginian suggested as they crossed an intersection formed by the last cross street before the rise toward the pass.

"He's a little touchy about that. Considers *Mex* is as as bad as *greaser* and since his father was a Mexican—"

Harv spat forcefully at the street. "To hell with him, mister. He ain't nothin' in this town. Only got give his guns back on account of he was with you." He snapped a thumb and finger. "Could end for him just like that if he puts a foot wrong. On account of it wasn't him stopped the hunter killin' George. Now you, mister, you're a whole different proposition."

They had halted outside the livery stable, which was across the street from the town meeting hall. Next to the hall was a schoolhouse and another church. Up from the livery a bakery and a feed merchant's.

A man with a Winchester rifle resting across his thighs sat in a rocking chair on the shaded threshold of the feed merchant's. He had been dozing before the clop of hooves on the street roused him. And now he was struggling to keep his chin from drooping down on to his chest again after seeing the old-timer bartender from the Miner's Inn and one of the strangers.

"I am?"

"Sure you are. Hey, Red! Couple of mounts to tend to! Belong to friends of George! So best you move your ass to do your best or could be you'll get your ass in a sling!"

While one of the big double doors in the livery facade was creaking open and a short, emaciated, stoop-shouldered, red-haired old man emerged, Adam Steele decided he had reached a wrong conclusion about Harv. Decided the bartender was not acting a part because he was afraid of anything. Instead, was putting on an act: purely and simply to try to bask in the reflected glory of the man who had saved the life of George Blood.

Red Gatling was scowling and shared the expression in equal measure between Harv and Adam Steele as he took the reins of both horses and rasped: "Up your friggin' ass, Harvey Cox. I always do a good job with horses and you friggin' know it. Don't matter who rides the animals. Why, even if you had a horse, you ass kisser, I wouldn't hold it against the animal for belongin' to a sonofabitch like you. Horses can't help who owns them."

He had led the two geldings into his stable, let go of the

reins, and come to the open doorway as he concluded what he had to say. Now deepened the lines of his scowl and again faced each man for an equally long second. And slammed the door.

Harv Cox was unconcerned by the sting of insults that had been rasped at him. Spat into the dust and checked that Elmer Flexner's opposite number at this end of town was listening before he said, with a tone of sadness: "Red's gonna get himself killed one day when the new folks lose patience with the way he is. He just ain't never made no effort to get along with George and the others. All the time pretendin' he likes horses better than—"

"I don't have to run around after them, kissin' their asses!" Gatling yelled from just the other side of the doors. "On account of I'm a liveryman who knows his job. I ain't the friggin' town drunk given the saloon to run because he's an ass kisser!"

Cox was on the verge of fury now, as he looked at the guard in the doorway of the feed merchant's and saw the man was dozing again. Then at the Virginian, who was frowning his impatience with the exchange. The bartender swung away from the front of the livery and this helped him to control his anger at Gatling. And he even managed to show a brief smile as he pointed a forefinger at his temple and rotated it in a gesture to indicate that Red Gatling was crazy.

Steele asked, as he came up alongside the old timer, "What's at North Pass now there's no more silver to mine, feller?"

The smile returned to the bearded face and was brighter and stayed longer now. "Some skunks livin' in hovels is all, mister. Never was a town, really. Just the claims with the shacks of the grubbers on them. Then Mr. Jack Volney, he built that processin' plant I told you of. And a street of tin-roof shacks for the men he brought in to work the place. Foreigners mostly. Chinese and greasers and even a handful of niggers. Just the one store to supply the needs of them kinda people. And a saloon of sorts with a couple of whores in rooms out back. So them niggers and foreigners had no call to come over the hill into South Pass."

They were retracing their footsteps back along the center of the street. Not, as Steele now knew, so that there was opportunity for low-voiced talk that could be seen but now heard by people in the flanking buildings. Instead, so that Harvey Cox could flaunt his close association with the favored stranger.

"So there wasn't much there in the old days, mister. And even less today. On account of the processin' plant built by Mr. Jack Volney fell down."

"Fell down?"

"Sure did. After the lode was all worked out and most folks had left town—everyone gone from North Pass and just a few of us left here on this side. Folks reckon it was on account of so many mine workin's bein' dug in the mountain. Like a rabbit warren over there, it is. Foundations got weakened and the plant just fell down. A heap of rubble is all it is now."

"Blood mentioned a feller named King who robbed the Englishman in North Pass—"

A rifle shot cracked through the hot, still air that was pressed heavily down on the street. And the bullet exploded a spray of dry dirt from the ground some six inches in front of where the Virginian set down his leading foot. His gloved thumb instinctively cocked the hammer of the Colt Hartford canted to his shoulder, but he was able to stay the move to bring the rifle down and his free hand up as his unblinking gaze located the man who fired the shot.

It was Floyd, his jaws working as he chewed some more candy. Having stepped on to the doorless threshold of the former Chinese laundry between the doctor's office and a boarded-up print shop. The Sharps rifle with black-powder smoke wisping from the muzzle still aimed at the spot where the bullet hit—but wavering a little because of the chewing motion of his cheek against the stock.

At one end of town, the drowsy guard jerked up out of the rocking chair and peered up toward the pass, disoriented by sleep and not yet able to get a bearing on the direction from which the shot came. At the other end, Elmer Flexner stumbled out of the shack, dressed in just his long johns. With his genitals exposed. He was gripping his Remington revolver.

Between, footfalls hit floorboards, curses ripped from throats, crockery and glasses smashed, doors were wrenched open, and guns were cocked.

Cox had frozen as rock still as Steele a moment after the Colt Hartford was cocked and Floyd was seen. But now the old-timer thrust his trembling hands high into the air as he shrieked: "I ain't said nor done nothin' wrong, boy! And I'm sorry for what I yelled at—"

Men with drawn revolvers or double-handed grips on rifles angled across the fronts of their tension-rigid frames showed at the corner of the street on which the Miner's Inn was located. And another group appeared out front of the neglected mansion now used as a bunkhouse. Elsewhere, other men with guns at the ready stepped from doorways or leaned out of windows. Not in groups. Here and there one with a woman in back of him. Glimpsed, or heard as she rasped an urgent plea for caution.

But it was not the sight of any of these gun-toting men that caused Harv Cox to curtail his groveling to Floyd. Instead, the crashing open of a door at the front of the house in which George Blood lived, and outside of which the rifle shot had halted the old-timer and the Virginian.

"Okay, so what's the shootin' about?" the enormously fat man demanded as he stood on the crumbling cement of the house porch. His small eyes spotting in a second that there was no danger to himself in the situation that had Steele and Cox trapped at the apex of a triangle with Floyd at another corner and the men out front of the bunkhouse at the other.

Blood had a napkin tucked into the neck of his shirt. A glass of wine in one hand and a hunk of bread in the other. He had sprayed some soggy fragments of partially chewed bread as he made the demand for an explanation. Now bit off another piece and worked it around with his tongue as he waited for a response.

"The dude was pumpin' the old-timer about North Pass, George," Floyd supplied eagerly. "Was just gettin' in to askin' him about King, so I figured to put a stop to it. We all know what a blabbermouth Harv Cox is, so I didn't want it to go any further without—"

"What d'you want to know about King and North Pass for,

Steele?" Blood interrupted after swallowing what was in his mouth.

The Virginian had shifted his gaze from Floyd to Blood, to Floyd, and now, as he returned his attention to the fat man, glimpsed a familiar figure near the group of gun-toting men on the corner. Edge, with the Winchester canted to his left shoulder and his revolver still in the holster. An amused expression on his lean face as if he were looking forward with eagerness to hearing Steele's answer.

"Just that the Yank and I like to know what we're getting into, feller," Steele answered evenly.

"Into?" the fat man posed, suspicion inscribing a frown into the bulging flesh of his face. "Just what you tryin' to say, mister?"

"Reckon Edge and I like it well enough around here, George. Because South Pass seems to have almost everything men like us are looking for. Except a little action. Of the killing kind."

"We was gonna have a hangin' before you butted in, dude!" Floyd snarled. "Gonna hang another dude."

"George would've been dead if this guy hadn't—" the old-timer with his hands still stetched toward the cloudless, sun-glaring sky started.

"Shut your damn mouths and let the stranger get said what he wants!" Blood snapped.

Steele calmly nodded his appreciation of the opportunity. And went on: "Thought that if you and this feller King were not the best of friends—which from what I've heard you are not—there might be a chance of some real killing action."

The fat man nodded, but there was still a trace of the frown of mistrust on his face as he asked, "Why him, stranger?"

"Why who, George?"

"Harv Cox." The hand fisted around the wineglass was waved in the direction of the old-timer, and this set him to trembling again. "He's just a drunken slob I let run the hotel because I got a soft spot for old guys."

From way along the street came a short burst of shrill laughter. Which was quickly curtailed when the sentry posted at the pass side of town ordered Red Gatling to shut up.

"He ain't one of us."

"Nobody who is with you is much of a talker, George," Steele pointed out. "Hard to get Harv here to stop for long enough to ask a question."

"Ain't that the truth?' the fat man posed rhetorically and a little pensively. Then emptied the wine from the glass down his throat. And spoke louder. "Okay, you guys. Put up the guns and get back to eatin' or sleepin' or whatever. Seems I got my lunch interrupted for frig all."

As the men who had not been directly involved in the incident did as instructed, Steele heard Harvey Cox vent a long sigh of sweet relief and saw Floyd scowl his bitter dissatisfaction with the outcome.

But it was a short-lived expression on the face of the candy-chewing young man who had lowered the Sharps rifle to his side in the doorway of the Chinese laundry.

George Blood called, "Arch?"

And the dour-faced Baxter halted his move to withdraw from an upper-story window of a house at the opposite end of the block from the one in which the fat man lived. As the woman's hand into which he had given his Winchester thrust the rifle back at him.

"Yeah, George?"

"Pay him off, Arch," Blood answered and made to turn back into his house as he pushed the last of his hunk of bread into his mouth.

"Young whippersnapper," Harvey Cox murmured happily.

The terror of suddenly coming to a violent end wiped the scowl from Floyd's face. And the kid gagged. Kept the bile from erupting the vomit of nausea, but lost his soggy piece of candy in the forceful expellation of his breath.

Adam Steele was not so certain about Blood's intention and came within a fraction of a second of bringing the cocked Colt Hartford down from his shoulder and whirling into a crouch to aim and fire at the fat man. Like the Englishman in the Miner's Inn, intent upon taking the chief of his tormentors with him if he was to go. And there was just a hint of a smile along his mouth line as he glimpsed Edge—standing alone on the corner now— tense to react in a similar manner, but with his head turned fractionally to show that his potential target was Arch Baxter at the window.

"George?" Baxter yelled.

"Yeah, Arch?" Blood countered, a little impatiently.

The Virginian experienced no sense of the warmth of gratitude toward the half-breed because of his readiness to start shooting. Th smile was simply in response to the predictable nature of Edge's instincts. Which were the same as his own. If he were to die, the half-breed would not be far behind in the plunge to purgatory. So he was poised, too, to take at least one of the enemy with him.

"Which one you want paid off?"

"The one who talked his way out of the soft spot I had for him, Arch."

A shrill laugh burst from the lips of Floyd and he had to lean against the doorframe to keep from falling over from the weakening effect of relief that he was not to die.

At the same moment, Harvey Cox vented a groan of depthless despair and took a backward step as his hands came up again—but to be held out in front of him. Toward Baxter instead of the sky. Like Ed before him, the old-timer made no attempt to draw the gun from his holster.

The Winchester exploded a shot that drilled into his skinny belly just above the belt buckle. And knocked him flat on to his back. The scream that came from deep inside him sounded of terror rather than pain.

Steele looked back and down at him as he hit the street and clawed at the center of the rapidly expanding stain on his lower shirt front. Muttered, "Seems in this town it's not so much who you know but what you know that counts, feller."

Cox had stopped screaming, but he could not hear the sardonic sentiment expressed by the grim-faced Virginian. For Steele spoke against the sharp cracks of two more rifle shots. The first of which tunneled a bullet into the center of the old timer's face and knocked his head violently to the side. While the second angled between two of his ribs to find his heart. He was already dead then, the spasmodic jerking of his body and limbs triggered by an involuntary reaction of his out-of-control nervous system.

Then he was still, and the blood ceased to pump out of the three bullet holes in him as he lay like a broken puppet on the center of the street.

Baxter gave the killing rifle back to the woman and withdrew from the window, the familiar expression of indifference to everything and everyone on his face.

Floyd, still looking a little weak at the knees, unwrapped a piece of candy and popped it into his mouth as he moved off the threshold of the former Chinese laundry and went along the sidewalk to enter the office of Doc Watkins next door.

Edge came up the street from the corner.

George Blood called out, "I'll see you two guys at the celebration party." And went back into the biggest house in town, slamming the door behind him.

A fly buzzed in to settle on the beard of the dead Harvey Cox, and began to gorge on the blood that had oozed from the hole at the side of his nose.

Edge said: "I don't know if I should be seen around you, Reb. Way you're getting to be the death of men in this town."

Steele directed a grimacing look down at the corpse of Cox with the rapidly drying patches of dull red on his belly, chest, and face. And drawled as Floyd emerged from the doctor's office, "The crazy old bastard got what he wanted, in a way of speaking."

"How's that?" the half-breed asked.

"He wanted to run with Blood."

Chapter Twelve

The dull-eyed, badly complexioned Floyd had the smell of liquor on his breath and it was obvious he had gone into Watkins's office to take a snort of Dutch courage. For there was a swagger of bravado in his gait and a braggart's sneer on his youthful face as he came to the center of the street to take care of the body. Which he did by stooping to grasp a booted ankle, then turned to drag the remains of Harvey Cox unceremoniously along the street to deliver it to the mute preacher.

He had seemed to want to snarl something to the Virginian and the half-breed, but had not taken a large enough slug of liquor to fill the cracks in his courage opened up by the ice-cold gaze of Edge and the penetrating stare of Steele. So vented his feelings in other directions. Began to shout when he was still a long way short of the church: "Hey, gravedigger! We need another hole! Preacherman, there's another guy needs prayin' into heaven! Cause maybe hell's all filled up and that's the only place—"

"Hey, Devlin!" a man called from a onetime gun store with its sign of a skillfully cut-out wooden revolver still hung over the door.

"Yeah?"

The man sounded weary and sour tempered. "If you don't keep the friggin' noise down, kid, you could wind up like the preacherman."

Floyd Devlin muttered, "Up yours, Rix." But just loud enough to reach the unhearing ears of the corpse he was dragging.

At about the same level, Steele asked Edge, "Was she worth the two dollars, Yank?"

"Figure that's between her and me, Reb."

It was the half-breed who took the lead in moving away from

118

the spot where Harvey Cox had been gunned down. And he ambled north—back the way Steele had come with the old-timer. The Virginian fell in at his side, both men with their rifles canted to shoulders, hands fisted around the frames. Eyes watchful.

"Bench out front of the stage depot is shady, feller."

"Sure."

They angled off to the west side of the street and stepped up on to the low run of boarding across the front of the derelict depot where stages of the Trans-Territorial Line had once halted. Edge sat on the bench and held the Winchester between his knees, its stock on the sidewalk, as he took the makings from his shirt pocket. Steele leaned a shoulder against an awning support and said:

"You never struck me as the shy kind, Yank."

"It's okay, feller, the walls here don't have any ears. The whore wants to give me all her future earnings less eating money to get her out of here."

"His expression posed a tacit question.

Steele answered: "A history of North and South Pass is all I got. In the days before the silver ran out. You saw what happened after I tried to pry something useful out of him."

Edge struck a match on the barrel of the Winchester and lit his cigarette. And on a stream of tobacco smoke said, "Always have figured a feller can learn more from going with a whore than he can walking out with another feller."

"Reckon if we hang around together too long here, you and I will get talked about," Steele warned. "Or worse."

"The whore doesn't know of any other way over the mountain except through the pass. But there has to be one because your prisoner couldn't have come through here without being seen."

"I have an idea about that."

"Your walk wasn't a complete waste of time then?"

A nod. Then: "Not like this time."

The half-breed grinned. "Sharp, feller."

The Virginian also grinned as he came back, "And I reckoned I was being blunt."

"Okay, I'll get to the point before the hard men around here get the needle from not knowing what we're talking about."

"And before you lose the thread of what you were saying, Yank."

"You cotton on fast, Reb."

"You want to start talking that way?" Steele asked, humor gone from his face and tone of voice now, as he saw two rifle-toting men appear from the bunkhouse. One to turn to the south and one coming north. "Change of guards, you reckon?"

Edge nodded. "I figure. Seems a feller named Casey was first to bring a bunch of wanted men to town. After everyone except for a handful of deadbeats like Harv Cox left when the pay dirt stopped being dug. Army deserters and one of them was King. Casey was top man because he was a sergeant. King was second in command with two chevrons.

"Had the run of the whole town, if they wanted. But there's nothing but a couple of rows of shacks and a fallen-down ore processing plant on the north side . . ." A tall, black-bearded man of about forty with a twisted left leg he had to favor was the relief sentry for the pass side of town. As he limped within earshot of where Edge was talking, the half-breed made a smooth change of subject. ". . . and she damn near cracked my spine the way she wrapped her legs around me, Reb.

"But she wasn't as strong in that part of her body as a whore I had in New York City. Story went that if she really wanted it and the man wasn't making it for her, she was likely to break his back."

The limping man had been glowering at the men on the sidewalk out front of the stage-line depot. But now, as he picked up on their talk, he showed a set of darkly stained and misshapen teeth as he contributed, "Man, I bet no guy sucked her off, uh?"

"Reckon not," Steele agreed.

The man stopped and ran a shirt-sleeved arm across his sweaty brow. Said: "I mind the time we and some other boys went to this fancy cathouse in New Orleans and—"

"Mo, for frig sake!" the sentry by the feed merchant's yelled as he rose from his rocker. "I could friggin' starve to death before you got here!"

"Keep your friggin' wig on, Rich!" Mo snarled. And went on along the street with a smile on his face as he recalled good memories.

Rich, who had a bad knife scar on his right cheek and a very thick, auburn moustache, left his post before Mo reached there. And glared at his relief. Then showed the same feeling of ill will for Edge and Steele as he passed them and the Virginian was saying:

". . . New Orleans has more cathouses than San Francisco. And the best whores in the entire country."

"Man would have to try screwing them all in every town to say that for sure, Reb," Edge said.

"He'd have to be some man, Yank."

"Couldn't be done by one, Reb. Take a whole army of them."

"And chances are they'd all end up with a dishonorable discharge."

"Okay, Reb, he's gone on by. We can quit talking claptrap now."

"Fine. The old-timer told me about the North Pass side of town."

Down at the southern end of the street the fresh guard took up a position in the rubble of the building that had once stood across from where Elmer Flexner and the Chinese whore remained in the shack.

"Casey didn't stay the top man for long. Because a couple of months after the deserters made South Pass their hideout, Blood and his bunch of bank robbers rode in. With saddlebags filled with money and a wagonload of whores."

Edge flicked his cigarette out into the sunlit street and laughed loudly.

"I miss a joke in there?" Steele asked.

"We were supposed to be having a good time when Mo went by," the half-breed reminded.

The Virginian turned against the post to look along the street. And let his boyish grin suffice when the guard glanced at him.

"Casey tried to make Blood and his bunch pay rent money to stay here. And Blood knocked him down. With that big gut of his, the whore said. Just banged into him and knocked him down. Then jumped up and down on him. Stomped him to death.

"Preacher tried to stop it. When he couldn't, called the wrath of God down on the fat man. So Blood had a couple of his boys hold the preacher still while he cut out his tongue."

"What were Casey's men doing while all this was going on?" the Virginian asked, as unemotional in listening to the story of past horrors as the half-breed was in telling it.

"Lined up against the front wall of the Miner's Inn with rifles aimed at them. Ten of them, as she recalls. Including King. And the local citizens who had stayed around after the silver ran out. Fifty or so of those, including the whore. Blood had just five men then, including Baxter and Flexner. And that feller Ed Rouse he had shot in the saloon.'

"He's a real nice person, the fat man."

'Gave everyone the option to stay or leave. Just the bartender left. And Blood had Baxter shoot him in the back as he got on his horse. King and three of the other deserters snuck away the next morning before sunup."

Edge rose from the bench and stretched and yawned. Began to pace up and down.

"Walt King has more than three men with him at North Pass now, if what I've heard is—"

"Not through yet, Reb. All this happened nine or ten years ago. The whore knows it for certain because she was a part of it. Saw and heard what went on. What comes next is just what she's picked up from overhearing talk in the saloon.

"Men come and go all the time here. To raise money or hell or both. Sometimes those that go don't come back. Sometimes strangers come and stay, but always they're known to somebody already here. Occasionally brought in by an old hand. Whichever, when one of the bunch comes back from a spree or a job, he's always pumped for news of King. Because King let it be known to all who cared to listen that he intends to make Blood pay for killing Casey and taking over South Pass. And all he's waiting for is to have enough men to do it. Reason he was riding around in the open for you to put the arm on, Reb? Recruiting drive?"

"Reckon so," Steele allowed absently. Then, pointedly, "She know how many men he has with him now?"

"That's all hearsay, feller. Estimates vary from a handful to a hundred. With a lot less than a hundred, he'd have already made his try for a comeback, I figure. The English dude said he was robbed by just three men out of twenty who were the only ones he saw in North Pass."

"Does she know why he hasn't gone over the pass and hit first?"

"Be suicide for an attack to be launched on North Pass from the south if King does have a reasonable number of men. Because of the terrain in the pass proper, King's patch is virtually impregnable from here. If he has more than a handful of defenders."

Edge was silent and pensive for several seconds.

Edge said as he began to roll another cigarette: "We've been straight faced for a long time, Reb. Might get our invites to the party taken away if word gets around we don't laugh so much."

The Virginian shrugged and rasped the back of a gloved hand along his bristled jaw. "Reckon we're still talking about a whore, but you haven't told me anything funny she said."

"When Floyd Devlin took that shot at you or Cox?"

"The both of us."

"Whatever. The whore said she sure hoped it wasn't you who'd been shot. Because she thought you were the sweetest-looking guy that's been through South Pass since she came to work here."

Steele showed his boyish grin. "She sounds like a woman of taste."

Edge struck a match and lit his cigarette. "Talking of which, the cook's dead and we never did get to eat since we got here."

The cracked bell in the church tower began to toll. In a slow, mournful, funereal cadence.

"Not even the forbidden fruit?" Steele asked as they both stepped down off the sidewalk. Heading north on the main street again—toward the livery stable, where there was food in the saddlebags off the half-breed's horse.

"I told you. It was her put the bite on me."

Chapter Thirteen

The black-bearded Mo, who had assumed Rich's former position in the rocking chair out front of the feed merchant's, looked eagerly toward the two men approaching him, their pace matching the slow toll of the bell. Relishing the prospect of company during a long spell of monotonous sentry duty. And talk of whores they had all known.

But then he scowled in piqued disappointment when they halted at the livery and Edge tried to open one of the pair of big doors.

"You ain't gonna leave town unless George gives the okay!"

From in the stable, Red Gatling demanded to know, "Who the frig's that?"

"Feller that rides the black gelding brought in here a while ago," Edge answered. "Need to get some supplies from the saddlebags."

Mo grunted an acknowledgment that this served as a response to his warning too. And resumed his grimacing survey of the rocky, parched, sun-bright slope over which the trail ran into Silver Pass.

"Come back in an hour, why don't you!" Red Gatling growled. "I'm all closed up for lunch. Whole town's all closed up for lunch. If you weren't strangers hereabouts, you'd know that. Same every day."

Edge put an eye to the crack where the double doors met in the middle. It was murky in the livery, because just a stray shaft of sunlight penetrated here and there through gaps in the boards nailed across glassless windows. But it was light enough for the half-breed to see the emaciated, red-haired old man squatting down on his haunches at the rear. He was not able to recognize what occupied Gatling's attention in a stall that seemed to be stacked with hay bales.

The cracked bell continued to toll its melancholy message of the dead being buried.

"Exceptin' for the preacherman and Hubert Perry that digs the graves," the liveryman went on, still busy with his hands among the hay bales. Like he was burying something among them. "No rest for them until the killin's stop. And I don't reckon that'll be until the two strangers leave South Pass."

"Harv Cox reckoned he was crazy," Steele said.

This as Edge shifted the rifle from his shoulder and leveled it at his side, thumb cocking the hammer as the muzzle was rested against a knothole in a door. He squeezed the trigger. And Steele added:

"I didn't know insanity was catching."

Outside the feed merchant's, Mo wrenched his head around from scanning the slope and pumped the action of his own Winchester as he came up from the rocking chair. He grunted.

Inside the livery, Red Gatling howled in terror as he threw himself sideways from his squat. And rolled into a tight ball with his knees folded up to his belly and his chin tucked down on his chest, arms clutched over the top of his head.

The bullet had missed him by a foot to snick into the hay bales.

"Reason I'm down here at your livery, Gatling," Edge called evenly through the crack as the old man continued to stay in the same fetal position, "is that I'm so hungry I could eat a horse."

Mo's black-bearded face had been set in a frown of rage at being alarmed by the rifle shot. But suddenly he vented a roar of laughter. That acted to stem the noise and activity that the shot had triggered throughout the town.

The tolling of the bell was curtailed and Steele said to Mo, "He's a laugh a minute, isn't he?"

"It's okay, you guys!" Mo bellowed along the street. "No harm done!"

"And like I said," Edge went on as if there had been no interruption of any kind, "you have my saddlebags in there."

Gatling had shifted one arm from his head and now moved the other one, but seemed unable to turn his head as he stared fixedly into the stack of hay bales. Then, as he rose up on to his knees and to his feet, he called huskily: "All right, for frig sake! I'm comin' to open up for you! Just don't fire no more shots in here!"

Edge stepped back from the doors and saw that Mo was lowering himself into the rocker again while those men who had spilled out on to the street in the center of town were moving back into the buildings, sour faced and griping at having their afternoon peace violently disturbed yet again.

From an upstairs window of his mansion George Blood shouted: "You guys watch your friggin' step! It's siesta time around here and a guy my size needs all the friggin' rest he can—" The bell in the church tower began to toll out its cracked note again. And the fat man at the window jerked his head around to aim his heightened rage in another direction. "Quit ringin' that sonofabitchin' bell, you crazy preacher! Ain't nobody mournin' that scum you're buryin', so bury them quiet!"

He slammed the window closed.

Red Gatling slid the plank from two brackets and dragged open one of the doors. To glower out at Edge and Steele and demand: "Toss that smoke away, stranger! Can't allow smokin' in a place that'll catch light and burn down quick as blinkin'."

"Makes sense," the half-breed said as he dropped the partially smoked cigarette and stepped on it to kill the smoldering tobacco.

Steele went inside and Edge followed him, entering a livery that had a horse in every stall save two—the one which the hay bales were stored and another next to it which seemed to be where the emaciated old man slept.

The animals all looked to be in good condition from regular attention, which acted to emphasize the raggedness of the liveryman's work clothing, the dirt ingrained in his skin, and the unhealthy sparseness of his flesh. Probably the smell of the old man would have been close to overpowering outside the stable, which was redolent with equine scents.

"Over there in the corner," he said, nodding to a table where the saddles of the two men rested. "Almost through with one of them."

It was the Virginian's, highly sheened from a vigorous soaping of the leather. Some of the brasswork had not yet been polished.

"It looks like you're doing a fine job Mr. Gatling," Steele told him.

"It more than looks like," came the growling response as Edge went to the work table. "It is. Other one'll be the same if I'm allowed to get on with what I'm the best at."

He remained by the door, holding it open for the two men to leave.

Steele went to look into the stall where the bay gelding he had ridden from the burned-out sugar plantation stood. And saw that Gatling had not neglected the horse to work on the saddles. It seemed that it was only the man himself who failed to receive anough attention.

Edge took his saddlebags and canteens off the table and said, "It's a nice place you have here, feller."

"I know it."

He followed the half-breed with eyes that mistrusted the world. And was suddenly nervous when the tall, lean man stopped at the stall where the hay bales were stacked.

"Like to stay a while, if you don't mind? Have a bite to eat and maybe rest up some afterwards."

He said this as he jerked a bale off the top of the stack and dropped it on the floor

Intrigued, Adam Steele looked at the liveryman as he vented a gasp of shock. Then at Edge, who was impassive as he lowered his rump on to the bale and began to unfasten a saddlebag.

"You got no right to—"

"I don't think you're crazy like Harv Cox said you were, Red," the half-breed cut in as he took some sourdough bread and hard cheese from the bag. And signaled that the Virginian should come across the stable and join him.

"Folks only say that about me because they're lazy good-fornothin's!" Gatling retorted. "And I'm real good at anythin' to do with the horses. Work hard at bein' good and they can't understand how I can like workin'."

Still intrigued, the Virginian had moved to the rear of the stable and taken the saddlebag Edge handed him. Remained standing, without checking on the contents of the bag, as the half-breed, bread and cheese in his left hand, drew his revolver and cocked the hammer..

"Dear God, no," the skinny old man rasped, to capture the attention of Adam Steele for just a moment, before he looked back down at Edge again.

To see him chewing with relish on a mouthful of bread and cheese while he rested the Frontier Colt upside down across his right shoulder—aimed into the stall stacked with hay bales.

"Reckon there's something about this I'm in the dark on," Steele drawled and switched his puzzled gaze constantly between the calmly eating Edge and the petrified-with-terror Red Gatling.

The gulp of the half-breed swallowing the mouthful of food sounded vulgarly loud.

It served to jerk the liveryman out of his frozen attitude. And resignation to the inevitable mixed in with some sad disappointment pushed the look of fear off his face.

"So you saw, stranger?"

Edge took the revolver off his shoulder and rested it briefly against his face, with the barrel to his lips in a gesture for quietness.

"Not much, feller. But best if Mo didn't hear anything, I figure?"

Now Red Gatling was as puzzled as the Virginian. But contained his curiosity while he sneaked a look out of the doorway and across the front of the former bakery to where the sentry was slumped in the rocker with his rifle resting across his thighs, morose again as he gave his full attention to the hillside. Then the liveryman quietly closed the door and slid the plank into place.

"You saw enough?" he posed, and was like a different man from the one whom folks in South Pass thought of as crazy. He spoke in a different tone, carried himself in an altered posture, and even seemed to have changed facially. Was like a taller, younger, more cultured brother of Red Gatling.

Edge slid the revolver back into its holster and shrugged as Steele delved into the saddlebag for food. This after both of them had done a double take at the man crossing the stable from the entrance.

"Saw you act like you expected the shot to do more than just get lost in your haystack, Red."

"Getting hard to tell who isn't putting on an act in this town," Steele muttered as he selected sourdough bread and some dried meat for lunch.

"Yeah, and I thought I'd done that scene up in Montana a while back, Reb."

"Black powder is what's in there," the liveryman admitted as he dropped on to the chair in front of his worktable. "Twenty pounds of black powder. If your bullet had set that off, it would have blown up me, you, this building, and maybe the whole end of the street."

"You don't plan on trying to blast more silver ore out of this mountain, I figure?"

"You bet I don't, mister!" he answered vehemently. Then sighed and shared a look of sadness between the two men near the hay. "Suppose you'll really put yourself in good with that fat bastard when you tell him about it?"

"You've got us wrong," Steele told him, and it brought a tentative expression of hope to his filthy, bristled, sunken-cheeked face.

"You mean you're not in South Pass to throw in with—"

"In South Pass on our way to North Pass, Red," Edge interrupted. "And we'd have been passed through this part of town by now if the Reb here hadn't got himself in so good with the fat man."

"Or passed on, Yank," Steele added.

"So you won't tell about my store of black powder? I thought you didn't want Mo Spencer to know in case he stole some of your thunder for finding it, mister."

Both men had finished eating and now they drank from a canteen as Red Gatling became increasingly excited at what he was hearing.

"Long as you promise not to set it off while the Yank and I are still in town," Steele said.

"Prefer to rise in the world by my own efforts, feller," Edge added.

"You don't have to worry about that," the liveryman assured them, the excitement diminishing now. "Took me six months to smuggle it into the stable after I found it in a crate out back of what used to be the Miners Supply Company Store over on Crest Street. And all I been able to do with it since is take out a bag every once in a while and look at it. Knowing I haven't got any idea how I can use it. And knowing, too, that I couldn't handle any idea on my own."

He looked pointedly at the two men who were now both sitting on the hay bale.

"Through to North Pass is all," Steele reminded.

"There's a whore at the Miner's Inn agrees with your opinions of the fat man and his bunch, feller," Edge added.

Gatling nodded. "Nora Stebbings. Mel Diver at the notions store too. A whole lot of others who do business with the bastards. But everyone's too afraid of Blood. Of what he'll do to them if he finds out they're plotting against him. I haven't even told them about my black powder. Hey, how do you know about Nora, mister?"

"She told me I could be her pimp and keep most of the money if I got her out of town," Edge answered.

This completed the liveryman's slide into depression. "Running away from home is for kids. And why should we be forced into it by the likes of Blood and the rest of the vermin?" He shook his head, as if to deny the impulse to familiar anger over an age-old problem. "You going to help her?"

"Right now I'm helping him," Edge said, and jerked a thumb at Steele. "And the way that's shaping, it could turn out to be a lifetime's job."

"Better than pimping, Yank."

"Not so well paid."

"But you get to keep your self-respect."

"What are we talking about, Reb?"

"Talking around is what we've been doing, Yank. You listened to the whore and I didn't turn a deaf ear to what Harv Cox was saying. And we both know why we did that."

Red Gatling rocked his head from side to side as he looked at each man who spoke. His expression was of total confusion.

"Why search for one card when we have a whole deck waiting to be picked up."

"And dealt with."

"Less than fifty-two, but the odds look bad."

"A little powder carefully applied in the right places could work wonders for us, I reckon."

The start of a grin showed on the emaciated face of Red Gatling and he swallowed hard before he was able to rasp, "Are you guys saying what I think you're saying?" He clicked a thumb and finger. "Hey, card—that's King, ain't it? Walter King. You want to get to North Pass to get him?"

"Careless talk already cost one life today, feller," Edge reminded icily.

The liveryman had to gulp again. And then he nodded vigorously. "Okay. You're right. I won't say another word. Just listen and do whatever you want me to."

"Party night, Reb."

"You reckon we should make it go with a bang?"

"Maybe raise the roof."

"You guys have gotta be jokin'!" Red Gatling said in a hushed whisper.

"We're doing the best we can, feller," Edge growled.

Steele added, "In an explosive situation."

Chapter Fourteen

The man called Edge and the dudishly dressed Adam Steele left Red Gatling's Livery Stables at just before three o'clock that afternoon. Not that the time had any significance. If it had been important, either of them could have made a reasonable guess at what it was by glancing at the position of the harshly glaring sun on its slow slide down the southwestern dome of the cloudless sky.

But the time registered in their minds because the bare-chested and barefoot Elmer Flexner was in the saloon area as the two men entered the Miner's Inn. And he had his pocket watch out of his pocket and on the table where he sat with the pretty Chinese whore. And the watch chimed three times as the half-breed and the Virginian went up the stairway of the hotel.

The whore, who had been taken down the street in such terror to be given to the old-timer in his shack, was now happy and bright. Giggled with childish and genuine pleasure as she heard the watch chime.

Edge and Steele appeared to show no interest in this or anything else that was happening in the place as they climbed the stairway with apparent weariness, each with his gear from the livery hefted to his shoulder.

And a great deal was happening, although not in the saloon section. Instead, in the ballroom area, several men and women were working with lethargic ill will to make it ready for the planned party.

Not whores and Blood's men. But the original citizens of South Pass, who, like Red Gatling, hated what was happening to their town. But felt impotent about the situation. And at this moment worked with morose resentment or tacit anger to clean and decorate the ballroom and supply it with what the hard men felt was required for the celebration.

132

Cobwebs had already been removed from the walls and ceiling and the chandeliers were hung with freshly fueled lamps. And the floor had been swept. Now flags and pennants and colored paper were being strung around and across the room. While a piano was being manhandled on to the dais, where a cello and a guitar already stood against chairs. While on the far side of the room a row of trestle tables had been set up and plates piled high with food were being aligned along their tops.

Arch Baxter glowered as he supervised the preparations for the party, obviously not liking the chore and not relishing the party to come. Alongside him, Floyd Devlin was enjoying what he saw and looking forward to its outcome. Except for long moments when he glared with hatred at the two strangers as they crossed from the batwing entrance to start up the stairs.

Baxter growled against the chiming of Flexner's watch and the low sounds of the party preparation: "You got no call to look at them like that, kid. Hadn't been for them, wouldn't be no party."

He said it loudly enough for everyone on either side of the central stairway to hear. Which caused a wave of resentment to rise up toward the half-breed and the Virginian from the hapless group of workers reminded of why they were forced to give freely of their time and labor. While Elmer Flexner turned on his chair to grin at them and call:

"Hey, you guys! What you think of my new lady friend? Ain't she somethin'?"

A whore had replaced Harvey Cox as bartender and a few other women were seated in groups or pairs at tables. And all grimaced their revulsion for the skinny old-timer. Who, having expressed his delight with the Chinese girl, rose and leaned across the table to take her smiling face in both hands and kiss her on the lips.

"Something, feller," Edge allowed as he stepped on to the balcony.

"Reckon so," Steele added.

"She ain't nothin' but a customer in the line for Hubert Perry's service," the blonde-headed, lumpy-figured Nora Stebbings muttered bitterly from the doorway of her room, on her careworn face an expression that matched those shown by the rest of her kind down in the saloon.

"We're all going to be dead and buried sometime," Steele pointed out.

"Some a whole lot quicker than others, Reb," Edge told him. "According to the lady here, Flexner tires of his women pretty fast. And reaches a stage when he can only get a charge from them by brushing them off for ever."

"Empty rooms in this place?" Edge asked Nora.

"All over that side," she answered, gesturing with a hand toward the line of doors off the balcony above the saloon area. "On account of its pretty noisy there some nights."

"Be noisy all over tonight," Edge reminded.

"I gonna have anythin' to celebrate, mister?"

"Only if you take some advice you should have listened to your ma give a long time ago," Steele told her.

Nora showed a fleeting, sardonic grin. Asked, "What's a mother?"

"Stay out of dancehalls and saloons, ma'am," the Virginian cautioned softly, and followed in the wake of Edge across the rear section of balcony. After a glance down at where Elmer Flexner was laughing and the Chinese girl was giggling, asked, "Doesn't she know what's in store for her?"

"No, feller. Seems Blood always sends the old-timer the newest girl in town. Who hates the thought of being personal whore to a man who's just killed his old one. But it seems at the start, Flexner treats her real well. Sleep well, Reb!"

"You too, Yank!"

The cynically toned good wishes were spoken loud enough to carry down into the saloon as each man pushed open a door to enter neighboring rooms.

"But it didn't oughta be alone, you guys!" Elmer Flexner yelled. "Not with all these beautiful women eager for company. Course, there's one you can't have. The best lookin', best lovin', best—"

"So why don't you take her back home and screw her some more, Elmer!" a whore snarled "And keep your damn nose outta business ain't none of yours. Whores can be particular who they go with, you know."

"Some whores, anyway. And we ain't all like Nora Stebbin's that throws herself at anythin' with balls." This from another dejected woman in the saloon.

A third added in a similar tone, "Not for a lousy two bucks we don't."

The whore they were talking about wrenched open her room door wider and lunged to the balcony rail. To glower down at the scene below and shriek: "You dames better watch what you're sayin'! I do whatever the hell I want to with my pussy! Sell it or give it away or—"

"Pretty soon you won't be able to give it away, you fat cow!" a whore cut in.

To one side of the doorway, Floyd Devlin grinned his enjoyment of the quarrel as his jaws moved in their usual rhythmic chewing action.

On the other side, Arch Baxter leaned away from the wall and bellowed, "Shut your stinkin' mouths, all of you!" And when silence came to the entire hotel, every face turned toward him, he moderated his tone to add sourly, "Anyone wants to raise any hell of any kind, they just have to wait until tonight."

Up on the roof, to where they had climbed from the windows of their rooms at the side of the building, Edge and Steele squatted behind the projection of the impressive front. Shaded from the harsh glare of the sun and hidden to any chance glance that might be directed toward their position from any area of town where people still lived.

They were encumbered only by their saddlebags now—which were bulkier than when they were hung from the saddles on the geldings taken into the livery stable.

As they unfastened the straps and took out the first sack of black powder, Steele asked, "You fix for that disturbance, Yank?"

"No, feller," Edge answered as Arch Baxter's voice sounded as a mumble after his bellow had ended the row. "In this kind of town I'm not ready to trust anybody that much."

"Reckon we all deserve a little luck from time to time," Steele said as he eased down on to his hands and knees and began to lay a line of powder along the angle of the roof and the front projection.

Edge bellied across the burning-hot roof toward the rear and laid his charge from one end to the other. Then each took the top of a side wall. Moving slowly and silently, the sun beating down on their backs not entirely responsible for the sweat beads that oozed from their every pore, pasting their clothing to their flesh or dripping off the points of their chins. The tension of fear also the cause, now that there was no shrilly calling voices raised in angry argument to mask any sound they might make.

Back in the shade and cover of the front projection, Edge rolled over on to his back and rasped as he mopped at his face with a neckerchief: "Weather looks like it's going to hold, Reb. But I ain't gonna rely on my luck doing the same."

He had taken out a box of matches, and removed a half dozen sticks to drop into a shirt pocket before handing the box to Steele. The slits of his ice blue eyes glinted coldly.

The Virginian was seated on the roof with his back to the projection. And he frowned his ill feeling for Edge as he placed the box of matches on the line of powder at the corner—the corner diagonally opposite that at the rear where he had left his own matches.

"Long as Mother Nature keeps our powder dry, feller," Steele muttered, "I'll do what I have to to see it doesn't rain on our parade."

Edge nodded and took the lead in going to the side of the building and turning to lower himself down the wall, feet finding the ledge of the window of his room.

Because of his shorter stature, it was just the toes of Steele's boots that were on the ledge as he maintained his balance with both gloved hands hooked over the roof.

It was he who called, "Hey?"

"Yeah?"

"Thought we weren't going to hang around in this town, Yank?"

"I'm not, Reb," Edge growled, and was able to reach down with one hand, hook it under the top of the frame, and ease himself smoothly in through the window.

From where he watched with a smile of mild amusement as the shorter man accomplished the same end but with a great deal of awkward stretching. Then Edge touched the brim of his hat with an index finger and said along the wall, "See you later, little man."

Steele made a similar parting gesture and reminded, "This whole thing depends on me being a big shot."

"About the size of it, I guess."

Then, as they both withdrew their heads, Steele muttered: "Just you be sure to measure up, feller."

Chapter Fifteen

George Blood yelled, with a drunken grin spread across his fleshy and ugly face: "Like my Pa always used to say, we only pass this way but once! So we better have all the friggin' fun we can get! On account of we don't have no fun, all it gets us is into heaven. And unless a man likes playin' the friggin' harp, ain't much fun in that place!"

He roared with laughter and his jellylike body moved vigorously to give sight as well as sound to his mirth.

The Mexican girl he was embracing around the waist with one meaty arm winced with pain as the enormously fat man absently hugged her tight as a further sign of his enjoyment.

The fat man and his personal whore were standing at the foot of the stairway, watching two dozen or so couples dancing without enthusiasm around the ballroom floor. A few of them keeping time with the music played by the three-piece orchestra on the corner dais.

Elsewhere in the ballroom and saloon areas of the Miner's Inn, the celebration in honor of Adam Steele for saving the life of George Blood was just as subdued. As men and women, not yet drunk enough to overcome the discomfort of being cleanly and smartly dressed—or to forget they were unwilling guests at the party—watched and waited for something bad to happen.

For everyone in South Pass—except for the two guards who watched the valley to the south and the pass to the north—was at the party by order of George Blood. And it was a volatile mixture of people who did not want to be there—for a variety of reasons.

The businessmen and merchants and their wives who had made the preparations and who were afraid to even look up, let alone say anything, in case they offended in such dangerous company. All of them attired in their stiff and formal best clothes.

Like the hard men and the whores. Who resented having to wash up and shave or comb their hair and tie it with ribbons before they put on their finery for the sake of a stranger. Who had got in too good too fast with the fat man and had been the main reason why Ed Rouse and Harv Cox were killed. And who was an object of almost universal distrust—just like that tall, glinting-eyed partner of his.

From both sides of South Pass society, Red Gatling and Nora Stebbings shared a common cause for concern. A knowledge that Edge and Steele had plans for something to go wrong, but not trusting the strangers to warn them in time.

The Virginian and the half-breed were in the group to which Blood addressed his philosophy about enjoying life while it was available. Along with the Mexican girl, Arch Baxter and his personal whore, and Floyd Devlin, who was with a woman old enough to be his mother.

The fat man acted the drunkest of the group, but everyone knew this was not due entirely to the whiskey he had taken—all the men except for Adam Steele were drinking free whiskey, the Virginian sipping a glass of fruit punch, which had been supplied for the women who did not take hard liquor. In large part, the obese man dressed in another garishly colored outfit that served only to emphasize his gross bulk was drunk with power.

And now he enjoyed himself on account of this power as he scanned the ballroom and the saloon over a full circle, and saw his people and the true citizens of town respond to his laughter with bursts of their own or, at the very least, smiles and the lifting of glasses.

The celebration had been underway for just about an hour, had started at sundown when the chandeliers had been able to drop their glow over the two sections of the hotel's lower floor. The lamplight less penetrating than that from the Colorado sun, tending to play down the signs of neglect and to stress the bright colors of the decorations. So that, if anybody had been so inclined, it might have been possible to visualize the scene as paralleling many in the past when the Miner's Inn had its heyday. But if any of the longtime citizens of South Pass did half close their eyes, to see in soft focus the party sights being played out against a background sound of music and talk and laughter and clinking classes, it would surely have been possible to remain detached from the reality for just a short time.

For the stink of evil and the menace of hovering violence was too thick in the atmosphere of this town. Had become impregnated into the very fabric of the buildings so that no amount of the fragrance of perfume and talc, soap and pomade, of cigar smoke or of freshly poured liquor or fruit punch could keep the stench of rottenness long from the nostrils of anyone who possessed a grain of decent human feelings in his or her being.

Edge and Steele smelled nothing, simply sensed the hatred that was generated toward them from almost every pair of eyes that glanced at them.

"What do you two guys say?" George Blood asked after he had completed his survey of the room and drawn the desired responses from everyone. "Seems to me you ain't much in agreement with me. Always joking back and forth, but you don't laugh too much. And round about siesta time, it was just Edge here that had himself a woman to give him an appetite for sleep, way I hear it?"

There was an implied question in his tone of voice.

Edge said: "Tried her out for tonight, feller. And didn't find her wanting."

"Or leave her that way I friggin' hope?" Blood answered, and vented another frame-shaking burst of laughter.

"Only woman I had a yen for was taken, George," Steele said.

The fat man's face was abruptly darkened by a frown. And the Mexican girl grimaced again as his arm tightened around her narrow waist and his hand cupped and rose to caress her breast in the taut-drawn fabric of her high-necked white dress.

"You better not be meaning this one, mister," he rasped. "Owe you or not, no one but me gets to break in the virgins that come to town."

For the first time, Edge and Steele noticed that the young girl who was never allowed to leave the fat man's side was the only woman in the Miner's Inn who wore a white and unrevealing dress.

Steele answered: "The Oriental, George. One you gave to the old man to replace the Indian squaw he killed."

Edge let out his pent up breath in a low sigh nobody else heard.

The fat man was mollified, but still not happy with what Steele had said. He growled "Gives me a problem. Elmer and me go back a long time. Longest of any of us around here. Patched me up real good and nursed me back to health way back when I took a belly bullet from the guard on a stage we held up. Saved my skin, did Elmer just as much as you did."

The skinny old man, with a shirt and tie and hose and shoes on tonight, was out on the ballroom floor with the Chinese girl—she trying to get him to keep time with the beat of the music. She was still giggling and he was enjoying the lesson too. The fat man watched the couple sadly as he went on:

"Elmer, he don't ask for much. Just young girls to ease his old age. Never have taken one from him after I give her to him. Don't reckon he'll take kindly to that."

"Forget I asked," Steele said evenly.

Devlin said with a broad grin, "In case it's just that you're curious, dude, them Chink girls are cut the same way ours are."

George Blood's face became more deeply cut with the lines of a frown as he snapped, "Floyd!"

The dull-eyed youngster's jaw stopped chewing as fear took a hold of him. "George?"

"I think you should go and get another round of drinks for us, kid. And while you're doin' it, look around you and see how other people are behavin'."

"I don't get it, George."

"It's a nice party, Floyd. People havin' nice fun. Dancin' and talkin' and drinkin' a little. Soon be eatin' some nice food. No place for gutter-type talk, I'd say. I'd also say that if I hear you talk that way again while the party's still nice, you won't be around to see how things turn out."

Devlin swallowed hard, and almost choked on his piece of candy. The whore he was with beat him on the back as his pale face turned crimson.

The mercurial-tempered fat man laughed long and loud through the youngster's coughing fit. And blurted at it's end: "Don't worry kid. It ain't the cough that carries you off, it's the coffin they carry you off in." Then his tone of voice altered abruptly when he saw Steele and Edge turn to leave the group at the foot of the stairway. And he demanded to know, "Where the hell do you think you two are goin'?"

"Need to get rid of some of this punch, George," the Virginian answered, as he set his empty glass down on a nearby table in the saloon.

Edge said coldly, "This is some party you've thrown, feller." And drew glowers from Blood and Baxter—and Floyd Devlin when the youngest man saw the expressions of the others. "The Reb has to get permission to leave the room and take a leak. And I have to tell you ahead of the lady I'd like to dance with that I'd like to dance with her."

Blood came close to plunging into a deep pit of boiling rage, pushed to the very brim by the criticism, its tone, and the knowledge that it was well merited. But with everyone in the room still looking at him after his snarled demands just as the orchestra finished playing, he brought himself back to the fringe of sanity and began to clap in the same way as an elderly woman who had been dancing to the music. Then, as everyone in the ballroom except for Edge and Steele joined in the polite applause with its undercurrent of high tension, the fat man rasped: "You go for a piss. You go dance with your whore. You go get the drinks."

He tipped his head sharply to each man in turn. Then ceased clapping, took a firm grip on the upper arm of the Mexican girl, and pushed her forward.

"Mr. Blood?" she asked.

"Food, girl, I want some food," he instructed, as the orchestra struck up a faster tune and the dancers began to whirl— Edge and Nora Stebbings not among them as the whore protested that the dance was too fast for her. Talking as much with her hands as with her mouth. So that Blood and Baxter could read from her gestures what she was saying. And then the two men who were left alone at the foot of the stairs—Baxter's and Devlin's women having gone with the Mexican girl to bring food from the trestle tables—saw the half-breed agree that Nora was right and then sit down at her table.

"You want me to go check that the dude is doin' what he says he is, George?" Baxter asked.

The fat man allowed his own party manners to slip again and spat forcefully at the floor before he growled: "What else would he be doin' in the privy, Arch? Jerkin' off, maybe, because he can't have the Chinese ass? If you get a charge outta watchin' another guy jerk off, sure. Go take a look at what he's doin'!"

Baxter showed a chastened expression while Blood looked at him. And scowled his hatred of everyone after the fat man had switched his attention elsewhere—to draw grins and waves from the guests even though he was no longer showing any sign of enjoyment himself.

The three musicians—the mute preacher playing the piano, an elderly woman on the cello, and the black-bearded Mo Spencer with the guitar—continued to provide a cheerful tune to which a great many couples were gavotting. So many that the three women had to half circle the ballroom with its whirling dancers to bring the plates of food to the men at the foot of the stairway.

"I think I brought you all that you like, George," the Mexican girl said in her heavily accented English.

She thrust a plate at him, piled high with bread and cheese and relish and cold meats and salad. And he snarled as he knocked it aside:

"Shut up, girl! Can't you see I'm thinkin'?"

The plate hit the floor and shattered, spilling the food among the feet of the group. And, familiar with the irascibility of the fat man, no one in the group or outside it paid more than passing attention to his latest tantrum. And his expression was pensive as he asked:

"Arch, you think I should let the dude have the Chink? Just for a couple of hours? You think Elmer would go for that?"

Baxter and Blood took drinks off the tray Floyd Devlin had brought from the saloon. Then the three women. Everyone in the group save the fat man began to eat, and for several seconds a stranger suddenly arrived might have viewed the scene at the foot of the stairs as a normal part of a normal party. At least until he drew close enough to overhear that the garishly attired fat man and the taller, leaner, more sour-faced man at his side were discussing the taking of a woman from one guest to give her to another.

"Up to you, George. But like you say, you and Elmer go back a long time. This guy Steele, I don't—"

"He can't still be in the privy," Floyd Devlin growled as the music ended and the applause began, the dancers starting to clear the floor.

Blood did a double take across the room and said, "Shit!"

"Even to do that, George," Devlin put in, with the start of a grin. Which he abandoned when he saw the expressions of trepidation on the faces of the three women in the group, who were better placed to see what kind of new mood was signaled by the look spread over Blood's fleshy features.

"His friggin' partner's missin' too!" the fat man roared, and his voice raised in shrieking anger sounded above the diminishing applause and opening notes of a new tune. To bring silence to every corner of the Miner's Inn. And expressions of either puzzlement or alarm to every face.

Emotions that took a tighter grip on the minds and a firmer hold on the faces of all when Edge called, "Hey, Reb, come have something to eat before it all goes."

Blood wrenched his head to the side. And saw that the half-breed and the blonde Nora Stebbings were not where he had last seen them because they had moved to the food tables. Then he had moved to the food tables. Then he had to turn his entire bulk around to look in another direction. When Adam Steele answered from the saloon, where he was weaving among the tables and carrying a cup of coffee:

"Be right there, Yank."

George Blood grinned then, but his tone of voice was harsh as he rasped to Baxter and Devlin, "You guys get me thinkin' wrong about them two again and I'll—"

More music had been struck up, people grinned and laughed to the trigger of the fat man's expression, and there was movement again.

Then the roof blew off.

Steele hurled himself to the side of the stairway, tossing away the cup of coffee and folding both arms over his head. And snarled at the floor to which his face was pressed, "Who the hell stole our thunder, Yank?"

On the far side of the ballroom, the half-breed curled an arm around the waist of the whore and threw her to the floor. Went down on top of her and rasped: "Don't get any ideas, lady. No time or inclination for any more bangs tonight."

Chapter Sixteen

Before the explosion, two men were already dead in South Pass. Sprawled in the dust at either end of the main street with knives in their backs. The sentries, disgruntled at having to miss the party at the hotel, who had been gazing out in the wrong directions to catch a first glimpse of strangers who might or might not mean ill will to the men who had taken over the town.

Then the strangers who had evaded their watchful gaze lost three of their own number dead. As one of the trio who had climbed silently up on to the roof of the Miner's Inn made to put out the cheroot he had been smoking. By pushing it into what he thought was a heap of dirt.

His entire right arm disintegrated and he was dead from shock before his body was hurled off the roof by the blast. While the two men with him died from being hit by flying debris or smashing to the ground as they were blown, limp and helpless, off the top of the building. All three had their clothing and hair seared from their bodies by the great tongues of flame that writhed across the roof.

In one direction from the first blast and then in others as this flame touched off fresh explosions. All coming so close together that they sounded as one, which lasted for stretched seconds.

And shocked the men outside the hotel as much as the shouting and screaming people within the building.

Black-powder smoke billowed down as well as up and to the sides. And dangerous debris flew unseen through it in every direction.

There was not a single person, inside or out, who did not instinctively take cover. Then not more than a second spanning the recovery by all those who accepted violence and death as a part of normal life.

146

Outside, this included Walter King and seventeen other men from North Pass. Who could not understand what had happened and why. Knew only that three of their number had died on the roof and had to assume Blood's men were responsible. So it was in anger at being surprised, when they thought they possessed this element of attack, and fear of being trapped by Blood's counter, that the men outside began to blast rifle fire through the thinning smoke of the explosion.

Which doubtless saved the lives of Edge and Steele, as the initial bolt of shock was negated at a faster speed than the choking smoke. And hate-filled eyes raked the room, disoriented minds seeking those who were surely to blame for this havoc. The dudish Virginian who was picking himself up from beside the foot of the stairway. And the taciturn half-breed who was rising from behind one of the food tables. While at least a dozen people—men and women from both strata of South Pass society—remained down and still. Bruised or bleeding. Unconscious or dead. Hit by pieces of flying or falling debris.

The old woman who had been playing the cello. The Chinese girl who was doomed to be murdered by the lusting Elmer Flexner. The man called Rich who had been the killjoy guard at the north end of town earlier in the day.

These and others seen clearly in the flames that danced from the oil spilled by the chandelier lamps that had been dropped and smashed in the wake of the roof explosion.

But then the fusillade of rifle fire thudded bullets into the outside walls and cracked them across the interior through the doorway and windows.

And Blood roared: "It's friggin' Walt King! It's friggin' gotta be Walt King! Go get the friggin' bastards, you sonsofbitches!"

The insanely raging fat man made to get to his feet, but Adam Steele lunged at him to send him sprawling back to the floor. And snarled above the barrage of gunfire:

"You're a big target, George!"

This as, across the ballroom, Edge rasped close to the ear of Nora Stebbings: "No deal on your future earnings, lady. You're on your own from here."

Then he rose on to his hands and knees and went at a fast crawl away from there. Under the food tables and emerging from them at intervals to get around the trestles supporting them. Staying on the blind side from the dance floor with its sprawl of dead and wounded and terrified among the pools of burning oil. And the many snarlingly angry men with revolvers drawn who were making as fast a time as the half-breed in similarly ungainly crawls to stay under the bullets that cracked across the hotel to pit far walls. But who were heading in a different direction. Going to the front of the building from where men already by the doorway and windows were returning the fire of King and his men.

At the rear of the room, across from where the mute preacher was down on his knees on the dais, hands together and head tilted, lips moving to form the shape of pleading words, Edge came out from under the tables and climbed up on top of one of them. Muttered, "Say one for me, feller," and sprang upwards.

Saw with a fleeting frown that the praying man was smiling—as if it was thanks rather than an appeal for help that he was offering. Then Edge put the preacher and everyone else out of his mind as he hooked one hand over the floor of the balcony, grasped a rail support with the other, and swung to the side, legs swinging to find a foothold.

Bullets cracked from gun muzzles and thudded into timber. Maybe some flesh here and there. But not that of the man called Edge. Who hauled himself up and over on to the balcony. Heard footfalls at the top of the stairway and drew the Frontier Colt from his holster, hammer thumbed back, as he dropped into a crouch and turned sideways—towards a target that was lit by flames from below and moonlight streaming in through the holed roof above.

The Virginian rasped, "You sure come up in the world the hard way, Yank."

The half breed's tension was vented in a sigh and he countered, "How you doing, you unsocial climber?"

"Not so good without my rifle."

"So let's go."

No bullets were reaching the upper-floor balcony as the two men moved along the rear stretch and turned to the side, above the saloon area of the hotel. But they were in instinctive crouches against the constant rattle of gunfire. And in the knowledge that somebody inside the Miner's Inn could spot them and decide to blast at a hated and visible target he could see instead of firing wildly out into the muzzle-flash-streaked night.

Here and there the rafters continued to hold up sections of roof. But not above the rooms which were all around the outside of the hotel and had therefore taken the most intense blast from the accidentally exploded black powder. And what had been the side and rear and front walls of the building had also been badly hit—seared black and left jaggedly ugly against the night sky.

Each man in his own roofless and smoke-smelling room located his rifle and gear. Checked the action of the Colt Hartford and the Winchester before taking the time to locate saddlebags. Adam Steele to hurl his away with a grunt of frustrated anger as he recalled the gear was not his own. Edge locating a carton of shells in the toe of a bag before he dropped it back among the litter of the explosion on the floor.

Thus was the Virginian first to go to what was left of the window frame of his room, peer out, and take a bearing on the positions of the men firing at the hotel.

"What you got?" Edge yelled from the bottom half of the window frame of the next-door room.

"All of them across the street unless there's some playing possum!"

"What d'you figure?"

"That we get the hell out! Watch from the sidelines!"

"Take care, Reb! I got money riding on you!"

"So I don't have a thing to worry about, Yank! Reckon you'll take care of me!"

Again it was the Virginian who led the way: swinging a leg over the windowsill and wedging the Colt Hartford under an armpit and over an elbow before he drew up the other leg and leaped to the ground. Knees bent to absorb the main force of the impact.

Edge tossed his Winchester out first and then jumped. Just as they were rasping the exchange at the windows, the constant barrage of gunfire, crackle of flames, and din of yelling voices masking the clatter of the rifle and the thudding of feet against the hard-packed dirt in the alley beside the hotel.

From the shadows Nora Stebbings snarled, "Don't bother to tell a girl you got a friggin' army backin' you up!"

A man shrieked: "I friggin' knowed you was with them bastards from North—"

Edge and Steele whirled in unison toward the enraged man. The half-breed needing to snatch up his rifle from the ground as he came erect from the crouch after landing. The Virginian taking just as long to get a two-handed grip on the Colt Hartford.

They fired simultaneously at the sound of the man's voice. Which was on the other side of the alley from where the whore was standing, back pressed to the hotel wall. In the double muzzle flashes saw him staggering backwards with holes in his chest and a revolver hanging unfired from his opening right hand. It was Elmer Flexner. His watch began to chime eight times.

Steele snapped, "You have a big mouth, ma'am."

"He's just jealous because he never got to get the girl before it was the end for her."

"And you're not the only one around here spends time talking when there are more important things to do," Steele drawled, the anger of tension drained from him by the killing of the old-timer.

Then almost got himself killed. In the same way as Edge and the whore. As a fusillade of shots sent a hail of bullets into the alley from the street—drawn by the two reports from the rifles that blasted the life from the skinny frame of Elmer Flexner. At the same time as voices were raised in fear and rage at the other, rear end of the alley. Blood's men, some whores, and some noncombatant local citizens having lunged out of the back of the Miner's Inn in the wake of Flexner and Nora.

The half-breed and the Virginian again hurled themselves down and again Edge had to curl an arm around the thick waist of the whore and knock her off her feet, under the line of fire.

An answering barrage exploded from the other end of the

alley. The bullets aimed along its length and out on to the street, Blood's men ignoring the sprawl of forms on the ground. Who by drawing fire from King's men were obviously not the enemy. And who were probably dead.

But only the old-timer was that. Edge, Steele, and the whore were merely deafened for the moment by the continuous volley of gunfire and speckled with splinters from the flanking walls off which bullets had ricocheted.

"Let's go get them bastards! Let's kill them all! Man, do I wanna blast the friggin' sonsofbitches into—"

The man came along the alley at a lumbering run. Working the action and firing a repeater rifle to punctuate each shrilly voiced sentence. And a group of other men came after him. Less hysterically eager to do long-range, blind battle with the enemy. But taking advantage of his covering fire to reach positions where they would be able to shoot at the North Pass men with better effect.

The whore attempted to rise after the too eager man had leaped over Edge and herself, but the half-breed kept her pinned to the ground until the six or so men behind him had gone by.

And then they went down, as a barrage of shots from the street cracked into the alley to tear bullets into the flesh of the shouting man—to silence him and his repeater and to stop him in his tracks and knock him sprawling on to his back, limbs twitching and blood gushing.

"That Chas Rix always was a dumb, crazy bastard," one of the men who had gone down to get under the hail of bullets muttered.

"But a good buddy."

"Sure."

"So let's pay them for what they done to him."

"I got his rifle."

"Count of three."

The exchange was whispered in harshly rasping tones by three of the seven men who were on the ground between the dead Rix and where Edge and Steele and the whore played at being dead.

"Frig that, we go!"

This was the one who had found the repeater. And he pumped the action and fired it as he lunged up into a crouch and dashed forward. The others were just part of a second behind him in rising and blasting bullets to either side of him with revolvers.

Again Nora Stebbings struggled to get up. And again Edge held her down. This time moved a hand to cover her cursing mouth as he sensed somebody approaching out of the darkness at the rear of the alley. Could not hear footfalls because of the cacophony of gunfire. Which was doubled and tripled as the seven Blood men reached the street and drew the fire of the North Pass men—which in turn sparked a more intensive series of fusillades from those still in the hotel and others who had got out on the other side of the building.

Then the lone figure was close enough to be seen. Running with a light tread despite being in the grip of terror. Because she was a slightly built woman. Her white dress showing up more starkly than her face, which despite being bloodless was stained dark by her Mexican heritage.

Nora recognized her fellow whore and sank her teeth into one of the fingers over her mouth.

Edge snatched his hand away with a grunt of pain.

The fat man's personal whore tripped over the outstretched leg of the dead Elmer Flexner and vented a cry of alarm as she stumbled. But remained upright and running.

Nora called hoarsely, "Zamora!" and stretched out a hand to reach for the girl.

Whose terror expanded at the prospect of being held back—being clutched by the clawed fingers of somebody she perhaps thought was dead. And she shrieked a denial that went on and on without wavering from its shrill pitch as she plunged along the alley and out of it. Across the street and into the doorless entrance of a building on the far side. Evading the cross fire of bullets when she first showed herself in the open. And causing the gun battle to be briefly interrupted while she completed what should have been a suicidal dash. North and South Pass men alike taken totally by surprise at the sight of her—so plain to see in the white dress—and the sound of her: the scream venting from her widely gaped mouth having an eerie quality.

Especially in the surrounding silence after the gunfire was curtailed. Then came perfect silence.

A silence which was ended by George Blood. Who, a second after the girl's scream was cut off, howled, "Zamora, you crazy bitch!"

The acrid taint of gunsmoke had begun to be negated by the freshness of the mountain night air. But now every Silver Pass man with a gun in his hand fired it again. And the smoke was like an evil-smelling mist of early morning hanging and twitching to the passage of bullets between the opposing forces.

Edge and Steele and the blonde whore with the lumpy figure did not see this. For they had turned their backs on the abruptly more fierce gun battle. And made use of it to withdraw from the alley. And from town.

Circled around to the north side and started up the rock-scattered slope toward the pass between the high ridges. Moving fast at first, but needing to slow the pace on the upgrade. Then to pause to catch their breath. Sprawled out on their backs in a dusty, rocky hollow. Out of sight of South Pass, where the battle was not so frenetic now. The distant gunfire sounding in brief, sporadic bursts.

After perhaps thirty seconds of being spread-eagled, sucking in deep breaths of cool night air and feeling the sweat on their flesh become coldly dry, the two men rolled over and bellied to the rim of the hollow. Where they could peer down on the former ghost town, which from tonight would harbor a fresh supply of tormented spirits.

From their vantage point, the half-breed and the Virginian could see just one corpse—that of the sentry who had been watching this slope to warn of just such an attack as had been launched. But they could see several men who had survived the battle of the Miner's Inn. Withdrawing from the engagement in the same manner as Edge and Steele with the whore.

Heading west, though, from the far side of main street. A dozen of them. And they had a South Pass whore with them—George Blood's Mexican girl in the virginal white dress.

Nora Stebbings crawled between the half-breed and the Virginian and said in a shocked tone, "That's Zamora!"

"Your eyesight's as sound as your teeth, lady," Edge growled around the wounded finger he was sucking.

Steele displayed his boyish grin as he murmured, "Reckon that must've made your eyes water, Yank."

"It did, Reb. And put her teeth on Edge."

Nora grimaced and uttered a sound of impatience. Then demanded, "Where are they takin' her?"

There was no more frantic shooting in the town now. Just an isolated gunshot every few seconds. None of these fired by the group of men with the Mexican girl. Who went into a a clump of mesquite and abruptly disappeared.

"Wherever, she looks happy to be going, lady," Edge answered.

And together with Steele and the whore had his attention captured by three men who suddenly showed—running full tilt across the three hundred yards of open ground between the end of a South Pass cross street and the stand of mesquite.

Walt King's rear guard, who did not make it. Because they got no covering fire from the men whose escape they had secured. Were themselves too intent upon reaching their objective to take the time to blast at their pursuers. Who had ample time to take aim and fire at the moving targets.

"Mining country, Reb," Edge murmured, coldly glinting eyes peering out from his impassively set lean face as he waited for three more men to die. "Has to be a tunnel, right?"

"Reckon so, feller. Occurred to me that was how King got through town and over the pass. When Harv Cox told me about the ore-processing plant falling down because of subsidence."

"What's subsidence?" the whore asked with mild curiosity as she sensed the impending killings on the fringe of South Pass.

And they happened as the Virginian made to explain to her. But never got started against the sharp crackle of gunfire. By a group of Blood's men who had taken the time to go bring their rifles. Which they used to spray out a hail of bullets like a burst from a Gatling gun. Probably as many missing the targets as drilling into them. But enough penetrated into the backs of the running men and exploded out from their fronts to kill them on their feet. And pitch them into forward rolls, arms flailing and rifles arcing away from unfeeling hands. To become inert except for slow-oozing blood, several yards short of the mesquite in which the tunnel entrance was concealed.

"It's caused by—" Steele began.

"It doesn't friggin' matter," the whore cut in bitterly. "All that matters is that we should get the hell away from this place. Before we wind up like those three guys."

There was a brittleness in her tone that warned she was near the brink of hysteria. Her nervous system strained close to breaking point by fear of the death they had all been close to for so long.

"Easy, ma'am," Steele said soothingly.

"Yeah," Edge added in a growling tone. "We ain't in the business of saving fallen women to have them break up on us."

"That's your business, Yank," the Virginian drawled. "Mine's still unfinished."

He was staring fixedly down the slope at the mesquite where King and the others had gone from sight. Now rolled over on to his back to peer up at the pass.

Edge continued to rake his slitted eyes over the entire town and the area to the west of it. Where the fat man was personally engaged in the ill-tempered search to discover how the bulk of King's men had got away.

"Figure you were hoping your man would get his ass shot off down there, Reb?"

"Didn't have much hope of that, feller. Walt King's smarter than to be at the front when the lead starts to fly."

"Whole lot smarter than the fat man, I guess," the half-breed answered as he watched the obese George Blood in an almost demented rage. Obviously ranting and raving at his henchmen for not being able to find a trace of the escapers and the way they had escaped. His gesturing antics almost comical over a distance the sound of his voice could not travel. "George should have taken prisoners instead of gunning down those fellers."

"Reckon that proves what's said."

"What's that?" Edge asked as the search was abandoned and he turned over on to his back, digging into a shirt pocket for the makings.

"Blood's thicker than Walter."

Nora Stebbings continued to peer down the slope as the men moved into town from off the open area. And she shuddered before she rasped, "Shit, I figure Zamora's got a better deal than I do."

"How's that, ma'am?" Steele asked as he interlocked his fingers behind his head and yawned.

"At least she got took away good from that lousy town down there. All the friggin' way. And she ain't stuck with a couple of crazy guys who hang around all the time makin' lousy jokes."

Edge finished rolling the cigarette and said as he hung it at a corner of his mouth: "Look at it from our point of view, lady. Walt King has got youth and beauty on his side."

"Bastard," she rasped."

The half-breed shielded the flame with both cupped hands as he struck a match on the stock of the Winchester and lit the cigarette. This as the whore broke off her bleak-eyed watch on the now quiet and seemingly deserted town to slide deeper into the hollow and roll on to her back.

Steele glanced sideways at her stretched out beside him and drawled, "Grateful for the offer, ma'am, but no thanks."

"Go to hell!"

"We just came from there."

She sighed and a shudder shook her fleshy frame. "The real place, if there is such a place, can't be much worse."

"Everyone else seems to like it down there, lady," Edge said evenly.

"Uh?" She turned her head to the side and there were tears visible in the moonlight. She looked too emotionally drained to feel anything but exhaustion.

"Except for you and the fat man's woman. Didn't see anyone else leave town?"

"Maybe they were all killed in the shootin'. Them you didn't kill when you blew the place up."

Edge continued to gaze up at the star-pricked night sky as he said: "Meant to ask you about that, Reb. Way I recall it, we were supposed to be down the street. And you were going to fire that fancy rifle—"

Steele spat to the side and drawled: "Had my leak and then

went to the kitchen to get the coffee, Yank. Must've been set off by King's men."

"Yeah, I guess so."

"*You* were supposed to be down the street," Nora Stebbings said, and tried to inject some fire into her voice. "What about me and Mr. Gatling and Mr. Perry and Mr. and Mrs. Diver and the preacher and all the others that ain't with Blood and his—"

"And the Chinese girl," Steele put in flatly. "Been nice to have got her out of there."

"That part was down to Red Gatling, lady," the half-breed told the whore. "He knew who all those people were. And he was going to pass the word around."

"To leave when they saw the Yank and me leave."

"When we figured most of Blood's men were too drunk to notice."

"Those who had the guts for it to go to the place they use as a bunkhouse and get the men's rifles."

"Make a fight of it."

"But Walt King beat us to the punch."

Edge crushed out the cigarette against the rock-hard ground and eased up into a sitting position. Growled: "That's the thing, Reb."

"What is?"

"Whether we or King and his bunch can claim to be responsible."

"Irresponsible is what the hell you guys are," Nora Stebbings accused, but her tone still lacked force.

"Joint enterprise I reckon," Steele said.

"For blowin' the roof off a lousy saloon?" the whore murmured.

"Opening up the first topless bar in Colorado, lady."

Chapter Seventeen

It was a long, cold night on the hillside below Silver Pass. For none of the three had a topcoat to wear against the chill of the mountain air. And Walt King did not make his move until the dawn of a new day.

Edge and Steele and the whore were in better cover by then. Higher up the slope than the hollow where they had rested to recover from the race out of town. On the western rim of a curving ravine through which the trail ran in one of its snakelike turns to reach up into the pass. The point where they spent the night hidden from South Pass by the height of the ravine side and from above by a mound of jagged rock.

During the night the three huddled close together for mutual warmth and sometimes drifted into fitful sleep. Infrequently, there was talk.

Shivering, the whore said: "If I'd known it was goin' to be like this, I'd have stayed in town. A person could freeze to death out here like this."

This was ignored by the men who sat to either side of her, pressed hard against her, all three with their backs leaning on the base of the mound of rock. Both her taciturn escorts familiar with every kind of discomfort the elements could produce.

Later, Edge said: "We did this wrong, Reb. Should have got the horses and stole some gear and headed up over the pass."

"And if King had left some men guarding it, feller? Didn't somebody say North Pass is impregnable from the south?"

"Got horses and frig saddles," the whore put in. "And headed down the valley and to Stormville. Caught a friggin' train to Denver. That's what we should've done."

The subject was dropped because, by tacit agreement, it

was acknowledged that it was futile to discuss what might have been.

After a lengthy silence, Steele asked, "You awake, Edge?"

For an answer, the half-breed took his hands out from under his armpits and blew into them. Put them back.

"Why do you reckon that just the lady here and the Mexican got out of town while the Blood bunch were busy?"

The whore had seemed to be sleeping, breathing deeply and regularly as she half sat and half lay between the two men with their hats tipped forward over the upper part of their faces. But she spoke before Edge could answer. "Where would they go, mister? They live there in that no account town. They ain't like me and you guys. Beddin' down wherever we happen to be when the nighttime comes." She sighed. "Could've made a run for Stormville, maybe. Or even North Pass. But you seen them. Ain't none of them spring chickens no more. Doin' like we're doin' right now would most likely kill some of them. And the war down there didn't go on for too long, did it? Blood had found people were gone, chances are him and his men would've come out huntin' and killin'. Just from spite. Takin' it out on innocent people for what King done to them."

"Cover it, feller?" Edge asked after several seconds of silence.

"Reckon so. But you know what it means?"

"You friggin' blew it!" Nora Stebbings muttered.

"Now who's making bad jokes?" Steele said flatly.

"And old ones," Edge added. Went on: "So it didn't work out right for anybody, lady. King and his bunch spoiled our play. Then had his own plans altered by the fat man's whore switching sides."

"Hell, Yank, what do the side issues matter?" Steele growled.

"Wasn't me who brought up that one, Reb. I'm happy to sit here quiet and wait to see what happens next. Until morning. Then I'm going to get me a horse and head him for Stormville and the Denver train."

"Just like that, uh?" the whore said with a sneering tone. "Only horses around this friggin' neck of the friggin' wood are in North Pass and South Pass. Which in either you'll get your ass shot off on sight, I'd say. And you're gonna wait until daylight. And in broad daylight you're gonna—shit!"

She broke off her low-keyed diatribe and vented the expletive at the sound of a rifle shot. Which was fired up in the pass and echoed back and forth between the rock faces at the ends of the flanking ridges.

Both men knocked their hats off their faces and rolled away from her to either side, each tightening his grip around the frame of his rifle that lay by his leg. Then froze, on all fours, as unmoving as the terrified whore, as they listened to the distant echoes fade—and knew there was no immediate danger.

Nora Stebbings, as afraid of their instinctive reaction to a shot as she was of the shot, let out her pent-up breath in a sigh. And murmured, "Wow, you guys can move quicker than a rattler if you have to."

"We didn't have to, seems like," Edge said.

"Time we were up though," Steele answered as they both straightened and looked across the ravine and the slope toward the distant ridges in the far east. Where a band of gray daylight signaled the close approach of dawn.

The whore got to her feet and stretched. Then shivered and hugged herself. Eyed the two men bleakly for long moments. Grimacing at the sight of them in the slowly brightening light that showed the dirt and the bristles on their faces and the disheveled state of their clothes. But her response was not so much triggered by what she saw as by the image of her own appearance that was conjured up.

"God, I must look awful," she rasped, and spat on both her hands, then rubbed them over her face. Trying to remove the old paint and powder from her pores.

Edge had gone to the top of the ravine from where, hunkered down on his haunches, he was able to see in the brightening light the distant huddle of buildings that was South Pass. While Steele was crouched at the side of the rocky mound, looking down into the ravine, at the point, perhaps a mile away, where the trail curved out of sight. Which was where he would first glimpse anyone coming down from the pass on the trail.

Twenty feet between the two men, with the woman sitting on

the ground at a midway point, now using the skirts of her torn and stained party dress to scrub saliva into her face.

"Reckon we have to hope the situation gets to look better than all of us, ma'am," the Virginian said, and rasped the back of a gloved hand over his jaw.

"What do you think caused the shot?" the whore asked.

"A rifle," Edge answered flatly as he pushed a freshly rolled cigarette into the corner of his mouth. But did not even take out a match to light it. This as he cracked his glinting eyes to the narrowest of slivers at the sight of movement on the north side of the town, some four miles away.

"You're about as funny as the pox, mister!" Nora spat at the half-breed.

"Maybe I'll warm up with the day, lady. It's got them stirred up down the hill, Reb."

"Nothing in this direction. Ma'am, there's no point in us thinking anything yet about that shot. Maybe it was an accident. Maybe one of the men guarding the pass fired at a shadow. Maybe at a bird. *Maybe* to the future is like *if* is to the past."

Edge shot a backward glance over his shoulder and asked, "Is that as smart as it sounds, Reb?"

Steele replied, "Maybe, Yank."

The whore clenched her fists and beat them on her thighs as she shook her head violently and vented a constantly pitched sound of frustrated rage. Brought this under control as the two men gazed at her impassively, and accused in a tight tone: "You're both crazy, you know that? Terrible things are gonna happen around here soon. Up there or down there . . ." She jerked a thumb toward the pass and then the town. ". . . and still you sit around tradin' lousy jokes. You're both crazy."

The half-breed and the Virginian had turned their backs to her again, to watch for activity in the town and the ravine. And hard silence greeted the end of what she said, as the first warm and welcome rays of the rising sun reached down to the barren area of rock where the three had spent the cold night.

The whore snarled, "Oh, shit!"

Edge murmured, as he concentrated his glinting-eyed attention on a more frenetic scene of animation far below, "Said the first sign of craziness is talking to yourself, lady."

"Saw another sign once," Adam Steele recalled in the same detached tone as he heard a sound that heralded the appearance of men in the ravine. "Something about you don't have to be crazy to work here, but it helps."

"Oh, sh—" Nora began to repeat.

The Virginian rasped with venom: "Shut your mouth, ma'am!"

She stared at him in fear, bathed in warm sunlight but suddenly feeling colder than at any time during the night. Terrified by the split-second change from carefree calmness to somehow evil anxiety. Then she heard the clop of hooves and caught her breath.

Edge reported evenly: "I got what looks like the whole bunch coming up the hill, Reb. Mounted and in no hurry yet."

"You hear what I hear, feller," Steele said. "Sounds like more than a couple of riders, I reckon."

He peered fixedly down at the point in the ravine where the slow-riding horsemen would first appear. Just half the orb of the sun was above the rim of the world to the east and it was not yet shafting down to the bottom of the ravine. But there was daylight enough to show up every detail of the yellow rock walls which flanked the stone-littered trail. The dusty surface of which was marked by the sign of just one horseman riding through recently. From north to south.

The hapless Englishman named Smythe. Who could be said to have triggered the entire series of events which had led to what was happening at this moment.

The half-breed had a much wider view across the broad slope that was extensively bathed in morning sunlight, except where outcrops of rock laid long fingers of shadow across the barren dirt and motionless rivers of shale.

And as he watched, the men riding out from South Pass spread to either side of a centrally placed group, to form a broad line of advance across the slope. Which took no account of the snaking trail designed to take a lot of the lung-bursting steepness out of the hill. What such a strung-out and never-straight line did insure was that each man had a good chance to make it into cover of some sort should the enemy spring an ambush.

Despite the distance over which he looked at the slow-climbing riders, Edge could easily pick out the grossly fat George Blood as one of the group at the center of the line. Guessed that Arch Baxter was one of the other four men in the group. Floyd Devlin, maybe. If they had not taken a bullet during last night's gunfight.

He vented a low sound of self-anger. Like the Virginian had said, *ifs* and *maybes* served no purpose.

Steele also uttered a subdued sound at the same time. Of discovery, rather than surprise, as he saw the front riders of the group from North Pass come around the curve in the ravine.

Three of them, only two of whom he recognized. To one side the tall, fifty-year old, silvery haired, and ruggedly handsome Walter King. Beside him the pretty young Mexican girl named Zamora. Who no longer wore the white dress and who, it was a safe bet, was no longer a virgin. She was naked now, to reveal that her slender young body had been brutally assaulted in every cruel way possible by the man who took her. Or, more probably, the men who took her. For the extent of the rising and scratching on the flesh of her thighs, belly, breasts, shoulders, and arms seemed testimony to her having been brutally raped more times than one man could have managed in a single night.

But not her face in its frame of black hair that was freshly brushed and highly sheened. It was not marked at all. But was made ugly by what protruded from her mouth: held forcibly in place by a circle of rope tied to it and knotted at the nape of her neck.

A stick of dynamite with a detonating cap in place at one end. The other end jammed hard into her throat from the way in which she had to breathe in and out so hard through her flared nostrils.

Her wrists were tied together at the front and lashed to the horn of the saddle in which she sat.

Each time the exhaustion of her night of terror and pain caused her chin to droop toward her chest, the fresh-faced man of about twenty who rode to her left laid the thin thong of a short-handled whip across her back. Just painfully enough to bring her to full awareness of what she had been ordered to do.

The evilly grinning young man had to use the whip on three occasions while he, the Mexican whore, and Walt King rode from the curve to the end of the ravine. By which time Edge and Nora Stebbings had seen the three front riders and the dozen men riding behind them.

Nora was on the point of gasping her deep shock. But held the sound in. When Edge shifted his impassive gaze away from the scene in the ravine to find her with his hooded eyes. And she was hit with the same degree of terror as when Steele had snapped the order at her a few moments ago.

This as the Virginian left his vantage point at the mound of rock and came on all fours to where the half-breed squatted. The whore stayed flat on the ground on the spot from which she had peered down at the girl she said she envied not so long ago, pressing her face into the rocky surface and allowing the tears to flow silently.

At the end of the ravine, King signaled a halt and he and his thirteen men dismounted. Out of sight as yet of the Blood bunch, who were visible to the half-breed and the Virginian up on the ravine rim. The fat man and sixteen others still making slow time on the slope, often needing to dismount and lead their horses by the bridle or reins up the more treacherous stretches of the incline.

The bell in the tower of the South Pass church began to sound its cracked note in the slow cadence of a death knell. Which seemed somehow more mournful because of the brightness of the morning and the distance over which the clang, clang, clang, clang rang out.

The first time it sounded, both groups of men were alarmed by it. Those in the mouth of the ravine whirled toward the distant sound, snatching Winchesters from scabbards or Colts from holsters, frightened eyes seeking a target as thumbs cocked hammers.

A mile away down the slope, the line of advance was halted and men wrenched around in their saddles. Similarly brought out rifles and revolvers.

"Be that mad preacher burying last night's dead," Walter King said as the fourth cracked note of the bell sounded.

And there was a trickle of embarrassed laughter from several of the men who had reacted so fast to an alien but innocent sound.

Probably there was anger in the minds of George Blood and his men as they recommenced their advance, cursing the mute preacher and his faith that in the eyes of God all dead men were equal.

There was no need for the top man from North Pass to speak again, for his plan had been made and explained long ago. And his men moved into predetermined positions with eager confidence that the plan was a good one. Leaving their hobbled horses in the ravine and going on foot to the cover of rocks on the sloping ground to either side of the trail beyond the twenty-foot-high walls of rock.

Walt King was one of the last to go into cover. For he had accepted the personal task of fixing a length of fuse to the detonator cap on the dynamite in the mouth of the Mexican whore. Then he whispered something to her that made her shudder before he backed off from where she sat astride the horse on the center of the trail some thirty feet out from the end of the ravine. And pinpointed his own hiding place by making no attempt to conceal the fuse as he dropped down behind a rock. And further displayed the extent of his self-confidence when he lit a large cigar that gave off a great deal of smoke. Using a cigar cutter than glinted metallically in the sunlight— first to snip off the end of the cigar and then to sever the fuse.

Nora Stebbings gaped her mouth to vent her feelings about what she saw. And this time it was a joint cold and unblinking gaze from Edge and Steele that terrified her into remaining silent. Then she squeezed her eyes tightly closed and covered her ears with her hands.

But it was not yet time for Zamora to get her head blown off.

The half-breed, the Virginian, and the whore were twenty feet above and at least fifty feet back from the nearest of King's men. But in the tense, hot stillness of early morning with the far-off clang of the cracked bell the only sound to intrude, it seemed to the three of them as if the blinking of an eyelid would sound like an explosion and betray their presence.

George Blood and his men were out of sight from the top of the ravine now, as they came up the final step of the slope toward the spot where the naked girl sat astride her horse in petrified terror. Totally exhausted, but sharply aware of the dangerous part she was forced to take in this morning drama at Silver Pass. Her head held up despite the absence of the sting of the whip across her back. As she stared out over the obscene projection of the stick of dynamite to the spot on the trail where she expected the first of the South Pass men to appear. Without hope of salvation. Perhaps eager for death to end her suffering and humiliation.

Everyone in back of her was straining to hear a sound of Blood and his men drawing close. And many noticed that the labored nose breathing of the helpless woman astride the horse kept strict time with the ringing of the distant death knell.

Zamora breathed in, and did not let the air out of her lungs.

The bell in the tower of the South Pass church continued to ring out, coldly detached from the scene high above the town.

George Blood reined his horse to a halt on the trail. Likewise Arch Baxter to one side of him and Mo Spencer on the other side. Slightly behind these three were Floyd Devlin and a man Edge and Steele could put a face to, but not a name.

The youngest of the group said, "Jesus, George!" with such force that he involuntarily spat out his piece of candy.

The fat man, first to recover from shock, said: "I wish it was you, kid. All the time makin' with your mouth."

While he spoke, his small eyes moved in their sockets, following the trail of the fuse to the rock over which a pall of cigar smoke hung.

The others looked in the same direction, but then away, seeking signs of which other areas of cover hid men. But nobody shifted the repeating rifle which each carried aimed at the sky, with the stock plate resting on the right thigh.

Blood raised his voice to yell: "Hold it right where you are men! Looks like a parley is what we got here!"

The sounds made by the rest of his force were suddenly curtailed as Walt King grinned around the cigar clamped between his teeth, drew against it, and blew out a long stream of smoke. "You got it, Blood," he called from behind the rock against which he leaned his back. "A deal is what I got in mind."

"Men that make a deal gotta trust each other, King."

"So?"

'Me and four of my men are right out here in the open. You and your scum are hid like rats in—"

As the fat man was speaking, King looked to either side and nodded to the men who were watching him. Then the top man from North Pass gave a lead in slowly rising to his feet after first turning so that he was facing the group from South Pass. His men aimed their Winchesters from the shoulder at the mounted targets. While King held the end of the fuse in his left hand and his lighted cigar in the right.

Only the heads of the men astride horses moved, swinging slightly to left and right to gaze without emotion at the force backing Walt King.

Blood asked, with a glance up at the high ground to either side of the ravine, "How many more?"

"What you see is what I've got."

Blood grimaced his disbelief. "You think I'm gonna buy that from a sneaky bastard like you?"

"Why you calling me names, Blood?" He used his head to gesture toward his men, so that he did not have to move the cigar from its dangerous proximity to the end of the fuse. "Just the single shot was fired. To invite you to the meeting. If it had been a trick, would I have ordered my men to—"

"Way you come and went like friggin' ghosts last night, scum!" the fat man cut in, his tone still a snarl.

King remained calm in the face of his rising anger. "I've heard it said that you're so dumb you don't know your ass from a hole in the ground, Blood."

The fat man's fleshy face became crimson and almost glowing as the insult was spoken in an even tone from a mouth formed into a half smile.

Arch Baxter sensed an explosion of violence that would serve no purpose, and spoke before Blood was able to say or do anything.

"A tunnel, George. A friggin' tunnel from the old minin' days! We should've figured that!"

Edge and Steele peered down from the rim of the high ground, hats off to lessen the chance of being glimpsed, and hands fisted tight to rifles that threatened nobody. The whore had bellied backwards and now was by the rock against which they had all three spent the night. Sat hugging her knees and pressing her face into her thighs.

"Your boy has got it, George," King confirmed as Blood frowned while considering what Baxter had said. "Sure it was sneaky. But it was smart too. Not as sneaky as rigging the hotel to blow. But that was dumb, Blood. You got all the buildings down there rigged to blow? I figure you must have lost people the way—"

"What you sayin', King?" Baxter cut in sharply. "We didn't blow the roof off the damn hotel! That had to be you! Damn right we lost men when you—"

"Shit, that's friggin' right!" the fat man stormed. 'The way you got that woman rigged shows you're the friggin' expert with—"

"Steele!" Walt King blurted, no longer so calm. "Friggin' Steele and his friggin' buddy!"

Nora Stebbings jerked up her head. She had detached herself from what was happening down beyond the mouth of the ravine, seeking physical safety in mentally withdrawing from reality. But the calling of Adam Steele's name by King penetrated through the tenuous barrier she had erected around her mind. And as she heard the second part of what King snarled, she was certain the two men had been spotted.

She gaped her mouth wide to scream her terror.

And the half-breed and the Virginian sensed she was about to do something that threatened their survival. So simultaneously wrenched their heads around. To look back down the length of their prone bodies and across the open rock to where she sat. Still hugging her knees but with her head held high and her mouth and eyes pulled open to their widest.

And time seemed to stand still as a bead of sweat oozed from every pore on the face of each man, telling of the strain they were put under as they directed a tacit message to the near hysterical woman. A message spoken with bared teeth between drawn-back lips and with glinting eyes through narrowed lids. That told her to be absolutely quiet or the suffering which afflicted the Mexican girl would be nothing to what she would have to endure.

An empty threat in the circumstances. But delivered with such silent power that it served its purpose for the ticking seconds before George Blood asked coldly, "What about them two sonsofbitches, King?"

And Blood's voice, more familiar to the whore than sight or sound of Edge and Steele, reached through her barrier as strongly as the silent power of the men's stares. And in combination forced her to step back from the brink of surrendering to terror.

Walter King countered suspiciously: "You tell me about them, Blood." Untrusting, but ready to believe what he was told by a man he hated. Because he wanted to know the truth about a man he hated even more.

Like an argumentative child, the fat man snapped, "I asked first!"

Watching the scene below again, Steele jutted out a lower lip and blew a draft of cooling air over his sheened face. Edge pushed out his tongue and licked beads of salt moisture off the bristles of his moustache.

"Frig it, Blood!" King snarled, and moved the glowing tip of the cigar to within a half inch of touching the end of the fuse. "You got less reason to waste time than I have. Way you hate bounty hunters!"

"Hunters?" the fat man snarled, the single word powering from his mouth with almost physical force. And had not the situation been so tensely dangerous, his childish anger would have been laughable. "What the frig you talkin' about, King? The dude, he kept me from being shot by a hunter. The other dude—the English one—you fixed to come down to South Pass and use his trick guns on—"

"Walt don't know nothin' about that Smythe feller," one of King's men put in flatly, and drew the attention of the group astride the horses and King. "He weren't no bounty hunter, Walt. Hell, me and Eddy and Doyle known him from way back. A cheatin' gamblin' man is all he is. We took his stake off him and kicked his ass through the pass."

King nodded and returned his gaze to Blood. "There you go, George," he said in a tone of triumph that one of his men had scored a point off the opposition. "I wasn't over at North

Pass when this Englishman came through. First I've heard of him. Reason I wasn't there was because I was either in the Stormville jail or being broken out of it by a couple of my boys."

All the men on the horses were listening with concentrated attention. Their anger suppressed. But held in reserve just below a very thin surface.

"Put in jail by Adam Steele. Whose buddy showed up in town while my boys were planning to bust me out. Man called Edge."

"That's him!" Floyd Devlin put in excitedly. And was cowed into silence by the power in the eyes that briefly glanced at him.

"Both of them came after me and my two boys," King went on. "And they got lucky at the old Kingdom sugar plantation. But I got luckier."

He drew against the cigar. As much in need of the lift it gave him as to keep it alight and dangerous. His men continued to level their rifles and gaze fixedly at the Blood bunch on the horses. The naked Mexican girl with the punished body and dynamite stick in her mouth sat like she was already long dead—held rigid by the aftereffects of death.

Up on the rim of the ravine, Edge and Steele and the whore against the rock in back of them were just as unmoving.

"Never figured they got on my trail after they killed my two boys," King went on. "Came on back to town and fixed to finish you in South Pass once and for all, Blood. Figured it would be easy with all of you in the one place. But when the hotel roof blew, that threw me, Blood."

"So you stole my woman and ducked back into your hole, King!" the fat man growled, ready to be angry at him again.

"She came running to us. Told us some crazy story about being the daughter of a rich family in Denver. And that her father would pay a lot of money to have her back. Figured she was lying."

"I bought her in El Paso, King," Arch Baxter revealed flatly. "Gave her old man ten pesos for her. Don't figure he'd pay that much to have her back. Not the way she is now."

"Did figure you'd give something for her, Blood," King

went on after a nod of acknowledgment to Baxter. "Seeing as how she's your special piece of ass."

"She don't look so special to me," the fat man said dully, with a cursory, mildly rueful look at the captive girl.

"She still is, you have my word," King assured. "We had a little fun with her. But she's still the way you like your girls, Blood."

"You mean you didn't—"

A smile came and went very quickly across King's face as he glanced at Zamora sitting rigidly astride the horse, every mark of punishment on her slender body highlighted by the glare of the now fully risen sun.

"She was took a lot of ways. Gave us a lot of pleasure. But, like they say, she's still pure."

Nora Stebbings shuddered, but made no sound.

The Mexican girl interrupted her labored nose breathing to vent a kind of groan, which was all she could do to display how she felt about the memories of unspeakable torments.

"And you figured to trade her for the hunters?" Baxter asked.

"That's right," King answered. "After we'd had our fill of her, we asked her a few questions. Came out kind of accidental about you having a couple of new guys in South Pass. And now, if we're going to believe each other, George, this whole thing is for nothing."

He used the hand holding the cigar to make a gesture that encompassed the entire sun-drenched scene beyond the mouth of the ravine.

"What's that supposed to mean?" the fat man demanded, not sure whether he should feel insulted.

"He means that since Steele and Edge ain't with us, we can't trade them for the piece of ass suckin' dynamite, George," Baxter explained.

Blood nodded. "So what's gonna happen now?"

His small eyes raked over each of King's men with the leveled rifles, lingered ruefully on the naked girl for a second or so, then gazed expectantly at the man with the end of the fuse in one hand and a cigar in the other.

"They can't be allowed to get away with it, I'd say," Walt

King replied. "Word gets around that a couple of bounty hunters put it across on us and got away with it, every fast gun with an empty pocket could figure to come up to Silver Pass and try his luck."

The fat man considered this pensively for long moments. Then nodded. "A man's reputation can take years to make but maybe just a second to break is what my Pa always used to say."

"Like George said a while back, so what's gonna happen now?" Floyd Devlin asked, and flinched in anticipation of a rebuke.

But Arch Baxter simply added, "That's right."

"Like for there to be a truce between us," King answered, and hung the cigar between his teeth so that it bobbed when he talked. "So that we can join forces to track down and make Edge and Steele pay for what they done to us."

George Blood considered this for just a second before he nodded. "Makes sense."

None of his men made any sound or gesture of agreement with this.

"Were last seen in South Pass," King reminded. "So that's where we should start to look for them. See if we can pick up their trail."

"Them and a whore," Floyd Devlin put in. "They took that Nora Stebbin's with them."

The whore leaning against the rock drew in her breath sharply and held it.

"She ain't nothin'," the fat man growled. "Which is mostly what comes out when you open your mouth, kid. What about her, King?"

He nodded toward the naked prisoner.

King allowed the end of the fuse to fall from his hand and shrugged.

"She run out on us, Arch," Blood said. "Pay her off."

"Sure, George."

"A truce is what we have, King?"

"Sure, Blood."

"So okay, Arch. Do it."

The nose breathing ceased.

So did the distant tolling of the cracked bell to mark the end of the burials in the cemetery behind the South Pass church.

Nora Stebbings let out her pent-up breath.

Zamora stared directly ahead of her, at the muzzle of the Winchester rifle that was aimed at her and the face of Arch Baxter behind it.

He was a marksman. Just the one shot, the report of which was separated by the merest sliver of time from the duller but louder sound of the high explosive detonating. And in even shorter time, the punished young girl was a headless corpse, her shocked nervous system holding her body erect in the saddle for an instant as bone-speckled flesh flew in every direction through the smoke and flame of the blast.

Then the horse reared and wheeled and bolted. Panicked into the bolt by the sound of the explosion and then the stink of seared meat. Next the splash of warm, blood-wet fragments of pulp raining down on his neck and rump. The body without a head was unseated but still remained fixed to the saddle by the wrists lashed to the horn. And it was dragged along beside the galloping horse as the animal raced into the ravine, causing panic among the other mounts. Which could only toss their heads and snort, trapped by the hobbles on their forelegs.

When blood ceased to spurt from the terrible wound and lay a trail behind the horse and its burden, a less vivid crimson sign was spilled as friction against the ground opened up the skin of the dragged legs and feet.

But nobody saw this in the moments that followed the ghastly ending of the life of the young Mexican girl. For tension on this sunlit morning had risen to its highest point yet. While Arch Baxter kept his rifle to his shoulder, Walt King's men continued to aim at the mounted five and, without doubt, the men of Blood's force still in cover drew beads on exposed targets. When it would have taken just a single movement of any one of more than a score of curled trigger fingers to unleash a two-way barrage of lethal gunfire.

Edge and Steele were held in the grip of this same tension. Which the Virginian was about to break by blasting a shot into the sweating and bloated face of George Blood.

But an instant before he slid the Colt Hartford into position to place the shot into the target, Nora Stebbings saw the galloping horse dragging the bleeding length of flesh and bone that moments before had been a living young girl she had known and liked.

And she leaped to her feet to beat the air with her fists and to scream: "You bastards! You friggin' shithead bastards! You stinkin' rotten sonsofbitches of mother—"

Every man on and flanking the trail beyond the mouth of the ravine looked up at where the woman was shrieking at them. Blood and his men needing just to flick their eyes in the sockets. While King and his men had to wrench their heads around. And even then, the men from North Pass were too close to the cliff face to be able to see the ranting woman who was several feet back from the rim. Did glimpse, though, the barrel of Adam Steele's Colt Hartford, which had started to angle down over the top of the rock face. Where was instantly withdrawn.

By the scowling Virginian, who knew he had missed his opportunity to spark a deadly gun battle between the old enemies below. And now had to fight to subdue the reckless anger he felt toward the whore for her outburst.

Then had no time to feel anything except the need to survive. For a barrage of rifle fire exploded a hail of bullets at him. Fired by the North Pass men who had seen only the barrel of the Colt Hartford. And the men from South Pass who had glimpsed his head behind the barrel.

From behind him, the half-breed snarled, "This is another fine mess you got me into, Steele."

The Virginian, on his back now, used his heels to propel himself across the ground and came up alongside the half-breed. Drawled against the din of blasting gunfire and the pinging sounds of bullets ricocheting off rock, "Who asked you to come along, Edge?"

The half-breed's face showed an expression the Virginian had never seen before when he answered, "Glad it wasn't her, feller."

Steele wrenched his head around from staring at the man lying spread-eagled beside him under the spitting bullets. And saw the whore from South Pass. Who was in the process of dying. Less spectacularly than the Mexican girl, but with the same end result. Hit by a single bullet that had bounced off a rock, lacking the velocity to penetrate through the flesh into a vital organ, but with enough force to turn end over end and make an ugly, blood-gushing wound in her throat. So that she was against the mound of rugged rock again. Just half seated this time. Clutching at her throat with both hands. Trying to say something. Perhaps more invectives to hurl at the men below, or maybe pleas for help to those on the ravine rim with her. Whichever, no words came out between her frantically working lips. Just sounds. Then blood, held in by her hands but given free access through her mouth. And she died. Eyes and mouth wide. And legs. As she slid down the rock, trying to dig in her heels to support herself. But there was no hope for her and she finished up like a broken doll in the angle of the ground and the base of the rock, half tilted to one side and with the skirts of her dress hitched up around her waist, displaying legs that were as unattractive as her overblown figure and puffy face.

"Me, too, Yank. For a whore, she was all right. Maybe it wasn't made of gold, but I reckon she had a heart."

"And we don't have the time for sentiment, Reb." The half-breed's hard-set face now looked incapable of ever showing the kind of expression of sadness he had displayed while the woman was drowning on her own blood.

Steele nodded. Then drawled, "We going to stay here and do like she did, feller?"

"How's that?"

A hail of bullets continued to blast up from below. All cracking high above where they lay. But occasionally one ricocheted off the mound of rock to spin through the gunsmoke-tainted air at a random angle.

"Talk ourselves into an early grave."

"You're right. We should move before they fix for us to wind up like the Mexican girl."

"How's that?"

"Headed off at the pass."

Chapter Eighteen

There was no easy way up on to the western rim of the ravine. And while the combined forces of George Blood and Walt King tried to find one, Edge and Steele backed off from the enraged men. For a long time out of the line of fire of the blasting rifles but still in danger of being hit by a ricochet.

First down on their bellies, then on all fours, and finally able to stand erect. Initially making slow progress with the sweat of tension sheening their faces and pasting the clothing to their flesh. Then sweating more heavily from the exertion of retreating at a run. Protected by intervening rock formations from direct fire and ricochets then.

Their escape up into Silver Pass aided by the fact that the men who were so hungry to kill them served two masters and had been sworn enemies only minutes ago. So there was no coordination in the assault on the high ground, the wild firing at unfeeling faces of rock soon becoming more of a danger to the front-runners of the pursuers than to the quarry. And even when the first to recover from shock and rage realized there had never been any answering shots from up on the rim where Steele had shown himself, it took time for this to be communicated to every man in the disorganized and scattered bunch of angry men.

Edge and Steele were perhaps a hundred and fifty yards away from the mouth of the ravine when the final shot of the barrage was exploded, there was a momentary silence, and then a burst of raucous shouting. That was curtailed by the firing of another shot. Which heralded another silence which lasted perhaps two seconds. Before a single voice began to speak. Shouting, but not loud enough for the half-breed and the Virginian to comprehend what was being said against the ragged sounds of their own labored breathing.

They were no longer running, aware the thud of their heavy footfalls could reach down to the ears of the men beyond the ravine now that the constant barrage of gunfire was finished. But they moved as fast as they were able on the steep grade of the trail that zigzagged up to the pass from the far end of the ravine. Each holding his rifle in a double-handed grip across his belly. Needing to raise an arm every few paces to wipe sweat out of his eyes. Eyes which ignored the terrain flanking the trail, for they knew King would not have felt the need to post a rear guard. Instead peered down at the constantly rising ground ahead of them. At the sign left by the horse with its ungainly and grisly burden.

There were no longer any smears or spots of blood to be seen dried on the parched ground. But the rut in the dust and across the sign made by the large group of horses coming down the trail was easy to see—inscribed by the limply dragging lower legs and feet of the headless corpse.

Perhaps five minutes after the whore had triggered the explosion of gunfire, they came to the horse. Standing in the shade of a rock overhang. Head hung low and almost exhausted by the punishing bolt up hill. The drag of the awkward load having turned the saddle upside down so that it hung under the animal's belly, the cinch fastening at the center of the back. The hands of the girl with no head and flesh that was caked with a crusting of dried blood were still lashed to the saddlehorn.

Steele made to draw the knife from his boot sheath, but Edge was faster to slide the razor from the pouch at the nape of his neck.

The droning voice from below, which had occasionally been drowned by others that were raised in protest, was now lost amid a raucous cheer. This as the half-breed stooped to sever the rope that tied the corpse to the saddle and Steele lodged the Colt Hartford in the crook of an elbow so that both gloved hands were free to unbuckle the cinch. The gelding snorted his disapproval of being close to human beings.

The sounds of human approval for whatever had been decided between the Blood and the King bunches came to an end and solid silence crowded in on the two men, the corpse, and the gelding from all sides.

"He'd have trouble carrying just one of us, Yank," the Virginian said softly, stroking the horse and using his tone of voice as a further means of easing the equine mind.

"Even the littlest of us," the half-breed agreed. "Still got some steam left, though, I figure."

"Reckon so. I never did have any reason to go to North Pass except that it's Walt King's town."

"I go where you go, Reb. Until train time at Stormville."

The Virginian glanced up toward the sun. Not at it, because it was too high in the sky and dangerously bright now. "That means I have to put up with having you around for about another twenty-four hours, I reckon."

"If you live that long, feller. I'd say the last thing those boys down the trail are doing is getting further away."

Steele nodded. "Need to be sure they're close enough to hear him."

They were at the top of one of the sloping straights, close to where another sharp turn began. Below the turn the ground fell away steeply for some twenty feet, and it was down this drop that Edge cast a jaundiced glance as the Virginian gave his reply. Eyeing the boulder-strewn ledge halfway to the foot of the hollow, which was where they would have to wait until the pursuers rode by. Effectively hidden from the lower slope of the trail by a jagged ridge that intervened, but totally exposed should any of the riders look down from this stretch of the trail.

"If taking care of me was easy, maybe Samantha West would have handled the job herself, Yank," the Virginian drawled with a mild smile.

The half-breed spat down the slope and growled, "But knowing you were crazy, she hired another crazy man to do the job."

Steele pushed the saddle to the side of the trail and tipped it over in the wake of Edge's saliva. It impacted with the ledge with a far louder thud. And at the same time, the Virginian cracked a hand on the rump of the still nervous gelding. Which snorted at this latest example of ill-treatment by the human kind. And lunged into another bolt. Free of both the corpse and the saddle now. Determined to stay free and so racing as fast as the grade and his diminished reserves of energy would allow to put distance between himself and those who had caused him so much distress.

For stetched seconds, the thudding hooves of the retreating horse was the only sound to compete with the noisy slide of the two men down the ten-foot drop to the rock-scattered ledge. But then came a chorus of angry cries and the thunder of many hooves at the gallop from the other side of the ridge that reared up between the two stretches of the sloping trail.

Edge and Steele rose painfully to their feet after the voluntary fall, and pressed their backs to the rock face, rifles angled across their chests, heads turned to the side. It was the Virginian who stretched out a leg and hooked a booted foot under the saddle to drag it to the base of the vertical slab of rock. Just before the front-runners of the pursuers galloped around the turn. Heard but not seen by either man in hiding. Which was now it had to be if they were themselves to remain unseen.

The ground felt as if it were trembling under the moving weight of so many fast-ridden horses. But this was probably an illusion cause by the shuddering cloud of dust that was spilled off the side of the trail by pumping hooves. Against which the men on the ledge closed their eyes and compressed their lips until the final horse had been galloped by above them—the rider, like all the rest, not pausing on account of the headless corpse abandoned at the side of the trail.

The dust settled and the sounds of the galloping horses diminished up toward the pass. The half-breed and the Virginian wiped sweat and dust off their brows and out of the heavy growth of bristles on the lower part of their faces.

Edge growled, "Sure is dirty work we're involved in, Reb."

Steele ran the tip of his tongue along his lips and spat out the taste of them. Said evenly, "You can wash your hands of it anytime you like, Yank."

They came away from the rock face and tacitly agreed that the easiest way off the ledge was back up on to the higher stretch of trail.

The Virginian was first to rest his rifle and stoop—interlocking his gloved hands to provide the half-breed with a foothold.

When it was accepted, he straightened and grimaced as he was burdened with the entire weight of the bigger man until Edge tossed his Winchester on to the trail and then hooked his arms over the top of the low cliff and hauled himself up. Once up there, reached down to bring up the Virginian's rifle, which was handed to him, then the Virginian himself.

Then they started to walk down the hill on the zigzagging trail toward South Pass at the bottom. Not hurrying. Alert to the first sign that the riderless horse had been spotted and the hard men of the twin communities were headed in their direction again.

After a minute or so, Steele asked, "Not just because Stormville is back this way?"

Edge jerked a thumb over his shoulder, "Also has something to do with there being something close to thirty men who want to kill me being that way, feller."

"I was fixing to have them shoot up each other when the woman went crazy."

"Figured that, Reb. Fine idea that might have worked out fine."

The Virginian directed a sidelong glance at the taller man ambling along at his side. And drawled, "Soft soap I don't need."

"Not without Walter."

"Him I intend to get."

"Unless you do, you don't clean up."

"Thing is, now it could end up in a Blood bath."

"Just have to make sure it ain't us that gets plugged, Reb."

Chapter Nineteen

It took the two men walking more than an hour at their easy pace to get back to the north end of the main street of South Pass. And for all this time there was not a sound to be heard anywhere within earshot of them. Except for the regular thud of their own booted feet on the hard-packed, dust-layered trail.

After the uneasy exchange of light humor shortly after they began the return trip to town, the two men did not speak until they were crossing the most dangerous piece of ground. Which was the final hundred yards or so to the start of the street between the feed merchant's and the town's second church, which was no longer used. Dangerous because there was no cover for a long way to either side of this stretch of the trail.

Then Edge said, "You think we scared them so much they're still running, Reb?"

"I'd say they're trying to scare us, Yank."

"And I'd give them ten out of ten for effort."

"And five out of ten for the result."

"Got that itch between the shoulder blades, uh?"

"And if you took a bullet in the belly right now, you'd be ready to swear you knew exactly where it was aimed before the feller squeezed the trigger?"

Neither of them had looked over his shoulder, or to either side, for a long time. Certain that if an attack was to be launched from any of these places, it would already have taken place. Over a long range by somebody like Arch Baxter, who had already proved himself a crack shot with a rifle. Or from close in, by more than one man who, both Edge and Steele were certain, they would have spotted moving out on the barren, sun-bright terrain of the hillside below the pass.

Neither had happened, so now they concentrated their apparently nonchalant attention upon the town buildings. But, inevitably, could not fail to feel threatened from behind because they had seen so many men who wanted them dead go in that direction. And knew these men had long since found out they were tricked by the bolting horse.

In South Pass, scattered among several of the derelict buildings, were a group of whores who went with the Blood bunch. And some citizens of town from way back who supplied the hard men with goods and services of other kinds. Some of them as eager as Nora Stebbings and Zamora and Red Gatling to see Blood and his men driven out of South Pass.

But how many were not?

Shared the sympathies of old Harv Cox? Happy to turn a blind eye to the excesses of the hard men for the privileges that were sometimes extended.

It was midmorning now and the sun was glaringly bright and blisteringly hot—not affected by the few puffy white clouds that rode high against the infinite blue of the Colorado sky. And the shadows, in which it was not likely to be any cooler than out in the open, were correspondingly deeper. Particularly inside the buildings that had not yet fallen down and had their doors closed and glassless windows boarded up.

On Steele's side of the street, the church was like this. And the school next door. The meeting hall next to this.

On the side over which Edge raked his glinting-eyed gaze, the feed merchants doorway was open with the unoccupied rocking chair just outside the threshold. The bakery was totally closed up. He knew the livery stable was still in business, but at this time the double doors were as firmly closed as when he and the Virginian had first approached the building.

Spots on their sweating flesh high at their backs and low down at their bellies continued to twitch in expectation of the thud of a bullet. But conversely, while they sensed watching eyes following their progress, they did not feel a distinctive threat from any discernible point along either side of the street.

Hostility, perhaps. And resentment. But of the impotent kind.

On the center of the street between the facades of the livery and the meeting hall, they heard a sound. And became rooted to the spot as they swung down their rifles from the shoulder and turned from the waist to look at the source of the noise. Even before their eyes and the muzzles of their guns located the stable doors, recognized what they heard as an equine whinny.

Through the crack where the two doors met at the center, Red Gatling called without rancor, "Lousy feelin', bein' scared, ain't it, you guys?"

Almost like a military drill in slow motion, the half-breed and the Virginian sloped the rifles back to their shoulders. But kept their hands tight around the frames, and the hammers cocked.

Edge said, "Fear's an old friend, feller."

"Like a cousin to me," Steele added. "Hardly ever removed. You going to open up for us, Gatling?"

"No need. Your horses are hitched down at the hotel. Got dead men's saddles on them. Fresh water in the canteens and supplies in the bags. Everyone hereabouts would be real grateful if you'd get on them and ride them outta South Pass."

"Everyone, feller?" Edge asked.

"Everyone that's in town right now is what I mean!" the liveryman countered, his voice sounding of irritable impatience. "Course Blood and his bunch would like to have you stay, and no mistake."

"But you speak for everybody else, uh?" Steele asked.

The plank that fastened the doors was slid from the brackets with a screeching sound that was very loud in the otherwise silent town. Then both doors were pulled open wide enough to allow Red Gatling to step between them. Just one pace out into the glare of the morning sun. The brightness of which made him look older and thinner. And his hair seemed to be more gray than red today. His crinkled face showed a screwed-up expression that was a mixture of shame and regret and anger.

"Look, I got elected to speak up because we knew it would be my place you'd pass first when you come into town. After Hubert Perry seen you comin' through the spyglass the preacherman used to use for studyin' of the stars at night. Seen you way off up the hill." He waved a loose arm in the direction of Silver Pass. "Right after that, it was decided we didn't want no more help from you. And I was told to get your horses ready for ridin'."

"And if we don't want to go?" Steele asked.

"Then we're gonna have to hold you prisoners until Blood and his men get back. Because there ain't no way we're ever gonna be able to beat George Blood. Especially not now he's thrown in with the King bunch so there's near twice as many of the murderin' bastards as before. On account of that, we gotta stay on the right side of him. Hold you prisoners for him, or pretend we couldn't keep you from leavin' town."

Edge glanced back up the hill. "You know about the two getting together, feller? The preacherman's spyglass looks through solid rock?"

Gatling gave an irritable shake of his head. "Course it don't! But Hubert Perry kept pretty close watch up at the pass after we heard the explosion and the shootin', I can tell you. All of us wonderin' who was gettin' blasted and if it would make any difference to us down here."

He was briefly excited, reliving the time when hope had existed in South Pass. Then his heavily lined face resumed its former expression. And his tone of voice was even more morose than before as he again waved an arm to indicate the pass.

"Place high up there where anyone on the trail can be seen from down here with the spyglass. And Hubert Perry, he kept watchin' after the shootin'. And he saw a horse go by, draggin' somethin'. Or somebody?"

"The fat man's lady love," Edge responded to the implied question.

"King made her a prisoner and Blood had Baxter kill her," Steele added.

Gatling gave a grimacing nod, as if what he heard merely confirmed something of which he had been almost certain anyway.

"After that, seen you two go by. Walkin'. Then Blood and King headin' up their men. Together. Later, you two comin' back down again. That was when we decided it was crazy of me to throw in with you in the first place. Ain't no way we're ever gonna be free of that murderin' bunch of bastards. Unless you count when Hubert Perry digs our grave and the preacherman buries us."

"Take us prisoners, uh?" Edge said pensively, shifting his icelike gaze away from the liveryman to look along the deserted main street of South Pass, between the sorry facades of the mostly derelict buildings. "How you going to do that, feller?"

"Figured you might put up an argument," Gatling muttered sadly. And put his fingers in his mouth to vent a shrill whistle.

And along both sides of the street, many doors creaked open and men and women stepped through. Or, here and there, somebody emerged from a doorless gap in a wall. Just Hubert Perry known to Edge and Steele by name. Unless the clerically collared man called the preacherman were counted. But all of them known by sight from being seen in the Miner's Inn.

Whores and local people, the women greatly outnumbering the men. Everybody afraid, but resolutely determined to conquer it. All of them, from the youngest whore to the most elderly of the local women, holding a weapon of some sort. Be it a length of timber which could serve as a club or a pitchfork, a wrench, or an ancient and rusted cavalry sabre. One old man even had a skillet.

"Force of numbers is how, mister," the liveryman continued after the half-breed and the Virginian had surveyed the grim lines of people down each side of the street. "Knowin' that some of us will get killed by them guns of yours. But we'd rather die like that than be at the mercy of Blood and his bunch—them knowin' we'd helped you go against them."

Edge and Steele looked again at the twin rows of determined people who tightened their grips on their mostly unconventional weapons. And one of the whores called in a quivering tone:

"You know what happened to Nora, mister?"

"She's dead," Steele answered.

"Was that her the gravedigger saw being dragged by—"

"That was the Mexican girl that run out on Blood to go to King," Red Gatling answered, his impatience rising. "Look, if Blood shows up and finds us chewin' the fat with these guys, like we was good buddies of theirs, it won't go good for us!"

"Or us, Reb," Edge said.

"I think we should leave town like they ask, Yank."

"Ain't so much askin' as tellin', mister," Gatling growled. "And I'm right sorry to do it. But we ain't bein' cowards. Just bein' sensible."

"I'm with you, feller," the half-breed told the Virginian.

"Sure would hate to finish up beaten to death by a frying pan. After ducking so many bullets for so long."

"Grateful that you gave us the choice, Gatling," Steele told the liveryman and took the lead in starting along the street.

"There's some that didn't want to," Gatling murmured. "Blame you and me as much as Blood and King for the three decent people got killed in the hotel last night."

Edge moved off alongside Steele, both with the still-cocked rifles canted to their shoulders. Eyes moving back and forth to keep watch on the tense and sweating people who watched them.

Then they turned the corner to leave the main street and go toward the virtually roofless hotel. And were watched by just an old man and woman from the front of a barber shop across the intersection. The old couple, armed with timber clubs, eyeing them with shamefaced sadness as the two men approached the bay and the black geldings hitched to the rail out front of the bullet-scarred hotel.

"That horse looks real good after being on my feet for so long, Reb."

"You're not alone in that, Yank."

They unhitched the reins from the rail and slid their rifles into the scabbards. Then swung up astride the saddles with sighs of relief.

"If two fellers can be alone, that's what we are," Edge muttered and took out the makings. "You got anything planned I should know about?"

"We may be in a hole, but I reckon King's in a deeper one. So I'll ride out of town and see what I can dig up."

"West then?"

"Has to be. After all the trouble I've taken."

They backed their horses away from the hitching rail and turned them to go toward the intersection. Talking, as before, in an even, easy tone. Edge lighting and smoking the newly made cigarette.

"We aren't that important to Blood, Yank."

"Not like King."

"Which is why they're playing at being partners."

"King has to know that."

They rode on to the intersection. Still being watched by the old couple at the barber shop. And now by a few other people who remained on the sunlit street. Some with weapons and some without. More eyes watched from inside the decrepit buildings. Or ears listened to the unhurried clop of the two slow-ridden horses.

When they rode across the intersection at an angle to move on to another side street which ran west from the far side, a sour-faced whore at an upper-floor window above a print shop yelled, "Hey, that street don't lead no place, you guys!"

Steele turned just his head to squint up at her and answer: "You people directed us to leave town, lady. Didn't say in which direction it had to be."

The exchange drew the majority of people out on to the street again, all of them armed. And they began to move toward the intersection from both directions. To congregate into a curious and distrustful group and watch the half-breed and the Virginian ride slowly away from them. Between small, crudely built shacks where the poorest of South Pass citizens had lived in the good days when the silver ore was still being mined in the area. Now they were totally abandoned.

"King knows it," Steele continued, as if there had never been an interruption.

"Because we ain't that important to him."

"Excuses to both of them, Yank."

"To get close to each other, Reb."

"Finally end the feud."

"My money's on Blood."

"You don't have any money, Reb."

They reined in their mounts at the end of the street and looked out across the three hundred yards of open ground where last night three men from North Pass had died. Trying to reach the clump of mesquite by which the rest had escaped.

"I don't have enough help either."

"Anybody can win the easy fights, Reb."

"Hey, what you two guys doin' down there?" the toothless gravedigger yelled, a nervous tone in his voice. "You was told to get away from South Pass before—"

Hubert Perry curtailed what he was shouting, as his voice became drowned out by the frantic clanging of the cracked bell in the church tower.

And everyone on the intersection turned to look toward the source of the sound. Then, as the one-note warning carillon came to an abrupt end and the preacherman ran from his church to point frantically up at Silver Pass with both arms, all heads jerked around to peer in that direction. And voices were raised in a chorus of fear.

"Cutting out the preacherman's tongue didn't make him a dumbbell," Edge said evenly so that only Steele could hear him. And pinched out the fire of his cigarette.

"Follow his example?"

"How's that, feller?"

The half-breed put the dead, partially smoked cigarette in his shirt pocket for later. This as Steele slid the Colt Hartford from its scabbard, aimed it one handed toward the mesquite clump, and squeezed the trigger. Answered:

"Let actions speak louder than words."

Chapter Twenty

For stretched seconds, the shouting was silenced. And all eyes watched Edge and Steele in horrified fascination.

The half-breed went to the left and the Virginian to the right. Each man jerking a foot from a stirrup and using the other stirrup as a springboard to power his lunge from his horse. The Colt Hartford was already in the gloved hands of its owner. Edge had to slide his Winchester from the scabbard as part of the same smooth series of moves that got him from the saddle to the ground.

In unison, without any form of communication after the brief exchange following the sounding of the warning bell, each man duplicated the actions of the other. Reacting to the sights and sounds around him, yet strangely detached from his surroundings. Doing what he did instinctively. Like an animal ahead of a forest fire or sensing the coming of a storm, the proximity of other animals to which it was prey. Which was very near to the truth.

During the passing of those few tense seconds, they saw images which were transmitted to and processed by their minds. And their minds conveyed commands to motor muscles which obeyed in fractions of a second.

The ground was going to be hard, so as the men powered from their saddles, they began to turn into a configuration to hit the end of the street with their feet, knees bent to absorb the impact with the minimum of hindering jolt.

Somebody might be on the very brink of blasting a shot from an aimed gun. So the hammers of the Colt Hartford and the Winchester were thumbed back and fingers were curled to triggers.

Eyes—ice blue and coal black—moved along sockets between narrowed lids. Seeking the priorities of the risks to self-preservation. Which the minds catalogued while the muscles were prepared to swing the rifles on to whatever targets presented the prime threat.

The images were first seen as a blur, briefly examined in crystal clarity, then blurred again as a new component part of the scene was sought and surveyed.

Sounds were similarly distorted, heard in stark isolation from all others, then lost definition after rejection.

The mesquite which was silent and totally unresponsive to the shot from the Colt Hartford.

The trail from Silver Pass on which a string of horses was moving. At least two miles out of town yet.

The confused and frightened crowd of crudely armed whores and old timers milling on the intersection.

"What? . . ."

"Who? . . ."

"Shit . . ."

"Preacherman . . ."

"Blood? . . ."

"Where? . . ."

"How? . . ."

"Crazy! . . ."

"Look! . . ."

"God! . . ."

"Jesus! . . ."

Screams. Running feet pounding on the sun-baked streets of the town. The bell clanging again.

Edge and Steele hitting the ground and staying on their feet. Lunging away from their horses, which reared and bolted. Plunging into the last shacks at the end of the street. Whirling on the doorless thresholds. Wrenching their heads first one way and then the other. Looking first at the clump of unmoving mesquite. Then at the murderous mob of people that streamed off the intersection and along the street toward them. Shrieking their fury and brandishing the makeshift weapons.

Fear and resentment, shame and hatred, a thousand memories of suffering and a thousand dreads of worse to come—all these emotions and thoughts, and many more, fueled the flames of rage that impelled the screaming mob toward the two men.

The preacher kept up the constant clang of the bell. Denied the ability to express his feelings by the brutality of George Blood and prevented from indulging in violence himself by his faith, so using the bell as an outlet.

The half-breed on the north side of the street and the Virginian in the doorway of the facing shack traded a glance. At first were stoically impassive. Acknowledging there were no hard feelings about the mistiming of the move. And that if, as seemed more likely with each passing sliver of time, they were going to have to open fire on the mob, it was all just the way another cookie had crumbled.

Then a fusillade of gunfire cut across and momentarily curtailed the crazed shrieking of the crowd.

And three men and a woman were halted in their tracks and then corkscrewed to the ground. Dropping their crude clubs as dark crimson stains blossomed on their chests and bellies. The woman was the one who had been Arch Baxter's personal whore. One of the men was the old-timer who had been out front of the barber shop earlier.

The bell clanged.

"Turn on me would you, you—I'll teach you a friggin' lesson you'll . . . Damnit to hell . . . Stop that sonofabitchin' bell, Arch!"

The massively fat George Blood was at the head of a large group of his men. Sweating face almost purple with rage as he screamed at the shocked mob, many of the words lost against the sound of the bell.

Arch Baxter shifted the aim of his Winchester from the crowd on the street toward the distant church tower that dominated the rooftops of South Pass. And fired a single shot. The bullet hit the bell and ricocheted off into the hot air of late morning.

The preacher let go of the rope.

Some women began to wail and some men to moan.

Edge watched Steele and both men were grinning now. Expressions that were formed entirely by drawing the lips back from the teeth without any warmth being injected into the eyes.

The cold, brutal grins of killers—who awaited the signal to begin the killing. A signal which in the case of the Virginian was the thud of booted feet on sun-baked ground. And for the half-breed was a curt nod from the man across the street.

And, once more in perfect unison, the two matched their moves.

Swung out of the shack doorways with the stock plates of their rifles to their shoulders. Ignored the shocked and grieving crowd huddled behind the four sprawled and bleeding bodies. To concentrate solely upon the smaller but more dangerous group which came to a halt midway across the open ground between the mesquite and the end of the street.

Edge shot George Blood.

Steele shot Arch Baxter.

The top man and his first lieutenant. The half-breed and the Virginian selecting the target that was marginally closer to him.

It took less time to thumb back the hammer of the Colt Hartford than to pump the lever action of the Winchester. So Mo Spencer, who was alongside the crumpling Baxter, was the next man to take a bullet.

Chest shots, left of center, all three. But then Floyd Devlin tried to bob down out of the line of fire. Did not go low enough, though, and the half-breed's second shot drilled into his forehead, just under the brim of his hat. The youngster dead before the first three to be shot had fully measured their lengths on the ground under the rising dust of violent movement.

Voices were being raised again now. Confused against the barrage of gunfire from two rifles. And for part of a second the men who loosed off their third shots and saw blood-soaked holes appear in their targets were in a tight grip of ice-cold fear.

For from the confusion of shrill vocal sounds at their backs they recognized the tone of hysteria which had been in the voice of the doomed Nora Stebbings. When she was venting her suicidal diatribe up on the rim of the ravine.

She had been just one woman whose actions were dictated by a mind gone temporarily insane.

Now, mass hysteria was ruling the advance of close to fift

people who trampled their own dead in their insane craving for revenge.

But against whom?

The hard men who had ruled the roost in South Pass for so long started to grin and to bring their guns to bear.

And Edge and Steele wasted valuable time in wrenching their heads around. But were not so afraid of the mob that they ignored the danger of the hard men. And so folded back into the cover of the shack doorways.

No shots were fired at them.

A length of timber, three by three, crashed into the shoulder of the Virginian and he could not stem a groan of pain as the bolt of agony traveled the length of his arm. And perhaps there was despair in the sound too, as he felt the Colt Hartford wrenched from his grip while his eyes were forced closed by the powerful need to hold back tears.

It was a shovel that sent Edge staggering backwards into the shack. The flat of the blade thudded into his belly by Red Gatling, as an old woman who had to be more than seventy snatched at the Winchester. Which he had to surrender as the air burst out of his gaping mouth and he reached with both hands to comfort the center of his pain.

"They're ours!"

"We want them!"

"We're gonna . . ."

"They're gonna . . ."

"For every time they . . ."

"You shouldn't've killed . . ."

"God, if only we had Blood to . . ."

Just as had happened earlier, the half-breed and the Virginian heard just snatches of phrases. But no longer was the chorus of voices expressing fear and confusion. Venomous hatred dripped from every word now. Words that were heard by pain-assaulted minds against a steadily rising volume of thudding feet and shrieks of triumph. This added to by the clang of the cracked bell as the mute preacherman in his church sensed a turn in the battle.

Adam Steele was still on his feet, but needed the support of the doorframe to keep from falling down. He opened his eyes and it took several seconds for his vision to clear.

By which time Edge had rolled over on to his side and hauled himself on to the threshold of the shack across the street. But was not able to take his knees down from his chest yet, for it was only in the fetal position that he could be sure he would not vomit.

The two men ignored each other to peer out across the area of sun-bright ground where the six men they had killed were sprawled. To witness the putting to death of the rest of the men who had come through the mountain instead of over the pass. By way of the tunnel—or, more likely, series of tunnels—that had once yielded silver ore. Now, on two occasions, had spewed out men to kill and be killed. Yesterday's men expecting slaughter to be unleashed. Today's taken totally by surprise.

Blood and Baxter and Devlin and the other three shot down dying the easy way. Quick and as cleanly as ever a bullet could be.

The rest were bowled over by the human tide and became submerged beneath the men and women they had mistreated for so long. Women they had always considered weak and men thought too old to be a threat. Who now overhauled them in their terrified retreat and then, when they were down, began to beat them to death.

Not sticking them with the bladed implements or blasting at them with their own guns. For there would not have been sufficient satisfaction in that. Instead, using makeshift clubs of timber or metal, booted feet, and clenched fists. Screaming vitriolic abuse at the victims louder than they were able to plead for mercy. Arms were raised high and brought thudding down. Legs were swung and feet were launched forward. Bones crunched, skin burst, and blood sprayed. Faces became pulped and limbs limp. Screams faltered, faded, and were ended.

And not just the living were punished in this terrifying and agonizing way. For there were not enough men left alive for the greater number of attackers to beat up. So the unfeeling corpses of the gunshot men were assaulted and mutilated by the blood-hungry mob.

All the time the clanging of the cracked bell accompanying

the screaming and the cursing and the sickening thudding of heavy blows against defenseless flesh, as the preacherman celebrated the victory. Or continued to warn of danger approaching from another direction.

For perhaps ten minutes the beatings to death and the disfiguring of the dead continued at a frenetic pace. But the two strangers to town watched the evil scene for less than half this time.

By then their own pain had diminished to an extent where they were able to move away from the shacks, Edge bent a little at the waist and Steele leading to one side. And to retrieve the Winchester and the Colt Hartford from where the rifles had been tossed away after being confiscated for being used to mete out death too quickly.

With the rifles held in double-handed grips across their bellies, they turned their backs on the scattered groups of blood-crazed men and women and their victims. And walked slowly and painfully back along the street to the intersection.

"Hey, Reb?"

"Yeah, Yank?"

Edge paused to relight the partly smoked cigarette and Steele waited for him.

"You see something I missed?"

"When?"

"When you fired the first shot at the trees?"

"No."

They started along the sun-bright street again.

"Just plain dumb luck, uh?" He blew out a stream of tobacco smoke. "That Blood and his bunch showed up at the right time?"

"It happens sometimes, feller."

"Not too often."

"Never do rely on it."

"You see where the horses went?"

"No. But I reckon back to Gatling's livery stable is a good bet."

"I told you before, Reb, you ain't got the money to bet with."

They reached the intersection and came to an abrupt halt.

Stood stock still, guns held low and uncocked, not aimed. This as the preacherman stopped ringing the bell and, as if this was a signal, the beating up of the corpses came to an end.

Into the hard, tense, hot, dusty, brittle silence that smelled of violent death, the man at the center of a line of more than twenty who sat their horses stretched from one side of the street to the other drawled: "Sheriff Jonas Gale out of Stormville. You men better drop them rifles and reach for the wide blue wonder. Or die."

The whole bunch of them had badges pinned to their shirt pockets. And all had Winchester rifles which they aimed from the shoulder at the two men standing perhaps a hundred feet from them. Just some of them had horses on lead lines with blanket-draped burdens slumped over the saddles, the shrouds not large enough to conceal the hands and feet dangling down on either side of the animals.

"Figure there's been enough dying for one day, Reb," Edge growled, and opened his hands so that the Winchester fell to the ground in front of him. Then he began slowly to unfasten the holster tie from around his thigh.

Steele eased down into a half crouch to lay the Colt Hartford on the ground as he drawled, "If Walt King's under one of those blankets, reckon I have good reason to be blue, Yank."

"Some others got beat black and blue, feller," Edge reminded as he dropped the gunbelt and holster and raised his hands to the level of his shoulders, gestured with a slight motion of his head to indicate the scene at the end of the street behind them.

Steele matched his stance with raised hands.

Sheriff Jonas Gale, who was tall, powerfully built, about fifty years old, heavily moustached, and gimlet eyed, said evenly:

"Dye as in coloring stuff, uh? Well, mister, if you got any black, best get it ready to wear. Walter King got his."

"Ain't King he'll miss, feller," Edge explained. "The Reb was hoping to collect some folding green on him."

"A bounty man!" one of the other lawman rasped, and spat a globule of saliva at the parched street.

Gale jerked his rifle away from his shoulder and slid it in

the scabbard. Offered, "Okay, you can take the hands down now."

Steele did so and muttered, "White of you, sheriff."

Edge duplicated the move and rasped, "Nobody comes through with flying colors every time, Reb."

Chapter Twenty-one

The Territory of Colorado was scheduled to achieve statehood within the union on August first of that year, and such outlaw bolt holes as Silver Pass could not be allowed to remain as they were, one of the men with badges told a gathering of interested people at the meeting hall.

This was why Sheriff Jonas Gale was summoned secretly to Denver and ordered to head up a posse of professional lawmen with the express purpose of cleaning up the twin towns high in the mountains. The Stormville sheriff was given command because Silver Pass was in a part of the country he knew well.

The posse was within sight of North Pass when the King and Blood bunches rode into town from the gap in the ridges. And they attacked immediately. In the confusion, Blood and his men thought the King bunch had led them into a trap and there was as much fighting between the short-term allies as between the lawmen and the outlaws. In the aftermath of which, it was realized that most of the men from South Pass had somehow escaped.

A soon-to-die survivor told the lawmen about the series of tunnels that provided a secret route between the twin towns. Tunnels that had not been linked back in the mining days of Silver Pass. But which Walt King and his men had worked for more than two years to connect.

Riding out of town, between the pile of rubble and the shack where Elmer Flexner had indulged in his brutal sexual pleasures, Edge said, "You know how much the Stormville undertaker charges for his cheapest funeral, Reb?"

"For the gunslingers you killed at the railroad depot?"

"Right."

"The twenty dollars you got for taking care of me ought more than take care of them, I reckon."

When they started down the slope into the valley and t

town was lost to sight if they should look back, the cracked bell began to toll its familiar death knell. The mute preacher marking in the only way he was able the interment of those South Pass citizens whose passing had triggered the mob violence, aided and abetted by the dispassionate pair of men who now had their backs turned to the town.

The half-breed and the Virginian able to ride for Stormville far ahead of the posse, who had the gruesome task of identifying the viciously slaughtered Blood bunch before the individual corpses were consigned to the same mass grave into which King and his men had been placed.

They were up out of the valley, riding by the remains of the old military post, when an explosion sounded again in the town, now lost to sight amid the heat shimmer of midafternoon. The sound of the blast was muted by distance and caused no distress to the geldings. And neither rider looked back along the valley. Knowing that the tunnel into which the corpses of the hard men had been taken was now securely sealed.

"Owe a little money around town myself," Steele said.

"Guess you could've got in deeper, Reb. Way that Nat West gave you access to so much credit."

The Virginian spat as the half-breed lit a cigarette.

"Looks to be on the cards I may have to sell this horse, Yank. Pay off what I owe at the hotel and for my clothes and have enough left over for a ticket. Ride out on the train with you."

Edge shook his head. "Not with me, feller. I don't have to sell my horse. Soon as I've paid for burying my dead, aim to ride him to Denver."

"I can bank on that?"

"You still don't have the money to bet on it. Anyway, Reb, figure we balanced the book okay already."

"Reckon so, Yank. About time for another joint account to be—

CLOSED."*

But accounts of what happens to Edge and Steele after they go their separate ways will be told in the next books of the individual series.

More bestselling western adventure from Pinnacle, America's #1 series publisher. Over 8 million copies of EDGE in print!